STOLEN EMBRACES

How handsome he was, even now, with his face and beard covered with dirt from the dusty field. Her lips parted slightly. "You truly love me?"

"Oh, yes, my dearest! Is there any hope for me?"

She was smiling at last. "I love you with all my heart."

Suddenly, they were clasped together. She felt her lips press against his, felt herself rise from the ground and push against him. He brought her fingers to his lips. "Oh, how I have longed to hear you say that. My darling, I had almost lost the power to dream. Let me show you the love I have held within me so very long."

She clung to him with all of her strength, loving every sensation he stirred within her body. This was what she had been missing. This feeling of power—of surrender. This merging of her body with his, of her emotions with his. She felt her mind drifting, lost in ecstasy. And she knew at last that thought only matters when it can be abandoned to passion.

Rebel's Passion

Rebel's Passion

Andrea Layton

PLAYBOY
PAPERBACKS

Published simultaneously in the United States and Canada by Playboy Paperbacks, New York, New York. Printed in the United States of America. Library of Congress Catalog Card Number: 81-83260. First edition.

Books are available at quantity discounts for promotional and industrial use. For further information, write to Premium Sales, Playboy Paperbacks, 1633 Broadway, New York, New York 10019.

ISBN: 0-872-16994-4

First printing February 1982.

One

The great hall was crowded with festive guests. Far at one end of the room, President Washington stood speaking with a few members of his cabinet. The year was 1793, and the society of Philadelphia was gathered to celebrate the birthday of the first leader of the new nation and to share good wishes for the year to come.

A prosperous year, everyone hoped—a year of growing success for the young United States. To men and women of Washington's generation, the very existence of the new country was something of a miracle. But to Virginia Nelson and her friends, it seemed perfectly natural that allegiance should remain within the borders of their own land, that England should be considered a sister nation in the world community of countries and not the motherland.

Virginia had been born in 1777, a year after the Declaration of Independence. She had no memories of the hardships that had accompanied the fighting. The stories she had heard of the war, told by her father and Uncle Roy and her grandfather, Robert Salford, were tales of the romantic past to her. To her and most of her companions, liberty was taken for granted—a right every American possessed. Virginia differed only in that she had learned to appreciate her freedom a bit more than did some of her companions. Her grandmother, Elizabeth Bartlett Salford, had fled England and given up her heritage to live as a free woman in the new colony of Pennsylvania.

Her mother had carried on the love for freedom by her dedication to liberty—both personal and for her country. Virginia had herself been brought up with more liberty than was given many young girls of her day. She was a practiced horsewoman, as well as a skilled musician. She dabbled in art, but she also was interested in politics. Her father, George Nelson, wanted her to be aware of the world around her, even though her understanding of the political life of the nation set her apart from her friends.

She did not feel isolated from her peers on the night of the dance, however, though a few of her closest girl friends were already married. Her time would come, that she knew. She would be sixteen within a month, and then she would begin to receive suitors. Her presence at the President's ball was evidence of her change of position in the family.

She knew that many of the young men in Philadelphia wanted to vie for her hand. She had met some of them at the time of her grandmother's funeral, when the family and friends had gathered in the small cemetery just outside the city, to put Elizabeth Salford to rest beside the grave of her husband. Of course, at that time, Virginia had been too young to think of the boys as future suitors—and she had been too heartbroken to want to play when the funeral was over.

But that time had passed. She had seen the boys as they grew older, and with each passing year, she had studied them with a more critical eye. "You're fortunate," Carolyn Nelson had told her daughter. "You aren't facing this choice in the middle of a national struggle. No sooner did your father and I marry, than he had to go off to fight with General Washington."

Virginia nodded silently when her mother made such remarks. War meant little to Virginia. Separation was a word she did not understand. Her parents were with her all the time. And her husband would leave her home only to pursue his career. Yet she wondered often if war might not help her make her choice. She felt confused by the presence of so many eligible suitors.

"How will I know, Mother? How will I tell which man is the right one for me?"

Carolyn Nelson smiled secretively. "You'll know, my dear. Something inside you will recognize him, will say 'I've found the one who is right for me.' That's all you'll need. You'll just know."

"But will he feel it, too?" Virginia was puzzled. "What if I'm the only one to feel so sure that we belong together?"

"Then it won't be the right man!" Carolyn laughed. "Be patient, my darling. You're only fifteen. You'll find him—and you'll know."

Virginia had had to be satisfied with such an answer. But she had not been content to wait. From that moment on, she studied her companions with new intensity. Was Douglas the one? If not, then who?

These questions were foremost in her mind during the dance. Each partner was evaluated and mentally cast aside, until David Cavanaugh approached. He was older than the others, all of twenty-three or -four, a successful importer of fine liquors. He was a respected man in the community, not a child, like the other boys she knew.

She watched him as he stepped to her side. Was it possible that he was coming to speak to her? She glanced quickly at her dance card, which her mother had made up for her at the beginning of the evening. Yes! There was his name!

He bowed low and brought her fingers to his lips. "Miss Virginia! We have the next dance, I believe."

She felt a tingling begin in her fingertips and move swiftly up her arm. Helen Dunmore was standing nearby, and she sighed in open envy. Virginia glanced triumphantly at her friend as she took David's arm. What a coup. Now no one would dare to treat her like a child again.

She was aware, as she stepped onto the dance floor, of the striking appearance she made with such a companion. He was tall—all of six feet—with black, curly hair and skin a golden olive in color. The lace around his cuffs was of the most exquisite pattern, imported from Ireland. His coat was the finest brocade. His sharp brown eyes were fixed on her face.

She, on the contrary, was petite—only a few inches more than five feet. Her hair was a bright reddish blond, as her grandmother's had been when she was young. Her blue eyes sparkled with delight, and her ivory-smooth skin was the envy of all of her girl friends. She had the chiseled features of a patrician, the carriage of a lady of quality. She could feel the admiration in the eyes of the onlookers as she spun past them on the dance floor.

"A lovely ball, isn't it?" Her voice almost trembled.

David nodded, a warm smile on his full lips. "Not half as lovely as you, my dear. How have your parents succeeded in keeping you hidden?"

She laughed nervously. He was flattering her, she knew.

They had met before, on the docks, near Mr. Willing's warehouse, when she ran down there to play near the water while her father visited with his friend. But he had not paid any attention to her before. Now she was aware of the intensity of his gaze. *As if he can see through my clothes!* The thought sent a thrill down her back. She felt deliciously wicked—and excited. Was this, she wondered, how it felt to be in love?

The dance ended, and he led her to the side of the room. He stood before her, so graceful, so masculine. He drew a snuff box from his pocket and brought a pinch to his nose: just a tiny bit, not enough to make him sneeze. "I will speak to your parents. I must see you again, Mistress Nelson."

She lowered her head, too shy to respond. Was this inner excitement the same emotion her mother described? Did he feel the same way? She was almost relieved when he bowed and left her with her next partner.

He seemed to disappear then, for though she looked often, she could not find him in the crowd. He did not keep his promise to speak to her father, for he was not a guest at her birthday ball, nor was he at the harbor when she came to watch the ships arrive to unload their cargo. She decided, at last, that he was waiting for a signal from her, for some word that she was ready to receive him, and she vowed to make her position clear the very next time she saw him.

That moment never arrived. Summer came early to Philadelphia that year, and with it came the dread yellow fever, brought up from the tropics in the dark secrecy of some ship's hold. By mid-June, the city was reeling under the fiercest onslaught in its existence. Families not afflicted by the plague fled to safety. Social affairs were delayed and finally abandoned. The city was under siege, and the enemy at its gates was Death.

George Nelson and his family were among the few to remain—not by choice, but because the illness struck before they could escape. Carolyn Nelson was afflicted first. Virginia seemed to hover for a day or two on the verge of falling victim to the illness. Then her strength returned, and she was once again healthy.

George developed the illness suddenly, after a long day

working mid-city among the poor. By the time he reached home, his face was yellow and his skin was dry.

For Virginia the days that followed were a nightmare. Her father had dismissed the servants to save them from infection, and so Virginia was alone to nurse her desperately ill mother and her exhausted father. She did her best, following the directions of the overworked doctor.

Her mother died suddenly, resting in George's arms. He held her quietly and then put her down on the bed. The death cart had rolled past moments before, and both he and Virginia had shuddered at the sound. "We must take her to the cemetery ourselves and bury her beside her mother. I do not want her to be put in the common grave, despite the law."

Virginia nodded, too overcome to speak. She was at her father's side when he cut the wood for the coffin. He staggered when he tried to lift it to bring it into the house.

"Papa!" She rushed to help him. "Are you well enough to do this?"

He shook her away. "Yes, my dear. We must bring her to the cemetery tonight. Help me carry the coffin up to her room."

They stood together for a moment, looking at the still form of their loved one. Virginia took her father's hand. "Oh, Papa, if only I were the one lying there, and mother standing in my place. Then you would be together still."

"Hush, child!" George patted Virginia's shoulder. "You are a strong young woman. We have been blessed to love you these past sixteen years. I regret that your mother has left you before you were wed, but we cannot oppose God's will." He paused, a small smile on his face. "She was only eighteen when we first declared our love. Has she spoken of those days to you?"

"Yes, Papa."

"Good! Then you will understand my admonition. We endured many difficulties because we were both too proud to admit our love. Do not make the same mistake. Do not let your dream of wealth or position cause you to make a choice you will regret later."

"Papa! You will be here to guide me. You mustn't speak as if I will be alone."

"You may well be, my dear. Besides, we are alone any

time when we choose our love. I cannot do it for you, nor would your mother have been of any help. Your choice will come from your heart—and it will be echoed in the heart of the man who is right for you."

Virginia nodded. Her mother had used the same words and so had her grandmother when she was alive. Both had found their true loves in the wilderness, alone.

Of such stories had Virginia's dreams been built. Her reality had been very different. She had been born in New York while her father was still fighting the British. She'd lived at Fort Pitt in Pennsylvania briefly when she was still very young, and then George had been elected a representative to Congress. The family had moved to Philadelphia. It had been her home ever since.

"Papa"—she looked into her father's face—"when you talk of knowing my love, are you thinking of David Cavanaugh?"

"Possibly. He might easily overwhelm a girl as innocent as you. He is—" He looked down at his wife's face. "He does not show the temperament needed for the growth of true affection."

"Yet he is always polite—and he is very handsome."

"I see that. I fear, though, that you may be overly influenced by his importance in the community or by his charm." He paused. "He seems . . . somehow unreliable." He saw her expression change. "Well, my dear, I may be wrong! I should not judge him only by rumors—and by my unreasoning reaction to something I—" He bent and gently placed his wife's body in the coffin. "Come, my dear. It is dark. We must go now, for it will not be easy to dig the grave."

They paused first to muffle the wheels of the carriage and the hoofs of the horses. Then they moved slowly through the streets, alert for the sight of the death wagon. But they encountered no one. The moon was peering over the treetops when they reached the cemetery.

Virginia glanced about her in dismay. In one week, since the beginning of the plague, even this peaceful place had been defiled. Graves lay open, abandoned by unknown people who had themselves grown too sick to finish their work. At the bottom of the hill, on the side farthest from town, lay the open common grave, waiting for more victims.

Virginia turned in horror from the sight. Her father had shown unexpected strength during the afternoon and evening, working without rest to construct the coffin. Now he pushed himself even further. Panting from the exertion, he bent to the task of digging his wife's final resting place.

Virginia tugged at the handle of the shovel. "Please, Papa, let me do that. You are still too weak."

"No, my dear. I will rest if I need to, but I must continue until my darling rests safely beside her mother."

Virginia reluctantly released the shovel, but she stood nearby, ready to help. More than once she took over, giving her father a rest. Both she and her father were exhausted and covered with dirt before he was satisfied that the hole was deep and level enough. Then, gently, they slid the plain wooden coffin onto the ropes Virginia had carried from home, and together they lowered it into the ground.

George was breathing heavily as he gazed down into the dark grave. Then he pulled himself erect, supported by the shovel. With a sigh, he picked up a handful of dirt and tossed it into the gaping grave. "Rest in peace, my love." His voice broke. "Virginia, can you say a prayer?"

Virginia searched her memory for an appropriate intercession. She folded her hands and bowed her head. "The Lord is my shepherd. I shall not want. . . ." The comforting words flowed smoothly from her lips. It was her mother's favorite psalm.

Afterward, they worked together to fill the grave, and George rounded it off with his shovel. Abruptly, he turned and strode to their wagon. The muffled hoofs of the horses and the padding Virginia had wrapped around the wheels made their journey more dreamlike than real. When they reached the stable, she felt certain that no one in the city knew of their mission.

At the door to her father's study, Virginia paused. "Papa, you must go back to bed now. You are not well, and the night has taxed your strength."

He had lit a candle when he entered the house, and he held it up now so he could see her face. "You are right, my child, I am sick of body and of heart. Forgive me, my dear, and try to understand. I must be alone with my memories."

She gazed up into his face, her eyes wide with worry. "Are you certain you wish to be alone? I could sit nearby —just to guard you. I promise I will not disturb you."

"Oh, my sweet child!" He drew her close and kissed her brow. "You are so like your mother! But the emotions I feel now are very private." A look of pain crossed his face. "Go to sleep, my dear. You have not rested in days. And do not worry about me. I will be better in the morning."

When the first rays of sun touched Virginia's window, she woke with a start. What was she doing in bed? Her father and mother were sick! She should be nursing them, as the doctor had instructed her. She leaped to her feet and stood, trying desperately to gather her thoughts.

Then the memory of her mother's death and burial returned, and she shuddered with silent sobs. If only it had been a nightmare! She flexed her arms, aware that they ached from the exertion of the night. She would never see her mother again. And her father . . .

Her father! With sudden panic, she fetched a dress from her wardrobe, pulling it over her head as she raced to the door and down the stairs. She should never have left her father alone!

She paused at the study door. Another hot, humid day. The sun seemed to bake the city, turning it into a hell on earth. Already, despite having sponged her body before she went to sleep, she was covered with sweat.

She tapped lightly. "Papa?" There was no response. Was he sleeping at last? She pushed the door ajar and stepped inside.

She saw him, leaning back in his great chair, his head leaning slightly to the right where he had dropped off to sleep. He needed it so badly! She stepped to his side and felt his forehead. It was clammy with sweat and hot with fever.

Impulsively, she turned and ran up to his room, returning with a large, soft quilt. When the fever abated, he would need a cover, despite the intense heat of the room.

She realized with surprise that she was hungry. Would

he, also, wish for breakfast when he awoke? With a quick glance at his face, she headed for the kitchen.

There was little food aside from rice that had been prepared the evening before—or was it two days ago?: strips of dried beef jerky, a gift from friends in Fort Pitt, and a few fresh vegetables that had ripened early. Nothing like the lavish spreads that had issued regularly from the kitchen before the cook left.

She ate quickly and drew a flagon of ale from a large cask. Then she set about preparing a tray for her father.

She realized as soon as she entered the study that something was wrong. Her father had not moved in all the time she had been gone.

"Papa." She set the tray on his desk. His head dropped forward as she touched his shoulder. "Papa!" She was screaming, but he did not hear her voice. The exertion of the night had been more than his weakened body could endure. Caring for his wife's burial, he had drained himself of the little life force that had held him together during her days of illness.

Virginia caught his shoulders and pulled him into her arms. Tears streamed down her cheeks. There was no longer a need for her to concern herself with her father's welfare. He was dead.

Two

The sky turned a golden red, filling the study with an eerie light, but Virginia seemed barely aware of the passing of time. She stirred when the evening death cart rumbled past, and the sound suddenly made her aware of her dilemma. It had taken two to prepare the ground for her mother's coffin. She could never bury her father alone.

But where would she find a person who would help her save her father from the common grave? The officials had fled at the first certainty of infection in the city. Mr. Willing and his family—all of her friends—were gone, just as she and her parents would have gone, had her mother not fallen prey to the disease. If her neighbors were giving up their dead to the cart, they would only scoff at her sentimental need to bury her father beside the body of her mother.

Still, she would have to try, and soon. The heat was insufferable, and no corpse could remain long aboveground. She rose and moved swiftly from room to room, checking each casement to make certain it was locked. When she was sure the house was secure, she pulled the key to the massive front door from her father's pocket and stepped into the street. She felt strange turning the lock, for that had always been her father's responsibility. But now she was alone. She glanced back nervously as she reached the corner, then she hurried on.

She paused at the door of the first tavern. It was locked. Of course! Her father had informed her the day after her mother had fallen ill that the public houses had been closed throughout the city. But where would she find assistance? Was there anyone alive in this cursed city?

A noise behind her sent a shiver of fear up her back, and she turned swiftly. There was no one in sight. A rat, perhaps? The thought made her uneasy. She began to run, and it wasn't until she found herself before the door of another tavern that she realized there had been purpose in her flight.

She had neither seen nor passed anyone since she left her home. Was everyone dead? Had this city, the seat of the new government, been destroyed in five days of plague? What irony! To survive the terrible Revolution, to win freedom, and then to lose it all to a sickness that crept like a plague of Egypt, destroying all who moved before it!

Frantic now, she gazed up at the shuttered windows of the second tavern. Were there people hiding behind those blinds, watching her? Would they help if she called? She turned and lifted her head. "Please, someone—help me! I must have help!"

Her voice echoed up the street and faded in the distance. The houses showed no indication that anyone had heard. "Please! I beg of you! Open your windows and speak to me. I need your help."

There was still no response. Despair rested heavily on her shoulders. She was truly alone. No one would come to her assistance. Her feet dragging, she began to walk toward her home.

She paused at the corner. This lane was familiar. Up there, only a few houses away, was a place that she had visited often. Her friend, Helen Dunmore, lived up the street with her sister. Would someone be home in that residence?

Hopeful once more, she quickened her pace. She paid no heed to the hollow echo of her footsteps. There had to be help here. She was only vaguely aware of the distant sound of wheels on the cobblestones as she mounted the steps.

The noise of the wheels drew nearer. Was the cart coming past again, so late in the evening? Could she endure the sight of the abandoned corpses?

The wheels were behind her now, and she froze with horror. Then, with effort, she lifted the knocker. She had to get inside, away from this reminder of death.

"There's no one home there." She jumped at the sound of the voice, and turned to face the terror that demanded her attention. She saw, instead, a shiny carriage, pulled by two bays. A coachman, garbed in dark suit, sat erect on the box, his head turned in her direction. Was it he who had spoken? Then a head emerged from the shadowy interior. David Cavanaugh!

"David! Whatever are you doing in the city? I thought everyone had left for safety."

"I could ask the same of you. I thought you had gone with the others. Had I known you were here . . ."

Virginia took a step forward. "My parents are dead."

"The plague?" As he spoke, David drew back. "Are you sick with it, too?"

Virginia grasped the edge of the window. "No. The sickness seemed to pass me by."

"Well, how fortunate!" He emerged again. "What, then, is your trouble?" As he spoke, he pushed the door open. "Come inside. I find it depressing to remain idle in these plague-infested streets."

She climbed in and settled beside him. "Please, David. I need help to bury my father." She explained her wish. "Will you—and your servant—give me the assistance I need?"

He rested his hand on her knee. "Of course, my dear. Then you must come with me to a safe refuge. So far, this part of town has been spared the looting that has occurred elsewhere, but it will begin soon. You will not be protected, even by the strongest of doors and locks."

Virginia heard only David's promise to help. She perched nervously on the edge of her seat and waited as he gave directions to the servant. When they arrived before her house, she leaped out and rushed up the steps. And she breathed easily only when she saw that her father's body had not been disturbed.

Under his master's directions, Henry put together a rough coffin, and though he showed obvious reluctance, he nevertheless moved the body and laid it out as Virginia wished.

They drove to the cemetery in darkness, and Virginia remembered the journey she had taken only the night before. If only she had found David one day earlier. Her father might still be alive.

When the grave was filled, David took her arm. "Come, my dear. It's time for us to go."

She pulled free. "No, please, not yet. Let me say one

prayer. God only knows if I will live to return to this sacred place."

"Oh, you'll live, all right. If you have escaped infection so far, you are out of danger." David seemed annoyed, but he let her have her way.

Virginia knelt in the dirt, her head bowed. "Good-bye, Mother and Father. God bless you and greet you at the gate to Heaven." She raised her head. Then she remembered. "Oh, yes, Father, you must not fear for me. I want nothing more than to live as you and mother lived, together, surrounded with love and consideration for each other."

She rose then, and followed David down the hill to the carriage. They drove west, out of town, to a roadside inn that had not, in better days, been deemed worthy of patronage by the elite. Farmers, workmen who had to travel— and, rumor had it, highwaymen—were its most common patrons. Even in the darkness, Virginia could see that the buildings needed repair and that the stables were dirty.

David noticed her reaction as they stepped from the carriage. "My dear, you must forget everything from the past. This inn is frequented by all now, for it is one of the few where there is no sign of the sickness."

"I'm sorry. I didn't mean to be ungrateful."

"Think nothing of it." He was smiling again. "Come, I'll show you to our room."

Surely, she had not heard him clearly! "My room?"

"Yes, of course." He was already entering the common room and calling for Amos, the innkeeper.

The innkeeper led the way up the steps, but it was David who unlocked the door to the room and held it open for her. She stepped inside. David pushed behind her and closed the door. She turned, surprised at his action. "My room?"

"Ours, my dear. This has been my room—until this moment. I can think of no greater pleasure than to share it with you."

She drew away from him. "Please, David! What are you saying?"

"Nothing that is not logical, considering the circumstances. You must understand, my dear, rooms are at a premium. The innkeeper has no space for a woman alone." He stepped close and rested his arm on her shoulder. "But you should not let this upset you. I can protect you better if you are near. And I do want to protect you. Surely, the brightness I saw in your eyes at the President's ball last February was meant for me. There was no other man near me when our eyes met."

She blushed. "I— You must forgive me. I was foolish."

"Foolish? To find me attractive? You hurt my sensitivities."

"Oh, no! I find you very attractive." She blushed again at her boldness.

"Well, then, we should take advantage of this fortuitous event. It appears to me that the God of love has brought us together. He has paved the way for our union." He turned her as he spoke, and held her against his body. She could feel his strength—and his desire. The knowledge that he wanted her made her suddenly warm. His face drew near, and then his lips pressed against hers.

She sighed and relaxed into his arm. Could she have asked for a more kindly fate? She had met the man who wanted to marry her. What was it her father had said? He had warned her against too quick a decision, especially if it involved David. But her father had been wrong to doubt this handsome man. He was kind—and so very helpful. And he loved her. Was he not now saying that he wanted her to be his bride?

She was silent as he led her toward the bed. She felt certain, though she had had no prior experience with men, that he intended to take her for his own. Yet, she could see nothing wrong, since they were to be wed. Confident that this was the right thing to do under the circumstances, she let him draw her close once more, and she returned his kiss this time with the enthusiasm of a virgin, eager to taste the pleasure of love.

She felt, again, the heat of his passion, and her body responded to his nearness. Her senses reeled, and her mind seemed to open like a flower, touched by the sun. So this was love: this strange unrest, this desire to touch, to feel his lips against her bare shoulder. This sudden need to be close, closer than she had ever before been to any man.

She realized that she was trembling. Was this passion— or fear? Once she had heard two women speak of the first time, and they had mentioned pain and bleeding. But her mother had said it was wonderful. An unfolding of her inner soul, a melding of two individuals into one. What, she wondered, would it be for her?

David fumbled with the buttons on her gown, and she automatically reached up to push his fingers aside and open them herself. Her lips clung to his, her eyes closed. How lucky she was to find love so easily. Her father and mother would be so happy if they could know her good fortune.

Her dress dropped to the floor, and her chemise followed. The damp night air caressed her body. Would he be angry because she had not had a bath?

He stepped back suddenly and pushed her into the moonlight that filtered through the torn curtains. She stood still, too embarrassed to speak, her hands covering her breasts. He reached out and pulled them away. "God! How beautiful! And to think you have never had a man before."

She blushed. Did he think she would come to him so proudly had she let another hold her? He smiled, and she forgot her confusion. "You are the loveliest woman I've ever seen."

Her blush, this time, expressed shyness. Never before had a man seen her so exposed. Yet, in her innocence, she felt joy that so simple a thing could give her love so much delight. She did not pull away when he cupped her breasts in his hands.

"So delicate! So lovely!" His fingers touched her nipples, stirring them to hardness. The sensation crept over her body, setting her trembling with desire.

"You might be hurt, my sweet." His lips were close to her cheek. "Sometimes, there is pain the first time."

She nodded. "Mother told me. It's all right. I'm not afraid."

He led her to the bed then, and stood over her as he removed his own clothing. She watched him in amazement. A man's body was a mystery to her, one that would at last be unravelled. His desire was obvious, yet he moved slowly, caressing her gently, rousing her to want what had to take place.

She felt her heartbeat quicken, and she panted beneath his touch. "Tell me, David. What must I do?"

He kissed her gently. "Just do not draw back from me when I enter. Be prepared for the pain. It will be over soon." As he spoke, he rose above her and lowered himself down. She felt the tingling of his nearness, felt her thighs open as if they knew more than she did about what was ahead. And then the pressure began.

She cried out once, when he lunged suddenly. But then he grew quiet, as if waiting for some unknown change to take place. She lay under him, sensing the hurt, rising over it to enjoy the pleasure that she had been told would follow.

He moved only when he sensed her own wish for movement. He was not a newcomer to taking a virgin. He knew when to be forceful and when to wait patiently for her to grow to meet his passion.

He played skillfully on her senses, rousing her to new desire, building her capacity for enjoyment as he took his own pleasure. To Virginia, this was exquisite torture. The wanting was fulfilled at last, then built again to greater wanting. And again satisfied. Teasing, stirring passions she had never known existed within her.

She was aware once of his watching her as she twisted below him, lost in the rapture of the emotions that wracked her unresisting body. Never in all of her dreams had she expected love to be so magnificent, so overwhelming.

He met her eyes and smiled. "You like this, don't you?"

Her answer was a whimper of delight. She could not gather her senses together enough to speak. She could only feel that she wanted this joy to continue forever.

She realized he was speaking to her as he moved above her, but she barely understood his words. But later, when he rose at last and left the room, she recalled them, and she was troubled.

What had he said? Something about her being a "great find." "There's never been another quite like you." "You'll be a priceless treasure." "Bessie . . ." He hadn't finished that thought, because he had himself become suddenly tense. He had thrust himself within her and then, with a moan, collapsed on her breasts.

He rose then, and stood once more above her. "Go to sleep, my sweet. I must go away for a few days, but I will be back. Do not worry, my dear one. You are too valuable for me to forget."

She pulled herself up, suddenly frightened. "Please, David, don't leave me!"

He embraced her, and kissed her cheeks. "I must go, my sweet. But I will speak to Amos. He will provide you with food. You must understand, I am concerned for your safety. I will take what precautions I must to insure your being here when I return."

She dared not ask to go with him again, though she was fearful of being alone. Silently, she lay back on the bed. She watched as he dressed and packed a small valise. He was speaking again. "You will be safe in this room. Do not try to go out, for there are many dangerous men around, men who might do you harm or who may try to use you for their own pleasure. Do you understand?"

She nodded. "I will wait." She continued very quietly, "Please, come back soon!"

He kissed her once more, and then he was gone. She heard his boots thunder down the stairs, and then his carriage rattle out of the courtyard.

The dreaminess that had possessed her while he was with her returned, and she lay back, reveling in the memory of their love. When she fell asleep at last, she was smiling.

Three

Virginia woke with a start. How could she have permitted herself to sleep, when her mother and father needed her? She sat up and stared wildly about. This was not her bedroom! She was alone in a strange place and . . .

What a nightmare she had had, that her father had died after burying her mother. Suddenly she realized with an aching emptiness that it had not been a dream. It was real. They were both gone.

But she had found her love. David had been so kind, so loving. He had helped her and given her shelter.

If only he had not had to leave. She rose and pulled on her clothes. The oppressive heat had not abated during the night, and she was already wet with perspiration. She gazed out the window. The trees were still. The morning noises seemed muted, as if the air itself were a blanket.

Suddenly, overcome by the events of the previous days, she ran to the door and pushed on the handle. It did not budge. With a cry of alarm, she hammered on the panel.

A key turned in the lock, and the door swung open. "So you're awake, eh?" The woman who stood before her was short and heavy, with a toothless grin that cut across her face like a scar. Her eyes were narrowed and her hair was a mottled gray.

Startled, Virginia stepped back, and the old woman entered. "I wondered if ya would sleep all day!" She waddled across the room and pulled up the blankets of the bed. "Slept alone, did ya? Well, better luck next time! Mr. Cavanaugh's fussy about his women, he is!"

Virginia found her voice. "Fussy? His women? I don't know what you mean."

The old hag looked up from her work. "You'll find out soon enough, when he decides where ta put ya."

A cold fear gripped Virginia. She was not the first woman David had brought to this inn! And if she was to believe

26

this creature . . . She pulled herself together. "What do you mean, 'where to put me'?"

"Why, if ya don't know, ya're better off! Enjoy your moment of glory. Ya'll earn it, 'specially if ya gets sent ta some brothel near the city. Once the plague's run its course, there'll be lots of strappin' men lookin' for sluts with sweet faces ta share a night."

"Stop talking like that! Mr. Cavanaugh is an honorable man. He helped me bury my father—and he loves me. He told me it was God's will that I be his."

The hag dropped to the bed, overcome with helpless laughter. "God's will, eh? What an imagination that man has! Aye, a true bawd, he is. He can sweet-talk a saint into the life of a whore." She turned back the covers. "Aye. I see ya was a virgin. He make ya like it, dearie? I've seen him work. A real master, he is. Ya want it again, don't ya, sweetie? He's got ya, even if ya think ya're free. Ya want it, and he'll make ya pay for it dearly."

Virginia was overcome with panic. Could this old woman be speaking the truth? Her heart cried out to reject such a possibility, but her mind turned back to all that had transpired the night before, analyzing it with new insight.

He had said strange things when she was too wrapped in her own emotions to listen. Now the words came back again. "There's never been another quite like you!" "You'll be a priceless treasure." In the light of the old hag's words, what he had said made terrible sense. He had taken her deliberately, whetting her appetite for carnal pleasures, and now he planned to put her in a brothel.

She did not stop to consider whether her assumptions might be wrong. Instead, she sat quietly in a chair while the old woman prattled on. She barely heard what was said, but what did reach her consciousness only confirmed her worst fears. She had believed, in her innocence, that she had found her true love. What she had done was commit herself to a life of shame.

When at last the clean-up chores were completed and the woman gone from the room, carrying the chamber pot and the dirty sheets, Virginia rose and stepped to the small mirror that hung against one wall. She gazed silently at her reflection. "I was wrong, Papa." She stared at her wide, frightened eyes. "I was wrong, and you were right. I only saw David's handsome face and his smooth manners. You saw his soul." She dipped her hands in the pitcher of clean water and rubbed her face. Then she took her kerchief out and with it removed the stains of blood from inside her legs. When she felt clean, she looked about for a wiping cloth, but she found nothing, so she dried herself on a corner of the quilt. "And now . . ." She sat on the bed, once more close to tears. "Now I am ruined."

A sparrow landed on the window ledge. She watched it as it bounced around, chirping brightly. What, she wondered, brought so carefree a creature to this outpost of Hell?

The sparrow began to sing, its odd, crooked little voice sounding out of place against the noises of the courtyard. She watched it with growing curiosity. Was she wrong, after all, to abandon herself to despair? Was this God's way of reminding her that as long as life existed, hope should remain, too?

She rose and brushed the dust that clung to her skirt. The bird seemed to beckon her, and she moved in its direction. As she passed the foot of the bed, she picked up her slippers and put them on. Then she moved closer to the window.

The bird backed away as she approached, and she leaned toward it. "Please, little bird! Come back and sing to me." She reached through the open window, but it was gone.

She found herself looking at the flat roof of the cook-house, not more than four feet below her window ledge. Was the bird sent to show her the way to freedom? All she had to do was climb down, walk across the roof, drop to the ground, and vanish into the forest. The woods were all around. The isolation would serve as her shelter.

Before she had time to consider the dangers involved, she was over the sill. She dropped lightly to the roof, wavered for a moment, and then began to move away from her prison. She realized immediately that the roof was not as flat as it had seemed when viewed from above. It sloped upward to a peak, and she slid on the loose wood shingles as she climbed.

When she reached the peak, she saw a man step from

the barn, but he did not look up. She turned and almost ran down the slope. She must not be caught now!

Just as she reached the edge of the back of the roof, her foot caught on a loose shingle and she fell. She grabbed wildly for support, but the roof offered her none. She felt her hips slide over the edge, and instinctively she swung her legs down to break her fall. Then she hit the ground and landed on one side.

"Well, well! So Mr. Cavanaugh's woman has taken to climbing buildings."

A short, very fat man with a round, protruding belly stood above her. His hair was neatly pulled back in a braid, and his face, clean-shaven except for a small, pointed beard, was distorted by a leer. He wore a soiled apron that reached almost to the ground, and his boots showed signs of long, hard wear.

"Who are you?" She knelt, prepared to run.

"Who? Amos Durwood, at your service, madam!" He paused, but she showed no recognition. "The innkeeper!" He held out his hand. "Come along, now. It's hardly proper for a young lady to refuse the hospitality that has been offered her."

She backed up, well out of his reach. "Sir, I have been offered no hospitality for which I will not be expected to pay. I have been abducted against my will, and—" She stopped. Was that the truth? Had she objected to entering this place? She knew the answer, and she blushed.

Amos grinned, and she realized that his mouth was crooked on his face. "Please, mistress, spare me your tales. I am not a fool. I greeted you and Mr. Cavanaugh when you arrived. I can swear he used no coercion."

She flushed. "No, you're right. He did not, but—" Again, she paused. Could she argue her case with any success? No. All she had was the word of an ancient hag that David was planning an unsavory future for her. Still, she had to try to make this man understand. "He wants to force me into a life of sin! Please! You must help me get away."

He made no response, and she glanced up at him. He did not believe her. She fought to control her panic.

"You must be mistaken." Amos was no longer smiling. "I have known Mr. Cavanaugh for many years, and he is an honorable man. Mayhap you are distraught. He told me what you have been through. Only a day has passed since you buried your mother and father. I am certain if he locked the door to your room, it was for your own protection. He remarked to me as he left last night that he feared for your safety, since you were upset and nervous. This inn is far from any town or even a farmhouse. Were you to wander off, you might be killed by a wild beast or waylaid by highwaymen or Indians."

"No! Please! I do not want to be locked in a room here. I am afraid!" She grew quiet. When she spoke again, she used all of her charm. "Please, sir. I need your help."

He leered at her. "You are in no danger, miss. Do you think you are the first virgin who was surprised by the passion locked within her? Your family is gone. You are alone. You should be thankful that Mr. Cavanaugh has agreed to take you under his protection. He takes good care of his women."

She was shaking with terror. Confused, she took a step forward. Amos saw her move, and he reacted with unexpected speed, his fingers closing around her wrist. She cried out in alarm, but it was too late. She was caught, and she could not break free.

He pulled her through the common room, up the stairs, to the door of David's chamber. There he paused and fumbled with a ring of keys on his belt. The door swung open, and he stepped inside. As he pulled her behind him, he shouted. "Roger!"

A boy of no more than ten years appeared in the hallway.

"Get fresh water for the lady, and tell Marie I will have words with her before this day is out!"

Roger bobbed his head and was gone, taking the bowl of tainted water with him and hanging the empty pitcher from his wrist. When he returned, the bowl was empty, the pitcher filled with fresh water.

Amos still had not released his grip on Virginia's wrist. When Roger departed, he closed the door and let her go. But he watched her closely, and she grew uncomfortable under his unblinking gaze, knowing she had no chance of escape. Why did he not leave her, now that he had prevented her from reaching the nearby forest?

She realized that he was looking from her to the open window. Would he close it, leaving her to suffocate in the humid heat? Before she could speak, he stepped close and tugged at her dress. "Take it off!"

She stared at him in alarm. "No!"

"Do as I say." His arm swung out, and his hand smacked against her cheek, almost throwing her to the floor.

She cowered, angry at his brutality and frightened that he might hit her again.

"Take it off, I say!" He spoke more loudly, and his arm went up once more. Trembling, she began to unbutton her dress. It fell open, exposing her firm young breasts, covered only with the thin cloth of her chemise.

His eyes narrowed. "A beauty. A true beauty. He has found a prize winner this time!"

She could not endure his stare. Blushing, she turned away and then, reluctantly, she let the gown fall to the floor. She caught it as it fell and held it up before her.

He clutched at her shoulders and forced her to face him. Then she felt the dress being ripped from her hands. Her thin chemise barely shielded her most intimate parts from his view. Would he go now? Hesitantly, she raised her eyes.

He stood transfixed to the spot, his eyes bulging, his breath coming fast and heavy. One look, and she knew what he wanted. She drew back, determined to defend herself against this animal.

He did not approach her again but simply gazed at her with an intensity that made her restless. Then, abruptly, he turned and left the room. She heard him lock the door behind him and descend the stairs. He had taken her dress with him.

She stood immobile, still too overcome with relief that he had not forced himself upon her to think of anything else. But, at last, her awareness returned. She was, she realized, in an unendurable dilemma. She could climb through the window again but if she did, she would expose her nakedness to any man who looked in her direction.

Yet, the little that Amos Durwood had said served to reinforce her conviction that David intended no good for her, that he planned to put her in a brothel. Somehow, she had to escape before he returned.

She thought of Grandmother Salford, a noblewoman, descended from the best family in England. She could not disgrace her name, nor that of her father!

She felt dirty again, but even after she washed herself again it did no good. She could not erase the memory of Amos's penetrating stare.

Four

For the remainder of the day, Virginia sat close to the window, gazing dully at the small corner of the courtyard that was visible over the roof of the cookhouse. Carriages full of passengers pulled in. Gentlemen on horseback arrived and stamped into the tavern. Several times she half rose, ready to call out for help, then dropped sorrowfully into her chair when the man whose attention she had hoped to engage moved too quickly out of sight.

Only once did two horsemen arrive and remain within her view. She gazed attentively at the older of the two. Was it only her great need that made him seem familiar? She waved and shouted, forgetting for the moment that she had no covering over her body, and she felt a leap of hope when he looked up.

"Help me!" she cried out.

He cocked his head, and she realized he had not heard what she said. She called louder. "I'm Virginia Nelson. I'm being held captive here!"

He shook his head, and then he shrugged. Suddenly realizing that she was dressed only in a chemise, she backed out of sight. How humiliating! He must have taken her for a tart. Was she trapped already?

Her desperate thoughts were disturbed by the rumble of thunder. A drop of rain streaked past the open window. Then, with an unexpected rush, the storm broke. How wonderful to be cool, at last. The air had a fresh smell for the first time in more than a week. What was it her father had said shortly after the outbreak of the sickness in the city? "If the weather changes, it will be over." Was Philadelphia finally free of the terror that had gripped it?

As the downpour grew heavier she saw that the courtyard was empty. No one but a fool would be out in the heavy rain.

Or a woman—seeking to escape from a life of shame.

Searching for some cloth with which to cover her body, she pulled the quilt from the bed and clutched it to her. Once more, she climbed over the windowsill. Once more, she traversed the slope of the roof, but this time she was more cautious. She moved slowly down the far side, bending down to shelter the blanket from the rain.

At the edge of the roof, she knelt and slowly lowered herself over. She hovered a moment, fearful of falling again, and then she let go. As her feet hit the wet ground, she slid suddenly and landed, with a cry of alarm, on all fours.

She cowered against the building, searching the darkness for some sign that she was no longer alone.

The courtyard remained empty. Her shoes were soaked, and the quilt quickly grew wet, but she was free at last. Shaking her head to clear her hair from her face, she headed for the forest. There the rain seemed lighter, for the thick greenery served as shelter. But her movement was impeded by branches that tugged at her blanket, once almost pulling it from around her.

She came upon the road abruptly. In which direction should she go—toward Philadelphia, where the plague might still be virulent, or into the unknown—hoping to find help?

She hesitated for a moment, and then she turned toward the right, away from the city. She dared not think about what might lay ahead, nor could she contemplate the dangers she had left behind. She stumbled along, glancing occasionally over her shoulder, thankful only that she was truly free.

At dawn it was still raining, as if Nature were determined to wash the world clean of the horror that had come so close to destroying the city. Although the overcast sky hid the sun, and the air was still warm, it felt fresh and pleasant.

Virginia stopped suddenly. Horsemen were approaching ahead. Were they friends or were they men who would bring her back to Amos Durwood's inn? She dared not wait to find out. Sliding on the wet gravel, she hurried to the shelter of the underbrush.

The hoofbeats drew closer, and then a single horseman appeared around the bend in the road. He seemed to enjoy the rain as he traveled, for he made no attempt to shield himself. His wet hair clung to his brow, and his homespun clothing hung close to his body. When he reached a spot close to where Virginia was hiding, he paused and glanced back along the road.

In the pale morning light, his features were very visible. He had a strong face with a manly chin, an aquiline nose, and a straight brow. Here rode a man's man, sturdy and determined. His shoulders were broad, his arms muscular. Even from a distance, Virginia sensed an inner honesty in the rider. She was drawn to him instinctively.

She started toward him, confident that she could find in him a staunch ally. But at that moment, he spurred his horse and was gone. Disappointed, she settled back to wait.

The other riders now approached, surrounding a carriage in almost military order. She watched in fascination as the carriage drew abreast of her hiding place. For one moment, she caught a glimpse of the occupant, and she gasped in surprise. It was her uncle, Roy Salford!

She stumbled toward the road, but the underbrush caught her quilt and tore it away from her body. With a cry of alarm she fell back, embarrassed that one of the riders might have seen her, and in that moment's delay, she lost the opportunity. The small convoy was past, heading swiftly for the city.

Or for the inn! The realization that she might have left just when help was on the way brought tears to Virginia's eyes. Resolutely, she returned to the road and headed in the direction taken by her uncle. He could save her—even if she had to go all the way to Amos Durwood's inn to be by his side.

When she reached the inn, she retreated to the woods. Had she been missed? Was Amos waiting to capture her before she had a chance to speak to her uncle? She carefully studied the courtyard. The coach and the horses were nowhere in sight. Had the grooms already had time to stable the animals and put the carriage in the barn?

She had hoped to find her uncle in the courtyard, so she would not have to brave Amos in the common room. Now she knew she had no choice. She stepped from her shelter into the road.

At that instant, a tall figure emerged from the stable.

Amos appeared on the stoop at the entrance to the inn. He saw her stumbling toward the courtyard and shouted. The tall man responded like an arrow shot from a bow. He was across the yard and onto the road before Virginia could recover herself.

She saw him coming and she ran. As she reached the underbrush, she dropped her quilt but dared not retrieve it. Here the bushes were thick enough to hide her, if she could get far enough beyond him to find safe shelter.

Luck was with her. Just ahead was the path to the privy. Beyond it was a clump of thick brush, so thick she could not penetrate its depth with her eyes. She moved with sudden swiftness, pushing her way through the brush until, at last, she was hidden from the path. Behind her, she heard the tall man stamping through the woods. Amos was close behind him. Just when she thought they had seen her, they stopped.

"Let her go, Ben. She'll come out in time. I've never seen a woman who could stand the insects of the woods for very long!" Amos's voice came from close to the outhouse.

"I'm sure she's somewhere near here." Ben seemed unwilling to give up.

"Of course she is, you fool! And she'll be back where she belongs soon enough. We don't need to push the search now."

Ben stepped from the woods and stood near Amos on the path. "What if Master Cavanaugh returns before we get her back?"

"Watch your words, Ben Glasspool! It is not the business of others why we want the girl. Besides, she was left in my charge. If I deem her too hard to manage, I shall ship her to Bessie's a bit earlier. I'm sure Cavanaugh won't mind." He turned then, and headed along the path toward the inn, with Ben trotting docilely behind.

Virginia watched them depart with mixed emotions. She was glad they had stopped the search. But she knew that Amos had been right in his assessment of her feelings about insects. She was terrified when some small creature crawled up her arm or over her back. And she didn't even have the quilt to protect her.

She remained concealed for the remainder of the day.

The rain stopped at sunset, and the air grew cool. Virginia was frightened and terribly uncomforting. She had watched the gate to the inn throughout the daylight hours, hoping to see her uncle's carriage again. But though other travelers arrived and departed, he seemed to have vanished.

When darkness fell, she rose and crept toward the place where the quilt still hung on a bush near the road. She pulled it around her with relief, even though it was dripping wet. Then she moved cautiously toward the road. During her long wait she had reached the certainty that her uncle had not stopped at the inn but had continued on to the city.

She kept to the woods until she was well out of sight of the inn. Then, feeling a bit safer, she stepped onto the road, remaining near the edge even though it was slippery and often filled with puddles. She was hungry and tired, and the forest about her seemed almost unreal.

It was then she heard the horseman. Terrified, she crept back into the brush, waiting for him to pass. He was moving quickly, and he was opposite her before she felt safe. But he looked neither to the right nor to the left. The moon emerged from behind a cloud as he passed, and she almost cried out. It was the same horseman who had preceded her uncle that morning!

He was gone too quickly. Filled with despair, she stepped again onto the road. How close she had been to getting help—and again she had let the opportunity slip by.

Suddenly she heard a shot. What had happened? Were there highwaymen ahead? The silence that followed the firing of the pistol was too intense. Highwaymen would have started a fight . . . unless— She quickened her step, remaining close to the woods so she could hide if it became necessary. What if the highwaymen had killed the rider with that one bullet!

The road turned ahead, and she moved slowly forward. What she saw brought a rush of relief. The rider stood over his horse, a smoking pistol in his hand. He looked up as she came in view. "What . . . ?" He gazed at her in unconcealed amazement. "Where did you come from? What are you doing on the road?"

She stopped, uneasy again. Had she been wrong to show

herself? "My name is Virginia Nelson. I'm looking for my uncle, Roy Salford."

He stepped away from his dead horse. "Please, this is too confusing! I have just had a nasty fall, my horse has broken a leg, and I have had to shoot him. Now, out of nowhere, a woman arrives and claims to be Roy Salford's niece. I must be having a nightmare. But why would I invent you?"

She took a step toward him. "I'm not a nightmare! I—" She realized that she was crying and cursed her weakness, but she could not stop. She tried to speak, only to find her voice would not obey her.

He made no move in her direction. "I do not know who you are, though you claim to be Virginia Nelson. I am Anthony Burke. I am in Roy Salford's employ. And I happen to know that his niece is but a child. So, Miss Whatever-your-name-is, you can forget the pretense. What is it you want? Are you a decoy, sent out by highwaymen? If so, be advised, I have no money. Nor have I papers worth stealing. So you and your friends are wasting your time."

Virginia barely heard what he said. Her fatigue and hunger finally overcame her. She had no strength left with which to argue. Her knees sagged, and darkness folded in upon her. Then she was aware of nothing.

She regained consciousness slowly. She was lying on the road, with Anthony bending over her. "Good! You're awake, at least. Do you feel strong enough to speak?"

"Yes. Please, you must believe me! I am trying to escape a terrible fate." She stumbled as she told her tale, for it embarrassed her to speak of her shame to a stranger. Yet she knew she had to gain his assistance. As she finished, she clasped her hands together. "You must help me get back to Philadelphia. Please! You will see, when we reach the city, that I am Roy Salford's niece."

He rose and removed the saddlebags from his dead mount. From one pocket, he pulled a strip of dry beef and handed it to her. "Can you walk?"

She grasped his arm and pulled herself erect. "I'll try."

"Fine. For I can offer you no transportation. Salford has gone on ahead to visit with his sister—if she is at home. You say she is dead. If you are right, he will remain in her house. How far is it to the town?"

Virginia shook her head. "I don't know. I'm sorry. I cannot judge the distance."

He took her arm without answering. They walked silently together. Virginia chewed on the beef, thankful for some nourishment. She clutched the wet quilt close about her, surreptitiously casting a quick glance at her companion's face.

He was even more handsome up close than he had appeared when he first passed her on the road. There was a hidden gentleness to his expression that was not obvious at first. He appeared to be a bit younger than David, but his youth was not a weakness. His jaw was firm, his eyes steady.

She stumbled, and he caught her in his arms. She felt their strength and let herself rest there, too exhausted to pull herself free. His body, where it pressed against hers, was firm and hard, a man's body.

"You're too tired to continue." He did not release his hold. "And you're dripping wet. Forgive me for not thinking of your comfort." Lifting her in his arms, he carried her to the side of the road. "Is there another inn between here and the city?"

"I don't know. . . . I don't think so."

"Well, then, we'll have to make our own shelter." He stepped into the woods and pushed his way through the brush. He did not stop until he reached a small stream.

He busied himself with the task of preparing a camp. First, he cleared a circle of ground and made a bed of heavy stones on which he built a fire. The wood was still wet from the rain, and Virginia feared he would not succeed in starting a flame. But he was obviously a skilled woodsman, used to dealing with unpleasant conditions.

When the fire was roaring and hot, he stepped to her side. "Forgive me, but you must take off that wet quilt. I'll hang it near the fire, on a branch where it can dry." He pulled off his coat and held it out to her. "Have you nothing on at all?"

"Only my chemise." She blushed to speak of such intimate things. "Amos Durwood took my dress to keep me from getting away."

"You're a brave girl—and an ingenious one." He stood waiting.

"Please, turn around." He smiled but did as she asked. She dropped the quilt and slid her arms into the coat. It was wet, too, and she wondered what she had gained by her move.

"Now, sit here, while I make your bed." He pointed to a spot close to the fire. As she settled down, he took the quilt and draped it over a low branch.

With a sharp knife, he began to dig a hollow in the ground. Virginia watched in wonder. Her mother had described such a bed once! It was the same kind her father had made the first time he and her mother were alone in the wilderness.

Watching him, she tried to resist the sudden faintness engulfing her, but the one strip of beef had served only to increase her hunger, and her body rebelled at the continued strain. . . .

She awoke to find herself lying on a bed of dry leaves, her body pressed close against that of her companion. They were both naked. Her conscience told her she must pull away, but her body refused to respond. She was weak and shaking from cold. Then, to her surprise, she realized Anthony was sound asleep! His steady breathing was not interrupted, even when she stirred.

She lay quietly, afraid she might rouse him if she moved again. She could see that he had made careful preparation for the night's rest. He had gathered leaves to serve as their mattress. The quilt, dry from the heat of the fire, covered them. Over it, to shield them from the wind, were more dry leaves.

A new sensation came over her as her strength returned. Her skin felt alive wherever it touched his. For as long as she was able she held herself still, and then, fearful that she might wake him, she drew away and lay beyond his reach. She was filled with a tumult of emotions. Part of her was drawn to the sleeping man. The memory of the sweetness of love, of the pleasure that could be gained in a man's arms, pushed against her consciousness. But stronger than the memory of passion was the realization that she must keep her distance from this stranger. If she allowed his nearness to affect her, she would prove that David was right: that she was, in fact, suited to only one profession.

Her exhaustion at last overcame her uneasiness, and she fell again into a deep sleep.

When she woke, the sky was growing light. She had slipped into the arms of her companion, and this time he responded to her presence. He stirred, and his hands began to caress her breasts, to move gently over the flat of her stomach. His lips pressed on the lobe of her ear, and his breath was hot against her cheek.

She turned, a helpless victim of her passion, and her lips met his. A tingling sensation moved up her legs to her abdomen. She realized she was panting and pushing herself against him. This man, this stranger, seemed to know her innermost desires, seemed aware of her most sensitive, secret places. His lips moved down to the small spot at the side of her neck which she had discovered one day when, as a curious girl, she had explored her own responses. But her reaction was more sudden and more startling than it had ever been under her own fingers. Her body shook with sudden ecstasy, and she felt her legs wrap themselves around his hips. His male need was great, for she could feel his hardness, yet he was neither quick nor rough in his movements. He drew back, teasing her with his nearness, allowing himself to push at the gates of her passion with a gentleness that only added to her longing.

With a cry of desire, she raised her hips and pushed against him. And only then did he allow himself to move. She felt him enter her, and she moaned. Then he was moving slowly, relentlessly, arousing her responses, carrying her to a peak of pleasure she had never dreamed existed. She felt as if her body were floating, held down on earth only by his weight. He filled her body and her consciousness. Her fear vanished, and all she knew was the wonder of his closeness, the ecstasy of his embrace.

She was barely aware that her legs pulled him deep into her body, that her arms were wrapped around his back. Her breathing was ragged with desire and she groaned with each prodding lunge of his body.

She had wanted to prove to him that she was pure and innocent. The thought came to her, briefly, that she should be ashamed, that she should push him away and run to safety. But she could not. Shame could find no place in her mind or in her heart.

Then she felt him tremble. She opened herself to him, holding him, caressing his hair, his cheeks, his broad shoulders. Until she, too, was lost in the pulsing consummation of their mutual passion. And it was then she realized that he had been moving in his sleep.

He wakened suddenly, his eyes wide with alarm. A look of anguish twisted his features. "Oh, my God!" He drew back in alarm. "What have I done?"

She stared at him in confusion. What had he done? Was it possible that he did not know?

"I was dreaming. I thought it was a dream. Oh, mistress, can you ever forgive me?" She stared at him. Was this an act? Now, after he had taken his fill of her, was he trying to deceive her into thinking that he had not been aware of what had just happened?

She lay stiffly beside him. "How could a man sleep through such a . . ." She could not continue. She was too angry, too hurt, too outraged.

"I have been without sleep for four days of hard riding. Oh, I know I can offer no excuse that will make you forgive me for what I have done." He rose abruptly and pulled his clothing from the branches. When he was dressed, he turned again toward their makeshift bed. "Mistress Nelson, I am sure you want nothing so much as to be rid of my company. It was not my intention to have this happen, when I made but one bed for us last night. You were chilled to the bone—and I was almost frozen myself. I knew we would sleep better if we were warm, and so . . ." He stopped talking. She stared at him with wide, angry eyes.

He pulled his coat from where it hung on a branch and held it out to her. "Please, wear this. You might find travel easier if you're not wrapped so tightly in that quilt."

She took the coat in silence. It did little to hide her body, and her chemise was no help in covering her nakedness. In her outrage, she wanted nothing more than to be rid of this man who dared to penetrate her body with no thought for her feelings. She folded the blanket and wrapped it around her waist like a skirt. Sliding her feet into her slippers, aware that they were already worn from her walking, she headed for the road without looking back.

He caught up with her as they reached the highway. "You

will be hungry, Mistress Nelson. You must eat something."
He held out a stick of dried meat like the one he had
given her the night before. For a moment, she considered
refusing even that kindness, and then, aware that she would
hurt only herself, she tore it from his grasp. It tasted rich
and salty, and she relished each bite. But she refused to
give him the satisfaction of showing her appreciation. She
maintained her lead, staying a good yard ahead of him, for
she wanted to avoid looking at him again.

She forgot in her anger that he had said he worked for
her uncle. All she knew was that when she got to Philadelphia, she would say good-bye to him and never see him
again. She reached a bend in the road and hurried around
it.

The next thing she knew, a pair of massive arms lifted
her from the ground. She screamed in terror. Anthony
leaped forward, his fists swinging, but he had no weapon
with which to defend her or himself. As he attacked the
monstrous man who held her high above the road, a musket was fired. She screamed again as Anthony dropped to
the ground. She had recognized her assailant as soon as he
grabbed her. Amos's henchman, Ben, accompanied by another man, had somehow followed her.

It was not her capture that brought tears to her eyes.
She had seen Anthony fall, and she strained now to catch
sight of him as Ben hurriedly carried her away. Anthony
lay absolutely still. She could see a red stain spreading in
the dirt beside his shoulder. He was dead! And he had died
trying to rescue her from Amos Durwood's minion.

Fury possessed her. She hammered her fists on Ben's
back. She kicked at his legs and groin, but he merely
laughed and shifted her to one side, so that her blows fell on
his shoulder and his thigh. He took great strides, moving
with such ease that she lost heart. He was not human. He
reached his horse and threw her over his rump.

And then, at last, the full impact of her night crashed
down upon her. She had felt things in Anthony's arms that
even David, with all his skill, had not roused in her. David
had touched her like a master musician, striking life into
a fine instrument. But Anthony's touch had been strong and
driving, filled with true passion—perhaps even with love.

The wonder of her realization was overwhelming. Was

it possible? Could she have loved this man she hardly knew? And had he loved her?

She thought of his body, lying on the road, and she knew the answer. If he had not loved her, he had behaved in a most unusual manner. He had unhesitatingly given his life in an attempt to save her.

And the last words he had heard from her were words of anger. She was too miserable to cry. Nothing mattered to her, since she had no chance to repair the mistake she had made. Had he taken her in his sleep, as he claimed? She no longer cared. The alchemy of love had made them one, when neither had intended it.

Just before he was lost to her sight, he stirred. She glanced quickly at Ben, but he showed no interest in what went on behind them. They had accomplished their assignment. They had Virginia captive once more. A dead or dying man was of no importance to him.

Her despair was overwhelming. Dry-eyed still, she let herself hang limp. She had no wish to see the forest through which she had passed in her brief and unsuccessful flight. She had no wish to see the road. Her thoughts centered on Anthony and their brief, star-struck love. It had ended almost before it had begun, and it was her fault. Had she not given in to her anger, she would have been walking behind him, permitting him to listen for noises ahead that might mean danger. But she had been too angry to be careful. And in her pride and scorn, she had led him to his death.

As she was carried through the gate of the inn courtyard, she vaguely noted the noises of people making ready to depart. A well-dressed man was just mounting his horse.

"Sir! Help me, please! I am being abducted!" she cried.

Amos was immediately at her side. The gentleman had paused, one foot in the stirrup, and he gazed at Virginia with curiosity.

" 'Tis nothing, sir." Amos bowed and smiled. "Just a feisty wench who does not yet know who is master here. We caught her trying to follow a young gentleman who found her pleasurable but who certainly had no wish to keep her."

The portly man swung his leg over the rump of his horse and settled in the saddle. "I would think such a maid would not be worth keeping. Let her be on her own in the city for a time, and she will learn to appreciate the protection you offer her."

"Aye, 'tis tempting. But I promised her mother I would give her a home. She is my own flesh, though a bastard. I cannot disown her."

"A noble sentiment." The rider took the reins from the groom. "Well, I wish you success with her. It has been my experience that a willful female is best let go quickly or else beaten into proper compliance. No man wishes a woman who knows not how to submit." He did not wait for an answer. Wet dirt flew into Virginia's face as he spurred his horse and headed for the gate. Amos pulled her from the horse and stood her in the mud. "Did you really think you could escape Amos Durwood? Do not be so foolish again." He pushed her ahead of him. "Into the cookhouse! I will not trust you out of my sight until I can find a safer place for you."

She stumbled on the boards of the walk, but he made no attempt to help her. Relieved that she did not have to endure his touch, she pulled herself erect and clutched the quilt about her.

The smell in the kitchen of cooking vegetables assailed her nostrils. A roast, brown and covered with glaze, stood on the open oven door. Fresh bread rose on the back of the stove. She staggered and dropped to the floor. The smell of food nauseated her.

Amos pushed the cookhouse door open and entered, her dress on his arm. "Here—put this on!" He threw it toward her and, as she caught it in her arms, the quilt dropped to her lap and the coat Anthony had given her fell open, exposing her bare breasts. Amos leered at her, then slammed the door behind him.

When her dress was buttoned, she sat on the crate, wishing desperately she had treated Anthony better. She remembered that he had moved, and if some other traveler saw him on the road, he could be rescued.

The possibility that Anthony might be alive cheered her. At last, she turned her attention to the cooks. They were working furiously, filling plates, slicing bread, pouring pitchers of milk. How she wished someone would offer her food!

The cook at last turned in her direction. "Here! I cannot bear slobbering in my kitchen." He threw her a chunk of bread. A young lad who seemed to serve as cook's assistant brought her a mug of milk.

She ate quickly, for she feared that Amos would return and take her meal away. But he did not appear again until she had swallowed the last crumb of bread and drained the mug.

"Come along quickly!" he ordered.

She dared not disobey. Her fate, she felt sure, was sealed. But she might have a chance to speak to some traveler on his way to the city and warn him to look out for Anthony. She realized, suddenly, that only if Anthony lived did she have a chance of being rescued. If he lived . . . and if he felt toward her as she now felt toward him.

She was directed to a plain carriage which, to her relief, was empty. A stableboy climbed in and obeyed Amos's order to pull the blinds. The boy backed out, and Ben climbed in and sat beside her. Before Amos shut the door, he said, "Watch yourself, Ben. This one is to be delivered undamaged. If I hear you have touched her, I'll have your head!"

The driver cracked his whip and they were on their way. With Ben watching her, she did not dare lift the blinds. She would never know what roads they took.

She tried, at first, to be aware of their route. They turned right onto the highway. Did they turn again, or had the driver only swerved to avoid something in the road? There! That was a definite turn to the left! In what direction were they now heading?

The sun broke out from behind a bank of clouds, sending streaks of light through the cracks at the sides of the blinds. She dared not look at Ben, for she feared that any movement by her might be considered encouragement. Even more than Amos's touch, she dreaded feeling Ben's hand on her body.

He leered at her for a time, and then, evidently concluding that he had best obey his master, he sprawled across the seat and closed his eyes. When she heard him snoring, she timidly reached forward to peek under the blinds.

"I wouldn't do that, mistress! I'd have to blindfold you."

She drew her hand back. "I just wanted to see the sun-shine."

"Aye, and the roadsign it shines on!" He pulled a filthy kerchief from his pocket. "Shall I put this on you?"

She stared at it with revulsion. "Please, no. I won't do that again."

He settled back once more. She closed her eyes and leaned against the cushions. Neither spoke again until the carriage drew to a halt. She spoke quickly. "Please, can you tell me? Is the man who was with me . . . safe?"

"The master won't be pleased to know of him."

"Do you have to tell him? Please tell me, is he alive?"

"He might be. But, then, he might be dead. I don't concern myself with things that are not my business."

"But your companion shot him!"

"So ask him! I ain't Fred's keeper."

She decided to try another tack. "Did any carriages go toward the city after you brought me back to the inn?"

He thought a moment. "Aye. One, I think. But it might have turned around."

She decided his last remark was made only to torture her. A carriage had left the inn. It would take the road where Anthony lay. There was a possibility that he had received help in time. Worry still chewed at her consciousness, making what was happening to her far less frightening than it might have been under different circumstances.

She grew alert as she stepped from the carriage. The sun hung low in the sky to the west. The carriage had come from the south. Systematically, she reviewed every road that left the city. They must be, she concluded, far out on the northern highway, on the road to New York.

The inn they entered was maintained far better than the one owned by Amos Durwood. It was newly painted, with a neatly raked courtyard and a wooden walk wide enough for a lady to walk down without soiling her hem in the dirt.

The common room was much like that of any tavern with roughly carved benches arranged in rows and tables between them. A few men sat in the dim light, sipping ale or wine.

"Gregory!" Ben seemed uneasy as he greeted the tavern-keeper. "I must see Miss Bessie."

"Another one, eh? Well, you know where to take her."
Gregory returned to his work.

Ben took Virginia's arm and pushed her through a doorway shielded from the tavern by a heavy curtain. A thick
carpet covered the floor of the well-appointed room. A
large, magnificent chair occupied the center of the far wall.
Its back was carved with birds in flight, and the arms were
lions at rest. The cloth that covered the seat and the lower
part of the back was a vivid purple velvet of a hue Virginia had never before seen.

A woman rose from the chair as they entered. She was
tall, almost as tall as Amos, with brilliant red hair, green
eyes, and so much paint on her face that Virginia could
not but smile. Her gown was too elaborate, covered with
expensive lace and gems that sparkled as she walked. Her
lips were painted scarlet. She studied Virginia in silence.

"The master wants you to keep her here—for him."
Ben emphasized the last two words.

"Another one of his toys, eh?"

"Aye." He pushed Virginia toward the center of the
room. "I've done my part. She's your responsibility now."
He stepped backward into the tavern. "Gregory! An ale
to quench my thirst before I take to the road."

Virginia stood immobile. She had no doubt as to what
the woman was. Even in her sheltered life in Philadelphia,
she had heard of the loose women who gave themselves to
men who traveled.

The woman smiled. "Well, dearie, we might as well get
acquainted. My name is Bessie—Miss Bessie to you."

Without responding Virginia continued to stare at the
painted face.

Bessie frowned suddenly. "What's the matter with you?
Deaf? Dumb, maybe? Speak up, girl! You got a name, too,
I suppose!"

"Yes. Virginia."

"I suppose that will do, though I expect it isn't your
given name at all. Run away from home, did you?"

"No. I was waylaid on the—"

Miss Bessie gestured impatiently. "No matter. You're
here now. So Cavanaugh's taken a liking to you, eh?"

"I don't know— He's holding me against my will! Please,
you must help me get to New York or Philadelphia."

"Well, now, dearie, that can't be done. We don't travel much to New York, and Philadelphia's not safe for man nor beast." She chuckled. "Same old story! Why can't one of you girls think up something new? Holding you against your will. Maybe so. I suspect you might not have guessed where you'd end up when you lay with Cavanaugh. But you'll live a good life here. I treat my girls well. No beatings, unless they cross me."

"My uncle will search for me!"

"And he won't find you. Do you think Cavanaugh is stupid enough to leave a trail? Your relatives, if you have any, may hunt for you, but they will find no sign of your passing, here or anywhere else you've been."

"They will learn of my whereabouts. I almost escaped. An—" She stopped. If Anthony was still alive, she would be signing his death warrant to mention his name. "A man at the inn where I was first taken tried to help me get away."

Miss Bessie had lost interest. "Wait here. I'll send for you soon." She disappeared through a door close to her chair.

Virginia stared about her. The room was draped in long velvet cloths covered with designs that she recognized as Chinese. Her father, through Mr. Willing, had made many purchases of Oriental art pieces. A table near the great chair held more works of art, including a jade carving and an ornately carved ivory ball.

The chair, however, intrigued her the most. It was massive, designed for a king or at least for a large and very important man. The birds were easily identifiable as eagles, with their claws out to catch small rabbits that raced down the sides of the back. She studied it carefully. Her father had ordered just such a chair once, but it had never arrived.

Virginia suddenly became aware of two girls, sitting close to the tavern entrance. She backed away from the chair and she took a seat near them, but they did not speak to her as she approached. Was this what she would look like, if she could not escape? The girls were painted, as Miss Bessie was, and their eyes were dull.

Could she get away now? She rose and peeked through

the curtain into the tavern. Gregory stood close to the entrance, watching her.

Bessie reappeared at the far end of the room, beckoning Virginia to follow her. The girls giggled as she passed, but they said nothing and she averted her eyes. A man stood at the far side of the room, a glass of wine in his hand.

"This way, dearie! Up you go!" Bessie pointed toward the stairs. Virginia dared not disobey. If she had understood correctly, she was to be treated differently than the other girls. She would be left alone, at least until David arrived. In the meantime, she could try to make her escape.

She was directed into a room at the end of the corridor. Bessie closed the door and turned the key. Virginia heard her footsteps fade away.

This room was also ornately decorated. The bed occupied the center of the carpet, like a throne, and around it were chairs covered in deep red velvet and tables inlaid with fine woods. The one window looked out over a ravine. She stared out for a while, estimating her chances of escaping by that route. There was no way she could reach ground without risking injury. The woods as far as she could see were unbroken. Like Amos's inn, this place was isolated.

Overcome by despair, she threw herself on the bed and wept. Until this moment she had retained some faith in her future. Now all that was gone. She had said it herself, when she spoke to Bessie. Her friends would have no reason to believe she had lived through the plague, since her parents were both dead. Neither would her uncle have reason to expect to find her alive. If Anthony had not survived the attack, her last hope for help was gone.

Was Bessie right? Virginia had not been able to tell just how severe Anthony's injuries were. She had seen blood spilling from his shoulder. Had he been hit anywhere else? Had there been more than one shot? She could not be certain. She had been too upset to notice.

If Anthony was alive, she had some faint hope that she might eventually be saved. He had to be able to search for her. But he also had to *want* to find her.

Her tears increased. There were too many ifs: if he were alive . . . if he believed her . . . For had he not said he knew that Roy Salford's niece was a child? Whether he believed her claim to be Virginia Nelson or not, he still might search for her if he cared for her, if he felt the emotions she had felt as they lay together, if her presence in his dream as well as his bed had meant something to him.

She dared not pursue her thoughts any further. Just hidden below her consciousness was the awareness that she wanted him to live, even if he never came to her rescue. His life was dear to her for itself. She knew in her innermost heart that she had found the man she could love for the rest of her life.

Five

The door opened slowly. Virginia rose from the bed and moved to the window. She had no illusions regarding her whereabouts. She was in a brothel. If any attempt were made to force her to do what the other girls did, she was prepared to leap to her death.

A black face appeared around the door. The obviously very young girl was carrying a tray of food. She glanced up at Virginia but said nothing. Silently she put the tray on a small table, then disappeared, locking the door behind her.

The rich fragrance of roast beef stirred Virginia's appetite. She could see that the food was the best, possibly the same that was served to patrons of the brothel. She ate slowly, relishing every bite, aware that this might possibly be the only entertainment she would have.

The black girl came back shortly after she had finished eating. As she moved toward the door, Virginia stepped in front of her. "Please, don't go without talking to me. What's to happen? Why am I not set free?" She gathered her courage. "Do you know when David Cavanaugh is coming?"

The girl shook her head.

"Won't you say something? Please!"

With a swift step to the left, the girl moved around her, opened the door, and was gone. The key turned again in the lock. Virginia cried out in frustration, but there was no response.

There were no other visitors for the remainder of the day. Though Virginia was thankful that she was left alone, she still longed for someone to talk to, for someone who would answer her questions. She fell asleep at last on top of the bed, without removing her dress.

She woke suddenly, aware that the door was once more being unlocked. This time, she was determined to

54

get her answers. But when the food was placed on the table, she decided to wait until she had eaten.

As it had been the night before, everything she was served was fresh and delicious. Eggs, juicy sausage, potatoes, fresh-baked dark bread, and a steaming cup of tea. When Virginia swallowed the last bite, she prepared to confront her jailor.

The girl did not return alone. A black man with one game leg stepped into the room behind her, removed the chamber pot from under the bed, and stood at the door until his companion was out in the hallway. The change in routine was so unexpected to Virginia that she had no time to recover her thoughts. By the time she moved, she was alone again.

When the evening meal arrived, she had devised a different approach. As soon as the servant put down the dishes, she caught her wrist. "You must speak to me! I won't let you go until you do."

The girl's eyes grew wide with fear. She pulled back abruptly and then, with a twist of her arm, broke free. She was out of the room before Virginia could pursue her.

Discouraged and confused, Virginia sat down to eat. Why was the girl so frightened? Why wouldn't she speak? She had acted like a wild animal, afraid of being trapped.

There was a noise at the door. Virginia rose, prepared to face once more her servant-jailor. But this time the black girl was accompanied by a tall young woman, dressed in finery only a little less ornate than that worn by Miss Bessie. Her hair was a deep brown, hanging in fat ringlets around her head. Her eyes were dark and wide apart, and they were half-closed in anger.

"What right have you to frighten Clarabelle? Just who do you think you are?"

Virginia recoiled from the fierceness of the anger. "Why, I don't know what you're talking about. I haven't done anything to frighten the fool! All I have asked for is an answer to a few questions. She has refused to speak."

"Did it occur to you that she might be dumb?" Virginia's eyes widened in surprise. "Yes, dumb! The poor child is deaf. So far as we can tell, she had her ears boxed severely when she was a child, and it destroyed her hearing. She never learned to speak very well, and Miss Bessie does not want her grunting and making the strange sounds she thinks are decent words. So she says nothing. You have distressed her."

"Oh!" Virginia was overcome with shame. "I'm sorry! I didn't understand." She realized that the woman was turning to leave. "Please, don't go yet. I must know what's going to happen to me."

"I don't know that." The newcomer did not pause on her way to the door. "You'll have to speak to Bessie. But, please, don't frighten Clarabelle again. It's cruel."

"But you are all being cruel to me!" Virginia ran to the door. It was too late. Clarabelle and her protectress were gone. Virginia could not force the food down her throat. When Clarabelle returned to remove the plate, only a few bites had been eaten.

Clarabelle did not return that evening, nor did she appear with the morning meal the next day. Virginia paced the floor, aware that she was growing increasingly hungry. She thought longingly of the dish she had left untouched and wished fervently that she had not let her distress interfere with her appetite. What if no one ever came to the room again? What if she were kept a prisoner until she died of starvation?

Her frightened reflections were interrupted late in the afternoon. The key turned, and Clarabelle slipped into the room. The tray she carried was filled with food. She placed it on a table and hurried out without even glancing at Virginia.

Every morsel tasted delicious to the starving girl. She ate slowly, forcing herself to consider the burden she was placing on her empty stomach. And when she was through, she sat back and stared at the windows. She had once decided there was no escape. Now she had to try again.

She began by removing the sheets and the quilts from the bed. After pushing open the window, she saw that she would need to tie many pieces together in order to reach the ground. Drawing the quilt back inside, she began her chore.

It was not easy to tear the sheets for they were still very new, but she finally found a sharp edge on a metal clip that protected the edge of the wardrobe. With it, she cut the cloth at one edge. She tore wide strips to be certain that her makeshift rope would hold her weight, then she tied the strips together with firm knots. She remembered the pleasant days she had spent sitting on a rough board at the wharf, as her friends, the sailors who used the harbor, taught her the best knots for strength. Those had been such happy times, so free of trouble. Mr. Willing had seemed to enjoy her presence near his warehouse, and his own children had been her playmates.

Would she ever be happy again?

She pushed the question aside. This was no time to worry about the future. Her present was too fraught with danger.

She saw the empty plate and leaped to her feet. What if Clarabelle returned and alerted Bessie. Virginia glanced quickly about the room. Strips of sheet lay everywhere. Frantically, she gathered them up and stuffed them into a drawer of the chiffonier. Then she took the quilt, which she had found too strong to tear, and spread it back over the bed. Perhaps Clarabelle would not notice any change.

She had barely finished her cleanup when the key was turned, and Clarabelle entered. Virginia seated herself close to the table where her empty plate rested, and she remained still while Clarabelle completed her chores. The chamber pot had to be emptied. The pitcher of clear water refilled. And then, at last, the empty dish removed.

Virginia hardly dared to breathe when Clarabelle reached under the bed for the chamber pot. Would she notice the sheets were missing? She breathed again only when Clarabelle locked the door behind her. If this day were to follow the pattern set by the one preceding, there would be no more visitors.

Nevertheless, Virginia waited now until dusk. It would be dangerous enough when she slid over the sill and clambered down the sheet-rope. She wanted no other complications. Darkness would at least keep her from being seen by some guard watching from the road or from some unknown lookout post.

Darkness would also increase the danger from wild animals. She was not certain whether bears might not still roam the woods that edged the road. This inn, if it was the one she remembered from her childhood, was miles from civilization.

She shivered, and then deliberately forced the fear back. She had to take the risk. There was no alternative.

She checked the knots she had made earlier in the day. Each was firm and secure. The strips of sheet seemed strong enough to bear her weight. As she fed the length over the windowsill, she uttered a prayer. This had to work. She had to free herself.

And when she was free once more . . . would she dare to return to the city? She wasn't certain. Her father had assumed that a rain would clear away the plague. But had that, in fact, occurred? She thought of Anthony, lying crumpled on the road, and she knew that she would not first seek her own safety. She would search for Anthony in Philadelphia, then along the road going west, where he had been injured. She prayed that she would not have to go in that direction, for if he had not reached the city, she felt certain he would be dead.

Before she lowered the last three lengths, she tied the end to the leg of the bed. The sheet-rope stretched across the room, but she was reasonably sure that it was still long enough to reach the ground. If not, she might have to let herself drop the last few feet. It was not a pleasant prospect, since she was not sure of the ground below her, but she would have to try.

She pulled a chair close to the window and climbed through the opening. The sheet felt rough in her hands, and her weight was more than she had expected. Her grip was not tight, and she slid part of the way, burning the palms of her hands on the material. When she reached the first knot she stopped, clinging to the rope with her knees, and considered her predicament. Her hands were sore already, and she still had a good distance to go. Could she make it? Or would she fall to her death in the ravine below?

A new resolution gave her courage. If she gave up, then all hope that Anthony was alive would also be gone, for she would never have the chance to search for him. She dared not abandon the effort just because her hands were hurting!

Timidly, she let herself move down onto the next length. As she lowered herself, she knew she had no alternative. She did not have the strength to pull herself up. She must continue her descent, or she would have to hang helplessly until she fell or was discovered by someone in the brothel.

Ignoring her sore palms, she worked her way slowly downward. She counted the knots as she passed them. The first had been strong enough to save her from falling when her hands slipped. The others served as mileposts.

She had noticed before she began to move down that there were no windows directly below hers, but there were others close by, and she had no idea who might be in the rooms to which they opened. Another problem inhibited her movement. She dared not bounce against the wall, for fear the noise that she would make might rouse someone within. Even the rubbing of her clothing against the wood of the building might serve to alert someone.

She rested often. At one point, she hung close to a window, hearing movement inside the room. Footsteps advanced toward the casement, and she held her breath. Would she be caught after all this effort? She heard her heart beating, and she wondered if the sound was loud enough to cause whoever was inside to look out.

An arm pushed the casement open, and a feminine voice spoke close to the opening. "There! Is that better? We can't be heard here, you know, squire. Bessie knows the room you like."

The arm pulled back in, and the footsteps retreated. Virginia once more resumed her descent.

Her feet were still dangling when she reached the end of the rope, and she glanced down. The ground was only a foot below her. And it was level! She released her hold and landed lightly on the soft grass.

She dared not go to the road, for there she would easily be caught, but she needed to follow it so that she would recognize her route. Silently, she circled the inn and its stables, crouching when she saw someone approach the fence or turn in her direction. Voices wafted to her on the evening breeze, bits of words and phrases that were meaningless, but somehow they both comforted and alarmed her. There were so many people around the inn. Surely some of them might be friends, willing to help her.

She paused and considered seeking assistance. Then she remembered the gentleman who had advised Amos to beat her into submission, and she knew she dared not risk approaching even the most dignified guests. They would assume she was just a slut who refused to accept her place, or who was fleeing from some deserved punishment. And they would return her to Bessie.

Without a backward glance, she turned and skirted the road, moving parallel to it, yet far enough into the woods to maintain her cover. Now she began to feel the pain in her hands. Her arms ached from the effort she had exerted as she climbed down the rope. Even her legs were sore, but she dared not give in to her discomfort. This, she felt certain, was her only chance. If she did not reach safety, she would be lost for good.

Her spirits rose as she widened the distance between her and the inn. The branches of the bushes and trees she passed tore at her gown, but she did not care. She was free! And she would certainly find that Anthony had survived his injury.

Finally, she paused to rest. A thick bush served as her shelter, and leaves that had fallen in past years provided her with a cushion. Gradually she began to relax until, at last, she dropped into a deep sleep.

She woke with a start, aware of sounds nearby. A voice from the road seemed almost at her ear. "Dammit, Ben! Look again. She can't have gone far!"

She crouched back, afraid even to breathe. In the dim morning light, she could see that her shelter was far from perfect. Yet, if they did not expect to find her resting, they might pass her by.

Feet shuffled through the underbrush, pushing up leaves that had dried from last summer's growth. The men were obviously searching with little enthusiasm, for they hit at the bushes as they passed but did not seem to glance down. A pair of legs brushed past her place of concealment, and she prayed they would not stop or turn toward her. When they moved on, she exhaled in relief. Was she safe at last?

The voice from the road broke into her thoughts. "Try the other side. Hurry! If you can't find her, I'll have to get the dogs."

Virginia felt her courage drain away. Dogs! She had once seen a manhunt led by dogs when she visited a friend in Carolina. It had been terrible, even to an onlooker. The dogs had moved unerringly toward the culprit, following not his footsteps, but his scent. And when they finally located him, cowering in some bushes, they had come close to tearing him apart before they were called off.

The sounds of the search moved away, but she dared not depart. What if they saw her move? She would be carried back. And would she, then, be forced to join the other girls? Would she be assigned a customer and made to accommodate his desires?

No, she had to continue her flight to safety. No one seemed to hear her as she slowly crept forward, for they were all too busy and noisy themselves. She hurried on, until she passed over the crest of a hill.

If they planned to use dogs, speed was her only hope. Resolutely, she stepped onto the road. There had once been a carriage stop and another inn on the other side of the road from the Freedom's Arms. If it were still there . . . She began to run.

Then she heard the dogs. Frantic, she pushed herself to the limits of her strength. All that mattered was that she outrun her pursuers. She was panting, gasping for breath, when she saw the beasts on the rise behind her. She was beyond considering surrender. She had to fight for her freedom to the bitter end.

She quickened her pace, almost flying over the rough ground. At first she was moving downhill, and gravity assisted her in her race. But when she reached the bottom of the next hill, she lost her advantage.

Halfway up the hill, she twisted her ankle and fell. She lay helpless, watching the dogs advance upon her.

Six

"Brute! Hercules! Nero! Off! Stay off!" The shout stopped the dogs before they touched Virginia, but they remained close, blocking her from any chance of escape. They growled, baring their teeth and slobbering in their eagerness to bite into their target. Virginia stared at the sharp teeth and the curled lips. Her life was over.

When she opened her eyes, the dogs were leashed, and though they tugged at their restraints, they could not reach her. Ben towered above her. He tossed her over his shoulder and carried her like a sack of flour, back into captivity.

Clarabelle arrived with a tray of food shortly after Virginia was returned to her room. She moved silently about, not daring to meet Virginia's eyes.

Virginia stared at the bed. The torn sheets had been removed from the room and clean sheets spread on the bed. The window was closed but not nailed shut. The realization that her escape route was still open cheered her. She vowed she would try again as soon as she had the opportunity. But to succeed, she would need her strength.

She ate slowly, relishing each bite, thankful that she was not being starved as punishment for her attempt to run away. When the last bite was gone, she rose and returned to the window. Now that she knew what lay below, the drop into the ravine held no terror.

The key turned in the lock, and the girl who had defended Clarabelle entered. On her arm, she carried a clean, simple dress, much like those worn by farm women. "My name is Geraldine." She held out the dress. "Quick. Take off that torn thing and put this on."

Virginia made no move to take the dress.

"Do as I say! Do you want me to call Bessie?"

Virginia sighed and obediently did as she was told. There was no harm that she could see in ridding herself of the gown she had torn in the brambles.

When she had closed the buttons, Geraldine held out a brush. "Here—comb your hair." Virginia did not need a second urging. She had tried without much success to pull the pine needles from her hair with her fingers.

Geraldine locked the door when she left, but Virginia's spirits remained high. They could not keep her, she knew that now. She would succeed in her attempt to free herself or she would die. But she would not allow herself to be turned into a woman of convenience.

Then she gasped in alarm. Was it possible that Geraldine had helped her clean up so she would be ready for a "client"? Was that to be her punishment, that she be required to take a strange man into her bed?

She pulled the window open. If that was to be her fate, she would leap through the casement to her death. David would not have his will with her!

At that moment, Bessie pushed the door back and stood officiously viewing the room, as if to make certain all was in order. Virginia readied herself for the leap. And then a man entered. David! He ran across the room and pulled her into his arms. "Oh, thank God! My darling, I have been so worried about you!"

She accepted his embrace without responding.

He held her at arm's length, and gazed into her eyes. "Virginia, what's the matter? Why are you so quiet?" His eyes lit. "Has Bessie harmed you?" He turned to the other woman. "If you have forced her to join your girls . . . !" He did not finish his sentence, but his expression told the story.

Virginia stared at him in total confusion. She had expected him to want her to join Bessie's women! She had been told that he served as a recruiter for the brothels. Why was he rushing to defend her honor?

He pulled her close once more. "Oh, my love! I've worried so. Amos tells me you ran away from the inn. Why? Didn't you know everything I did was to protect you?"

She felt his strength, and her confusion grew. These were not the words of an outraged man who had almost lost one of his whores. These were love sounds, the voice of concern and affection. Why had she allowed herself to doubt him?

For the first time since his arrival, she began to relax. "Oh, David, I've been so frightened! Amos looked at me—"

"Damn him! His face would frighten the bravest woman. He should have left you alone."

"I tried to go back to Philadelphia. Oh, David, now that the rains have come, the plague is over, isn't it? I saw my uncle on the road to the city. I wanted to go to him."

"Your uncle? In the city? Oh, no, my dear, you must be mistaken. The city is still occupied only by the sick and the dying. If it was your uncle you saw, then he must have been headed elsewhere. To Charlottesville, maybe? I hear Mr. Jefferson is building a house there and is already prepared to receive guests."

What was it Anthony had said? Virginia searched her memory, but she could not remember his words clearly. He had acknowledged that it was Roy Salford in the carriage. He had said he was on his way to Philadelphia to visit his sister. But had he made it clear that the plague was over?

And what if David were right? Then Roy would have gone on, possibly inland to Charlottesville, as David suggested. But what had become of Anthony? "David, I was so frightened. Amos . . . Ben . . . this terrible place. . . ." Her words spilled out in a jumble, confused, barely understandable.

He closed her lips with his. When she was silent, he stepped back and once more gazed into her eyes. "I've been hunting all over for you. What happened? How did you come here?"

"I—" She hesitated. Suddenly, she had no wish to speak of her journey with Anthony. She had to clear her head first, had to decide which of these men she truly wanted. "Amos Durwood had me brought here. I was afraid that you were—" She could not continue.

"Afraid of me? Oh, my love! How could you be? Did I not show you how much I loved you?"

She nodded. "Yes." She barely whispered the word. "But . . . I didn't know. The old woman said—"

"What did she say?"

Virginia shook herself. "I cannot repeat it. Oh, David, forgive me. I was a fool to believe a foolish old hag." She was suddenly frightened that he would cast her aside because of her lack of faith. "I thought Bessie was going to—"

David turned to Bessie. "Is that what you had in mind?

You know you are to leave my women alone. This girl is mine!"

Bessie sputtered, and stared back at David with an outraged expression. "How dare you accuse me of such a thing? Have I ever gone against your wishes? Have I not, from the very first time we met, been honest with you? This child of yours is upset. She suffered from an excess of imagination. And no wonder. You told me yourself that she buried her parents only a week ago. You said she was exhausted from nursing them, and that was why you feared for her safety. That was why you thought she ran away. Why blame her madness on me?"

Bessie could see that she had David at a disadvantage. She continued without a pause. "Consider what the child must feel. You left her alone. And then Amos, the beast, frightened her, as you should have known he would. Can you blame her if she panics and tries to run away? And as for her fancies that I planned to put her to work—David! You know me too well to think that is true."

David turned back to Virginia. "Who brought you here?"

"Ben. He caught me when I tried to go back home, and Amos had him bring me here." She tugged at David's sleeve. "Please! Take me away from this place."

He seemed not to hear her. He was once more looking at Bessie. "Why did you put her in this room? Isn't it one you usually have occupied with one of your women?"

"We lost a girl a month ago, so the room was empty. But if you are suggesting that I intended to make use of her, you are mistaken. If I recall what happened the day she arrived, Ben came late in the day, unexpectedly, and he carried none of the instructions that you usually send along. We were very busy here, and I had no time to check on him. I believe it was Geraldine who brought her to a room. I doubt not that she thought I had received your messages."

David frowned at Geraldine when Bessie spoke her name, but he made no move of anger in her direction. Bessie's words seemed to assure him that none of her girls were at fault in the matter. He scratched the back of his head. "You know women far better than I, Bessie. If you say Virginia has broken under the strain of being alone, I must believe you. But what can I do to avoid more such imaginings in the future? I cannot take her with me yet. I have many duties I must tend to alone."

"Oh, leave her here. I'm sure there will be no reoccurrence of her trouble. For one thing, I will give her more freedom. Now that she is no longer afraid, she need not be locked in her room."

"Aye, but there's a difficulty." He glanced toward Virginia, and when he saw that she was listening, he lowered his voice. "She is still in great danger. I was told by Amos that she believes the plague is over, that it is safe to enter the city. Some man assisted her in her attempted escape. Now, whether he tasted of her honey or not, I have no reason to believe he lied to me about that. Fortunately, the man was killed when she was rescued and brought back to the inn. But I understand he had accomplices. I tell you, she is in danger. I know not why, but there are men who would steal her from me and do her harm." He looked again at Virginia. She had heard clearly only the things he had wanted her to hear. He turned again to Bessie. "You must understand something about Virginia Nelson. She is not like any other woman I have had. She is a lady. And she is my woman." He took Bessie's arm and moved away. "I must keep her hidden for another two weeks or so. I wish to set the scene for her 'rescue.' In due time, I will 'discover' her here and restore her to her uncle. There will then be no question of my worth as a suitor. I tell you, Bessie, she is a find. With her family associations, I will be able to open doors closed to us before. I will have access to shipping information, both by land and sea, that has been till now unavailable." He smiled. "Ah, we will all be wealthy beyond your wildest dreams."

He glanced quickly at Virginia. She sat where he had left her, her face buried in her hands. Either she was weeping or she was in a faint. Still, he must now make certain that she did not overhear his last discussion with Bessie. He touched her cheek lightly with his fingers. "Virginia, my darling, what troubles you?"

Virginia feared the question, yet she had to know for certain. "You said the man who assisted me when I tried to escape is dead?"

"My sweet! You are far too concerned for others." He turned to Bessie. "How gentle she is. The picture of thoughtfulness!" He bent over Virginia. "Why do you worry about him?"

"I—it was my fault he took me out. He did not want to do it, but I insisted. I assure you, he was not trying to abduct me."

David scowled. "You waste too much concern on the rogue. Let me tell you the truth, for I can see he did much to confuse you. The city is still infested with the plague. And if you did see your uncle—which may not even be true, for how easy is it to recognize a man sitting inside a carriage—then he was on his way elsewhere. But did you speak to your uncle? Are you certain it was he you saw?"

Virginia hesitated. Was she certain? Until that moment, she had not doubted that it had been Uncle Roy.

David continued. "My sweet, I locked your door to protect you from the rough men who frequent the inn. As for your being locked in *this* room, why, that is a mistake that will be remedied." He took her hands in his. "My dear, you must face the truth. I know not what his reasons were, but the man who befriended you on the road had some evil reason for his action. You can be thankful you were saved from him in time." He held her eyes with his. "You were rescued in time, were you not?"

Virginia tried to hold her eyes steady. Suddenly, she did not want anyone to know what had happened between her and Anthony that night in the woods. She no longer was sure it was something for which she could be happy.

The thought that Anthony was dead overwhelmed her. Ben had lied to her when he said he was not sure what had happened to her champion. She threw her arms around David's shoulders and buried her face in his shirt. "Oh, David, I feel so terrible. I have brought harm to innocent people because I was afraid—just because I believed an old woman. Mr. Burke died because he tried to help me. I didn't know it, but I did not tell him the truth about what had happened to me. I am sure he was sincere. He was kind to me, and I was so frightened. I didn't know when you'd return."

"Oh, my sweet!" David drew her close. Over her shoulder, he winked slyly at Bessie. "How frightening for you all this has been. I only pray that you will forgive me for my part in making you so unhappy. You can see now that the locked door was for your protection, though obviously, I can understand how you might have misinterpreted my intentions. You must see now that even though I did not order Amos to send men after you when you ran away, I would have done so had I been there. I am thankful that Amos saved you from reentering that death city." He released her and gazed into her eyes. "This man Burke was not to be trusted. Can you see that now? Who knows what terrible fate he had planned for you? There are men who steal women to put them into slavery. I thank God you are safe again!"

Had she misjudged him so badly? She pressed against him once more. "Oh, David, please don't leave me again."

He stepped back, his face solemn. "I must go, my dear. You will be safe here with Bessie. I must find any accomplices your abductor might have had, for as long as any of them are alive, you are in danger. Trust me. As soon as life is possible in the city, I will return you to Philadelphia and to your uncle, when he arrives. Be patient, my sweet. Remember that I love you and want you for my own."

She met his eyes, and for the first time in over a week she felt truly safe. How could she have misunderstood him? And Anthony? Difficult as it was, she would have to admit that he had acted strangely. Obviously, he had pretended not to believe her so that she would insist on going with him. How deceitful was his story about her uncle!

But why would anyone try to abduct her? For money? Her parents had not, so far as she knew, been overly wealthy, though they lacked for nothing and lived well.

David seemed to understand her confusion. He took her by the shoulders. "You are wondering why Burke would abduct you, are you not? Well, consider this. There is great unrest in parts of the state over taxes. Would it not be possible that some of the leaders of the revolt might want to keep you prisoner so as to force your uncle to do their will? They might have planned their attempt before the plague, to use it against your father. But it still would be effective. Your uncle, I am certain, values your life all the more because your parents are gone." He bent and kissed her on the lips. "You are safe now, I promise you."

"Take me with you. I fear what Bessie might do to me if I stay here without you to protect me."

"Please, my love, enough of your imaginings. You are very distraught. Can you not see such fears are only caused by your loneliness and the recent death of your parents? Bessie has worked with me for many years, and though you might not approve of what she does, the girls are happy here, and they have no other place to go. I let her—and them—stay as a kindness. She will take good care of you, for she knows how much she owes me."

"But"—she clutched at his sleeve—"I—" His lips closed over hers, and he held her close. Then, suddenly, he was gone. She stood swaying, too startled to move. Moments later the sound of his horse's hoofs thudded on the hard-packed dirt, and then she heard them no longer. Overcome with dismay, she dropped into a chair.

Bessie stood above her. "Now! You would have caused me much trouble had you succeeded in making your escape." She was furious, and Virginia wondered if she was going to be beaten. But Bessie restrained her anger. "Cavanaugh will be gone for a fortnight. In that time, my fancy creature, you will work to pay me for the cost of the sheets you destroyed."

Virginia felt her anger rise. "David said you would take good care of me. You cannot be trusted. I will tell him—"

Bessie slapped her viciously. "You will tell him nothing. I'll have you killed if you dare to say a word. Remember that, my sweetie. I may spend my time here, but I have long arms. I will reach you, no matter where you try to hide. No matter who serves as your protector." She turned toward the hall and shouted. "Gregory! Come here this instant!"

A broad-shouldered man appeared in the doorway. He wore a loose shirt and a pair of fitting, rough brown breeches. Over them both, he wore a large, dirty apron. His voice was deep, and heavy with an accent. "Yes, ma'am?"

"Here!" Bessie threw Virginia into his arms. "Take this tart and put her to work!"

"Aye, mistress." He caught Virginia's arm and began to move toward the steps.

"Wait!" Bessie held up one hand. "Geraldine, do what you can to change the bitch's looks. Tie her hair back, put some paint on her cheeks and lips. I want no rumors reaching Cavanaugh that I have put his doxy to work."

Geraldine approached Virginia. Gregory had to keep a tight grip on his captive, for she fought any ministrations by the girl who had seemed to be a friend. When Virginia's face was painted and her hair pulled up into a tight bun, Geraldine stepped back. "Is she all right now, Bessie?"

Bessie smiled. "Excellent! Aye, Geraldine, you have a knack. 'Tis no wonder you are so valuable to me." She turned to Gregory. "Take her now. She will sleep in the storeroom. I'll send Henry down with a mattress. Watch her carefully. She must not be allowed to escape, nor to speak too long with any of the patrons."

"Aye, ma'am." Gregory half-bowed and pulled Virginia behind him down the stairs.

She had to go quickly, for she was in danger of losing her footing on the steps. But this was not what David had ordered for her when he left. She took comfort in the realization that David would return, and there would be an accounting. I'm not afraid of Bessie! Virginia thought furiously. I'll tell him, no matter how much she threatens me.

She listened in silence to Gregory as he explained her duties. Life would not be easy, for there was much work put on her shoulders. But she would endure, and she would not try to get away. She would wait for David to come back.

The memory of Anthony's handsome face disturbed her still. She was responsible for his death. Yet he had deceived her. Would she ever be able to judge a man correctly? She wondered if she could ever forget that for a few brief moments she had thought that she loved him.

Seven

Virginia silently watched the foaming ale pour from the barrel into the mugs. When the last was filled, she lifted the tray in one hand and moved through the crowded room. She approached a table where three men sat talking. They barely glanced at her as she put the drinks before them. Then one man drew out some coins and dropped them into her hand. "Begone, now. We have much to discuss—in private."

"Yes, sir." She curtseyed but lingered nearby. Had she ever seen any of them in her father's house? Had they been guests at the President's ball? She could not remember. It had been her first official function, and she had been far too excited to notice anyone but those young men who had danced with her.

She could not ignore the fact that these men appeared to be headed for Philadelphia, that they acted like statesmen, and that they were not the first to return to the city. Undeniably, the plague was over. David had lied to her when he insisted that the city was still unsafe.

Had he lied to her in other matters as well? She could not say. In the week that had passed since his departure, she had grown restless, and suspicious. She longed to find her father's friend, Thomas Willing, whom she felt certain she could trust. And she wondered if, as Anthony had said, she would find her uncle at her home in the city.

If Roy Salford was now at her home, then everything Anthony had told her was probably true. She could not yet confront the memory of Anthony without much turmoil and pain. The memory of his face, the manly smell of his body as he lay beside her, his presence, his kiss, his caress —all these stirred her deeply.

But the memories also confused her. Which of the two men did she truly love: David, who now seemed kinder than ever, but whose association with Bessie and Amos per-

74

turbed her; or Anthony, who, for all she knew, might have died on the road?

The man who had paid for the ale looked up. "Well, girl? Is there something you wish to say to us?"

"Yes, if you please, sir. The plague—are its ravages ended?"

"What a strange question! Of course, they are. Were you not aware of last week's storm? It put an end to the danger and cleansed the city of the filth that had accumulated during the worst of the pestilence. Yes, my young friend, the trial is over. The scars are healing in the city and in the earth that surrounds it. Graves left open have been closed. Houses abandoned by fleeing citizens have been secured and guarded, waiting for the arrival of owners—or relatives, if the owners are victims of the terror. Congress is meeting again. The president himself is due to return in less than three days."

Virginia curtseyed. "Thank you, sir. I trust I have not disturbed you."

"Ginia!" Gregory's voice boomed over the noise of the tavern, and Virginia jumped. "Move, lass, or I'll get you going with my boot!"

With a muttered "thank you," Virginia scurried away. She had felt Gregory's boot far too often in the six days she had worked in the tavern to doubt that he meant what he said.

She was careful for the remainder of the night to give the burly man no additional cause for anger. She moved swiftly, taking orders and delivering beverages and food to the guests. She smiled brightly at the men who sat at the tables, but few returned the greeting. Some did notice her comely face, and others patted her bottom as she passed. She ignored such liberties, for she knew they were common in taverns, yet she found them upsetting. Though the men touched her and often whispered ribald suggestions in her ear, they did not actually look at her or notice her response.

She suspected that in some other tavern, not so closely allied with a brothel, she might have been approached by the patrons. But at the Freedom's Arms, everyone knew that such accommodations were provided by girls procured for the purpose. For that, Virginia was thankful.

During the first days of her labors, Virginia had not been

concerned when the men ignored her. Now, suddenly, things
were different. If Philadelphia was healthy, if her uncle was
possibly in town searching for her, then it behooved her to
do what she could to free herself. And to do that, she felt
she needed the assistance of one of the many official guests
who passed through on their way to the city.

She glanced often at the three men who had been so
friendly. Maybe the one who had answered her questions
would also see to her release. She dared not approach him
until he called for more ale, and when he left without
finishing the glass she had served, she desperately inter-
cepted the three at the door.

The one who had spoken to her before smiled when she
curtseyed. "What interest have you in Philadelphia, miss?
Are you worried for the fate of your family?"

"No, sir. I know my mother and father are dead from
the illness. But I have an uncle, Roy—"

Gregory stepped between them. He said nothing to Virginia, but his look told her he would deal with her later. He
bowed slightly to the three departing guests. "My apologies,
sirs. The girl is not right in her head. She has strange ideas
about herself. Would you believe that she had never been
out of sight of this inn, yet she is convinced that she has
parents who died in the plague?"

"She is your daughter?"

"Nay, not mine, but the daughter of one of our girls.
Mayhap she feels unhappy because she cannot know her
father. May be that she has tainted blood and will always
show such weakness of the mind. Yet, she is a good girl in
all and carries on her duties with reasonable obedience."

"My sympathies. She is a lovely child. It always seems to
me such a shame when such a one is born without all her
faculties."

"Aye, 'tis a shame. But who are we to question the will
of God?"

Virginia heard the exchange, and in spite of her reserve,
tears came to her eyes. No one would ever believe her if
Gregory circulated such stories. She realized that the friendly man was smiling at her with open sympathy, and she
turned away. Gregory would beat her later, of that she was
certain, but the pain of his blows would not be half as
hard to bear as was the glance of her would-be benefactor.

She could see now that there had been many indications that things had returned to normal in the city, not the least of which was the steady flow of patrons from the north. It had been on the second day of her change in status when officials had arrived to inform Gregory that all bans designed to limit the gathering of many people were removed. The common room could again be utilized to full capacity.

One other circumstance revealed that the situation in Philadelphia had changed. People spoke with humor and optimism. There was laughter and singing again. And the fear that had surrounded residents of Philadelphia and the surrounding areas was gone.

When the last patron departed shortly before dawn, Virginia ran quickly to the storeroom which served as her bedchamber. She had watched Gregory carefully, and she realized that he had forgotten his promise to whip her. She prayed he would not remember later, for more than once he had roused her from her sleep to punish her.

As was her custom, she pushed a large barrel against the door. It would not serve to bar Gregory from entering, but it would at least warn her of his coming. Then she climbed onto her cot, hung her slippers on a post where they would be safe from cockroaches, and crawled under the covers. She did not remove her dress. It would provide some protection if Gregory did arrive to give her a whipping.

She stared at the pattern of light that shone on the ceiling through the cracks in the wall. The faint cry of a meadowlark told her the day had truly begun. Yet, tired as she was, she could not sleep. Her mind picked through the information she had received during the night, and she could not rest, even though her body was aching from the hours of lifting heavy trays.

She knew now that she could never trust David again. He had lied to her about the plague. Had he also lied to her about Anthony? A faint stir of hope lightened the weight in her breast. Neither Ben nor Amos had been able to tell her for certain that Anthony Burke had died in the ambush. Why had she accepted David's assertion that Anthony was dead without questioning the source of his information?

Had Amos and Ben both lied to David? For the first time, she recognized that possibility. She had been too despairing, too sick at the thought that Anthony was dead, to think clearly.

She was thinking clearly now. She knew she dared not wait for David to return. It was he who could not be trusted. "I must escape before he comes back. I dare not risk remaining any longer." She closed her eyes. Tomorrow maybe there would be a chance.

Her escape would depend on opportunity, not design. But she would be ready. When an occasion presented itself, she would be on her way to Philadelphia—and to freedom. Never before in her entire life had the word held such meaning.

Eight

The tavern was crowded, the atmosphere charged with excitement. These were not the ordinary patrons of the Arms. There were no wigged heads, no gentlemen in fine silks. The majority of the men were rough farmers, their hands callused and knotted from labor, their faces, even in the yellow light of the lanterns, ruddy from long exposure to the sun.

They milled about, their voices filled with anger. She caught phrases spoken in undertones: "Damn Washington!" "Damn Hamilton!" "Have we fought for our freedom from oppression by King George only to fall under the heel of another tyrant?"

A tall man with broad shoulders rose and leaped onto a table. He extended his arms. "Friends! Please! We can decide nothing if all we do is complain. Let us talk together and seek solutions to our difficulties."

Virginia backed toward the wall to avoid the rush of men. Once they were seated, she moved silently, so as not to interrupt the speaker, taking orders for ale and food.

"For those of you who do not live in this part of the country, I am Daniel Mason, proprietor of the Golden Ass. I think we can agree that this problem is shared by us all, both farmers and dealers. We have suffered in the last months from a blight far more deadly to our way of life than the plague that so nearly destroyed the great city of Philadelphia. Do you agree?"

A shout rose that echoed through the great room.

Daniel waited until silence again prevailed. "Aye, we have suffered a double blow. We have not yet recovered from the trials of the great war for freedom. Our sons and our brothers have shed their blood for the establishment of this great free land. We have ourselves fought for liberty and for the pursuit of happiness. We revolted against the levying of taxes that denied us the chance to live in freedom and prosperity. Tell me, what was it that served as the rallying point in our fight against the redcoats?"

The men answered as one. "Taxes! We rejected taxes without representation!"

"Aye!" Daniel's voice rose higher. "Taxes! And what is it we now seek, as citizens of free states?"

"Freedom from taxes!" The roar filled the tavern.

Virginia glanced about her. A man far across the room beckoned her, and she moved swiftly to his side. "Ale, and roast beef." He spoke sharply. "I've not eaten since morning!"

She curtseyed and scurried to the kitchen. When she returned with the food, a different speaker stood on the makeshift platform. He was not as tall as the first, and he had a belly that protruded far over his breeches. Virginia studied his face intently. Had she seen him before? She wasn't certain. Those who spoke were lost in the shadows cast by lanterns that flickered with each movement of the crowd.

Their words, however, were not lost. They spoke in anger of rights denied. They cursed leaders of the country who tried to take control from the states and put it in a central federal government.

The speaker droned on, and although Virginia lost interest, the men seemed eager to hear everything. ". . . and what has the whiskey tax done for us?" He raised his voice and glanced about the room. "I see you can find no good in it at all." He smiled. "Well, my friends, neither can I. We are being taxed by the federal government so it can become a monster that will steal all rights from our states. We are forced to pay for the right to do these things which even King George allowed us!"

There was an angry murmur, and he paused until it abated. "The men who propose to build a strong central government are not our friends. They care not for liberty. We must not permit them to turn the land we fought to free into another monarchy. I have heard a rumor that Washington has secretly ordered a crown from a goldsmith in England. Do not be surprised if one day he declares himself king."

"Nonsense!" The man who spoke rose from his seat. He ignored the tugs of his companions who tried to pull him down. "The Federalists do not threaten our freedom. They act to protect it. How can we defend our shores against invasion by Britain if we have no navy? How can we keep the armies of the redcoats from our farmland if we have no federal force to guard the borders? Will the state militia defend us? No! There are not men enough who will rally to a call to fight aggression aimed at some distant neighbor."

Cries of "Sit!" "Throw him out!" "Enough!" interrupted his speech, but he waited patiently until quiet was at last restored.

He spoke then, softly, so the men had to lean forward to hear. "I tell you, friends, what is being said here is treason. What proof exists of the claim that Washington wishes to be king? I know for a fact that he did not seek the position he now holds. If you strangle the federal government before it is fully born, you destroy our future. Is that what you desire? You speak of taxation without representation. How can you claim that you have no one to represent you in Congress? Each area has men who are sent there to voice their desires. What, if not that, is the meaning of equal representation?"

He sensed that the crowd was listening at last, and he raised his voice. "In the first months of this year hundreds of our men were pirated from ships on their way to France and impressed into the Royal British Navy. Do you want such thievery to continue? Do you not resent the British captains who dare to take free men and force them to live in bondage? Can you ignore the truth that no one state by itself can eliminate this blight? We *must* have a strong central government, with the power to maintain the freedom for which we paid so dearly."

The cries to silence him resumed, and this time he was dragged from the room.

Gregory grabbed Virginia's arm and threw her against the wall. "Pay heed to me, Ginia! We make no money when men sit and talk. If they do not order, you must move about them with filled mugs. They will buy when they see the brew. I will punish you if you fail to make this night profitable." He pushed some filled mugs of ale into her hands. "Move!"

She hurried to obey. As Gregory predicted, the tankards of ale disappeared and she returned with a pocketful of coins. She kept a few in her apron to pay for passage on the public coach were she to escape again, and she was relieved to note that Gregory did not bother to count those she handed him.

She thought again of her two attempts to return to Philadelphia. But she could not remain discouraged. She filled a tray with more mugs of ale and made another circle around the room, but she did not rid herself of her entire burden. The men were again listening to the first speaker, and she sensed a new determination in his words.

The mugs grew heavy, and she lowered them to a table. To her surprise, the men who sat there reached in their pockets and offered her pay. She saw Gregory nod, and she delivered the money to him. As she stepped toward the tap, a man engaged Gregory in talk. She recognized the face. He was one of the farmers from whom Gregory bought much of his whiskey. David Cavanaugh's fine liquors, imported from France, were far too expensive for most of his customers.

She stepped back from the tap without filling any mugs, but Gregory was too busy expounding his views to notice. The other workers who shared with her the task of serving the guests were nowhere to be seen. And the guests were too involved in their protest against high taxes to notice her.

She gazed about her. For the first time since her assignment to the tavern, she was unobserved. Cautiously, she backed away from the tables. She inched closer to the door, alert for any indication that Gregory was aware of her movements. He did not even turn in her direction.

She paused at the door, reaching timidly for the great handle.

Suddenly, the heavy oak panel swung inward and a tall, burly man stepped into the room. She did not wait for him to clear the entryway. Silently, she slipped behind him, letting the door fall shut. If the newcomer called immediately for ale, her absence would be noticed. If he did not . . .

"Kirk! We've been waiting for you!" The voices were dulled by the thickness of the wall, but she could hear that the man whose entry had opened her way to freedom had no time to order a drink. Amid the cheers of the assemblage he moved across the room to take his place with the other leaders.

Virginia did not wait to hear more. She darted around the shrubs that concealed the barnyard from the entryway. Then she was on the road, running swiftly in what she felt certain was the direction of Philadelphia. Her heart was pounding furiously. She was free at last. Now, if only she could reach her uncle, her safety would be assured.

Nine

The moon was creeping over the hilltops by the time Virginia reached a crossroad which seemed familiar. There had been a period when she was a small child, when she had traveled often between her home in New York and her grandparents' home in Philadelphia to visit them. She still carried in her memory the picture of the road they traversed. Nearby this spot was an old inn where the coachman changed horses and new passengers were accepted.

Was it still in use? She felt the first glimmering of hope as she approached the ancient buildings. Then she saw the burned roof, and her heart sank. She walked past the gateway without looking up. Then, suddenly, she saw tracks of carriage wheels on the road, and they turned into the empty courtyard!

She ran across the open yard to the half-destroyed building. Was it possible that this place still served as a rest stop for the intercity coach? A horse nickered, and she glanced around her in alarm. Then she saw the animals, confined in a corral. She had not been wrong! If she waited here, she could buy a ride into Philadelphia.

This would also be the place her pursuers would look first if they followed her. Could she trust the stableboy to believe she had good reasons for running away from the Freedom's Arms? She doubted it. Most men she had met seemed unwilling to believe her.

Cautiously, she bypassed the house, seeking shelter at least among a stand of trees, thickly circled by bushes. From there she could see the road without herself being visible.

She leaned back against a tree trunk. Would the coach arrive soon? She did not know. She was exhausted, and she had walked only a few miles. Her slippers were worn through. She was hungry.

A noise behind her brought her instantly awake. Someone

was hammering on the door to the shed that stood close to the corral. The moonlight shone brightly on the scene, and she immediately recognized Jonas, the black servant, and one of the male slaves who worked at the bar.

The stableboy stepped into the moonlight, rubbing his eyes. "What ya want? Hell! It's still night!"

Jonas spoke. Virginia could not hear his words clearly, but she could tell he was inquiring about her. Evidently, if she was not located before dawn, Gregory would not be worried. He did not know she had the price of a passage on the public coach in her pocket.

Jonas spoke to his partner. "She must have turned at the crossroads. Ned, you take the east fork. I'll go west. We ought to catch her soon."

She felt a momentary surprise. Why were they not searching for her in the woods close to the inn?

Ned grumbled as he moved away. " 'Tain't no sense sendin' us out like this! Dogs'll find her in the mawnin'!"

She glanced again at Jonas. He seemed to have an additional reason for giving her time to escape. She tried to remember the times she had seen him at the Freedom's Arms. He had carried her tub in the night she arrived. He had appeared often in the tavern, bringing drinks to Bessie's clients. And every time they passed, Virginia had smiled at him, aware that he was as much a victim of Bessie and Gregory's cruelty as she was. Had her smile meant that much to him? She could think of no other reason for his present consideration. The rest of the people at the inn seemed to ignore his presence.

She watched as the two men disappeared up the road. How she wished she could run out and thank Jonas for his kindness. But she dared not put him in further jeopardy.

The stableboy returned to his bed, and once again the courtyard grew quiet. Virginia put her head back against the tree and closed her eyes. Unless David himself returned to the Freedom's Arms and began to search for her, she was safe until the coach appeared.

She awakened suddenly. A pounding of hoofs on the road alerted her to possible danger. Had her worst fears been realized? The rattle of harnesses and the creaking of the carriage told her she had no need for worry. David's carriage was tight and new. The vehicle that approached had seen better days.

She ran from her hiding place as the horses turned into the courtyard. The stableboy began to assist in harnessing fresh horses to replace the exhausted animals. The driver was buckling the last strap and pulling the reins over the backs of the beasts when she reached the coach. "What's the trouble, miss?"

"Are you going to Philadelphia?"

"Aye! 'Tis strange for a female to appear in this God-forsaken place. From whence come you?"

"From a farm . . . nearby." She gathered her courage. "I go to take service in Philadelphia."

"Have you the price of a ride?"

She dug into her pocket. There was nothing in it! Panic-stricken, she looked up into the driver's face. "I had money! Truly I did." Her fingers continued the search but they found only a bit of lint—and a small hole. The coins had fallen through.

The driver shrugged. "Better go home and get your fare. I don't run this coach as a charity!" He swung up onto the seat, flicked the reins, and let out a shout. The horses leaped forward, showering Virginia with gravel.

Virginia stood motionless, too stunned to think. She had tried again and failed.

" 'Ey, miss!" The stableboy approached, his eyes narrowed, his lips turned up in a leer. "Why don't ya stay wi' me? I got a bed 'twould 'old two!"

She pulled away, startled that he had been able to catch her unawares. He caught at her dress. "Come on, miss. I ain't 'ad a woman in weeks!" He chuckled. "I know you ain't from 'ereabouts!"

She pulled herself free and ran into the woods. But when she reached the shelter of the trees, she paused, overcome with despair. What hope had she, after all? When morning came, Gregory would send for the dogs and she would certainly be caught.

She thought again of the hunt she had watched during her visit to Carolina. Hadn't someone said that if the fleeing man had headed for a stream, he might have confused the dogs and escaped from their pursuit?

She glanced about her. Was there a stream somewhere? And did she have time to find it?

The ground sloped away from the road. Did that mean there might be water nearby? Was it a stream that murmured in the distance? She wasn't sure. It might be the leaves, moving in the breeze.

But there was no strong breeze that would account for the continuous sound. Encouraged, she headed in the direction of the faint noise. She moved as swiftly as she could, for she had no idea how much of the night was left. All she knew for certain was that when the sun rose, the dogs would come after her.

Her dress was torn by the time she found the water, but she was too relieved to notice the rips in her garment. She stood for a moment at the edge of the stream, and then resolutely stepped in. Her feet slipped on the wet stones, and she almost lost her balance. Instinctively, she cried out and caught at an overhanging branch. It broke in her hand and she fell into the water.

Her dress was soaked by the time she rose to her knees. The water that had splashed onto her face mingled with her tears. She would be caught, for sure. Gregory would beat her, and Bessie might decide to give her to some client!

Her anger rose at the thought. She would not give in without a struggle. The stream bed seemed to be made entirely of rocks and pebbles, too large for her to keep her balance if she stood. The night air licked at her wet dress and chilled her body.

She could not crawl along the stream until she lifted her skirt and tied it about her waist, for it slipped and held her back. As she moved forward with knees unprotected, the stones tore at her skin, and the water stung her where the stones cut.

She glanced up at the sky. Was there a faint hint of blue? Her terror increased. It didn't matter if her knees and hands were sore. She had to move swiftly out toward the middle of the stream.

She lost track of the time. It had been, she knew, close to midnight when she slipped from the inn. How long had it taken her to reach the coach stop? And how long had she waited for the coach to arrive? She glanced up again. This time there was no question that the sky had lightened.

Suddenly, the sound of the water changed. Somewhere ahead, the water reached a fall-off—a cascade. She would have to leave her safety soon—and then?

She crept closer to the shore, straining to see ahead so that she would avoid the waterfall. but came upon it unexpectedly, despite her caution. Her hands slipped, and she had nothing with which to grab onto the stones. She flailed about, clawing at every stone, hoping to reach more shallow water before she was pushed over the edge of the precipice. Her fingers caught and slipped. And then they caught again. This time, they held tight.

Panting from the exertion, she sat up in the water and studied the falls. They were not half so high as she had feared. And on the far side of the stream a series of rocks turned the sharp drop into a sort of slide.

Crawling upstream on her hands and knees until she felt certain she was far enough above the falls to cross to the other side, she lunged and pushed herself over the deep center channel.

Again she half-floated, half-crawled .down the stream. The force of the water buffeted her against the rocks, but she continued to allow her body to move with the water.

Still the current grew stronger, and her terror increased. Had she misjudged the danger of the descent?

She screamed when the water threw her against a big rock, and then, afraid that her screams might be heard, she clenched her jaw shut. Had she gone far enough? Was it safe for her to move onto dry land? Until she was much closer to Philadelphia, she dared not leave the safety of the water. The sun was brightening the horizon. Soon the dogs would begin their hunt. Perhaps she had already gone far enough to escape them!

She wondered with a feeling of hopelessness just how far she had actually gone during her night's struggle. A mile? Two, maybe? Not far, of that she was certain. The dogs would cover the distance easily.

She stood up and gazed around her. Was the stream heading in the right direction? What if it brought her back to the inn?

What was it her father had taught her? Streams run into rivers and rivers run to the sea. Well, she was close to the sea. If she followed the stream the entire distance, she ought to reach the bay on which Philadelphia was located. And then she would be home.

The sun was high in the sky now. Virginia paused once to listen for the dogs. She tried to recall her moves after she had left the coach stop. She had run from the stableboy into the woods. Had she gone in the direction of the stream?

She wasn't sure enough of the answers to dare leave the safety of the water. She paused when she reached a wide area where a small pond had formed. She was so hungry, and so very tired. Did she dare to rest or take time to look for food?

For a few minutes she gave in to her despair. She bent and drank some of the water from the rushing stream just above the pool. She dared not eat anything, for she might poison herself with some dangerous plant. Water might fill her stomach.

A sudden thought brought her to a halt: At least she had learned enough about the wilderness to know that poison plants did exist. What if she'd had no such knowledge?

Needing to hear a human voice, if only her own, she said quietly, "Thank you, Papa, for all the things you taught me. Why did I let myself get so angry with Anthony that I forgot to be cautious? And why did I ever trust David when you told me not to?"

When the sun had reached its zenith, she stepped cautiously from the water. Desperately hungry, she had to find some food in the woods along the shore. A stand of blueberries was growing in a moist pocket of land close to the water. She gathered the berries, then sat in the middle of the stream, eating the succulent fruit. Each small berry was sweet and delicious. She continued, at last, feeling greatly refreshed and filled with renewed strength and courage.

Once, when she paused, she thought she heard the dogs in the distance. Was she still in danger? Not if her memory was correct. She had been told that when a scent is lost in the water, the dogs move alongside the stream on both sides, searching for the point where the fugitive turned back to land. And there was only one place where she had left the stream, near the blueberry patch. Unless they reached that point, she was safe. By the time she thought she heard the dogs again, they seemed farther away, and she had traveled miles from her one point of exit.

Dusk came suddenly when the sun slipped behind a hill. A chill wind cooled her body, and the shadows turned the woods into a murky haze. Did she dare to leave the water? She had to take the chance. She could not spend the night in the stream.

What was it Anthony had done to make a bed for them? She searched about for a sharp rock. She found one as the sky was beginning to turn dark blue. Time was running out. If she did not get settled soon, she would have to work in utter darkness.

She dug a shallow hole, as she had watched Anthony do and filled it with leaves. Many of them were wet, but having no choice she took what she could, until the hollow was filled. She was shivering now, for the breeze had picked up as the darkness deepened.

It was then she realized that she could not build a fire. She had neither flint nor firewood. She would freeze.

Abruptly, she began to gather more leaves. This was no time to give up. She had feared she would not escape the dogs, but she had done it. She could not quit when the worst was over.

When she had collected a large pile of leaves close to the bed, she stood up and removed her dress. Her chemise clung to her body, but it was thin, and she decided to keep it on. She lay down upon the bed cautiously, suddenly afraid of the insects that might hide in the leaves. Then she reached out and shoveled the remainder of the pile over her, until she was completely covered.

The sounds of the night closed in around her. Somewhere, too close for comfort, a small animal rustled the underbrush. A fox yapped, and she shuddered. Wherever the leaves touched her body, she imagined the insects there, about to bite her.

Despite her fears, she began to relax. Her makeshift bed grew warmer, and soon she felt the mild euphoria of sleep taking over her mind. She woke often as the night sounds intruded upon her sleep.

When dawn came she slid from her shelter. She put on her dress, which had dried during the night, feeling more hopeful than she had in a long time. She had avoided capture for one entire day—and a whole night! She walked in the middle of the stream again, this time for about an hour, before she emerged on the other side and headed back toward the woods that bordered the highway. When she saw the road ahead, she turned and moved parallel to it. Gregory might still send horsemen out to see if she were heading toward Philadelphia. Until she was safe at home, she dared not let down her guard.

She paused when the coach went by, heading from Philadelphia to New York. She wished she dared to step out and beg for assistance, but she remembered the man at Amos's inn. Strangers would feel no sympathy for her. They would pass her by or perhaps even bring her back to the Freedom's Arms.

The thundering of horse hoofs sent her rushing for shelter behind a bush. She watched in horror as Gregory rode past, followed closely by Jonas. They must still be searching for her. And if they were, how long would it be before the dogs were called back? Trembling, she crept away from the road, back to the stream. There, she felt safe.

She came upon the farm so suddenly that she was out in the meadow before she realized it was not simply an opening in the forest. Startled, she stepped back into the woods, and from her hiding place, she studied the land. The farmer was visible, far across the clearing, cutting wheat with a scythe.

A woman appeared at the door, carrying a pail of water. She crossed the barnyard and tossed the water into a plot of ground that Virginia knew must be her kitchen garden. Then she returned to the house without glancing once in Virginia's direction. Virginia carefully crept around the clearing. She realized that until she reached Philadelphia, she dared trust no one.

Her second night was spent much as the first. Hungry, she woke early, long before dawn, and hurried on her way. She knew she had to reach safety soon or she would grow too weak to travel.

When she did, at last, reach the outskirts of Philadelphia, the sky was growing light. Now she dared to take to the road, for she knew farmers would soon be arriving, and she could find shelter in the crowds that streamed into town with their produce. The bricks were cold under her feet, but they were smooth, not like the gravel of the highway or the stones along the stream bed. The sun peered over the horizon, bathing the buildings around her with the orange glow of dawn. A cat, on its way home from its nocturnal travels, paused to watch her pass. She smiled and called out to it, but it stared at her solemnly.

No longer did she feel the need to watch over her shoulder. It was what lay ahead that concerned her now. She increased her pace as she drew near the block where her home was located. Had her uncle taken up residence in his sister's house?

Her spirits rose when she saw the familiar brick front, the wide stone steps, the green roof. It seemed ages ago that she had closed and bolted all the windows. They stood open now, the curtains waving lightly in the faint breeze. She dashed up the steps, unmindful of her sore feet and her aching muscles.

The door did not open to her touch. She pounded against it. A dark face looked out. "Yes?" She could see the displeasure in his eyes.

"I've come to see my uncle. This is my house—let me in!"

"This is the residence of Roy Salford. He has no woman with him."

"I have just arrived. I tell you, he is my uncle. Call him and let me speak to him."

"You will wait." The face vanished, the door closed with a thump. Virginia stood alone on the stairs. She was overcome with disappointment. Why had she been treated so rudely?

A fly landed on her arm and drew her attention to her dress. She was filthy! She stared at her skirt. She looked more like a beggar than a lady of quality. Embarrassed, she rubbed her cheek. It was covered with a fine dust. Her dress was stained, under the dust, with ale and wine. And her hair!

Geraldine had tied it into a knot, and Gregory had insisted that she keep it up when she was at work. She had hated what it did to her appearance, yet she had welcomed the plainness that kept many of the tavern's patrons from showing an interest in her.

She reached up and pulled out the pins that held her curls. Half-finished, she stopped. Without a mirror, how could she improve her condition? The doorman reappeared, a somber expression on his face. "You go away, miss. My master's niece is a little girl, and she is dead. No one here wishes to disturb the master's mourning."

"Please! You must believe me! My uncle hasn't seen me in years. He doesn't remember how old I am."

"Go away! You only irritate fresh wounds." The man slammed the door in Virginia's face.

She stared at the carved panel. How often had she pushed it open and run inside? How dare they now lock it against her entrance? She raised her hands to pound again, but before she touched the wood, she let her arms drop to her sides. No amount of noise would draw her uncle from his grieving.

Slowly, she turned and descended. What should she do? Of what good was her escape if she could not reach her uncle?

Thomas Willing! If her uncle's household would not let her in, then certainly the Willings would make her welcome.

As she moved up the street, a thought came that filled her with despair. If she was turned away at her uncle's door, it was because Anthony had not reached him.

She knew Anthony had doubted her story at first. Yet she felt certain that before they were waylaid on the road, he had accepted her as his employer's niece. But if no one in the house believed her, that surely meant he had died.

She hurried forward, tears stinging her eyes. She had no doubt now that her lover was dead. It was too late to abandon her search for shelter. At the home of her old friends she would find assistance and friendship. And maybe, some day, she would learn to forget all the promise that she had felt when she lay in Anthony's arms.

Ten

Virginia was dragging her feet by the time she reached the end of the street. Never in her entire life had she been so exhausted. And then, to be barred from entering her own home, to be denied the right to rest on her own bed. She held back the tears that stung her eyes, convinced that her appearance was bad enough without the added disfigurement of weeping.

As she turned the corner, she heard footsteps behind her. Had David Cavanaugh or Gregory anticipated her, sending a search party straight to Philadelphia to apprehend her? Would they drag her back to her prison? She fought an overwhelming despair. Why was her uncle so unacquainted with the normal growth of a child as to believe that at sixteen she was still a little girl?

"No wonder he sent me a doll for my birthday!" She realized that she spoke aloud, and she glanced up at the open windows above her to see if anyone had listened. There was no one in sight. The footsteps continued. Her pursuer limped, as if he had recently suffered an injury to one leg. Had he heard her? Did he plan now to catch her while she wandered idly, talking to herself?

She ran the length of the block, but as she approached the next corner she lagged. Her legs were so very sore. She paused, gasping for breath.

During the brief flight, she had had time to consider her behavior. Why, she wondered, was she so suspicious? When her way was barred by her uncle's servant, she leaped to the conclusion that her uncle was trying to deny her her inheritance. And now, when certainly others might have reason to traverse the streets, she immediately assumed that whoever walked behind her was chasing her. How foolish . . . and how contrary to her normal reactions. Why had she not realized that the man who followed her might be sent to call her back?

She turned and waited for the figure to approach. He was moving swiftly, dragging his game leg along with determined speed, as if he had decided never to favor it any more than was absolutely necessary. She had been right, she decided, in her assumption that it was a new wound. A man who had endured such a problem for a long period of time was usually more resigned to moving slowly.

He was favoring one arm, too. Even from a distance she could tell that it was bandaged. He had been in a serious battle. But where? Not even the farmers she had encountered at the Freedom's Arms had been prepared to fight.

The figure drew closer, moving from shadow into sunlight. His dark brown hair hung loose, blowing slightly in the breeze. He looked up, and she gasped. "Anthony! Oh, Anthony!" She ran toward him, too overcome with delight to wonder whether he wanted so enthusiastic a welcome.

He caught her in his arms and held her close. For one moment it all returned—the passion, the warmth, the wonderful sense of *belonging*. Her arms crept around his neck.

Abruptly, he pulled away. His face was twisted with a mixture of emotions. But his voice was steady. "Thank God you are safe! Miss Nelson, I pray that you will forgive me for"—he refused to meet her eyes—"for . . . what happened. You had every reason to be angry. What I did was unforgivable."

She felt as if he had slapped her face. She had forgiven him many times over, and he was treating her like a stranger. She forgot, in her shock, that just before she was taken from him by Ben she had been too angry to even speak. She forgot that Anthony could not possibly be aware of how worried she had been about him.

She clenched her fists to hold back her tears of frustration. If he wished to be formal, she could comply. "Yes, it was. I trust you will make no further attempts upon my honor."

"I vow it. I have been so worried about you. And so ashamed of what happened between us." He saw the distress in her eyes and misinterpreted it completely. "I promise you, I will never speak of it again. If I could, I would save you the irritation of seeing my face, but I cannot leave your uncle. He depends upon my help."

She could stand the conversation no longer. "Are your injuries severe?"

"Nothing, compared to the injury I have done you."

"You seem to no longer question my identity. Yet I was not admitted to my own house." Her heart was aching, and she was filled with shame. What had made her run to this man's arms, when he so clearly regretted what had happened between them?

He avoided her eyes. "I saw the portrait of your mother that hangs in the parlor of your father's house. You bear a striking resemblance to her. I have spoken to your uncle about you, and we have had men scouring the countryside in search of you for the past week. And you say you were turned away at the door?"

"I thought it possible that my uncle had decided to disown me."

"For what reason?" Anthony seemed in control of his emotions. "No, he is just a very busy man, and he has given instructions to his servants not to admit strangers."

"Then you did not tell him about David Cavanaugh, or about"—she hated to think of that night she had spent with Anthony, now that she was sure he regretted it—"or about the other shame I have endured?"

He lowered his head. "No. I told him simply that you had been abducted from your home when your parents died, and that though I had tried to bring you back, men had overpowered me and dragged you off. Forgive me. I did not wish to shame you by speaking of all that happened between us."

For the first time since her escape from the Freedom's Arms, Virginia wished she had died. She knew that she had clung to the hope that Anthony was alive, and that the night they had spent together meant as much to him as it had to her. Now she knew her dream to be untrue. He had no respect for a woman who accepted him so eagerly on their first meeting.

She knew the standard that was generally accepted. A good girl might permit familiarities from the young man to whom she was engaged. Many of her friends bore their first children within months of their wedding. But only a whore took on one man after another.

She was convinced that Anthony must think the worst

of her. After all, had she not run into his arms in the middle of the street in view of all the neighbors? And had he not, instinctively, kissed her?

She felt overcome with shame. What right had she to seek shelter in her uncle's house, after all? He was an honorable man, a representative to Congress. And she was a . . . She pressed her lips together. She could not say the word. She hated even to think it.

She held her head erect. At least Anthony had been gentleman enough to keep her dark secret from her uncle. Now she would have to face it by herself. And that, she concluded, was as it should be. It was her guilt.

Anthony bowed very formally. "Please, Mistress Nelson. I must deliver a message to Thomas Willing. Would you care to go with me, or shall I bring you first to your home so you can clean up."

She felt the condemnation in his words. He was ashamed to be seen with her on the street. She was filthy. "Please, take me home." Her voice was strained, for she felt ready to weep.

He held out his arm, but when she did not immediately take it, he let it fall to his side. Once more, she misinterpreted his action, as he did hers. He walked sadly beside her, convinced that she would never forgive him for the evil he had done her. She held herself proudly erect despite her sore feet and dirty clothes, too proud to let him know how it pained her to know that he considered her unworthy of being treated like a lady.

The silence between them was strained. At last, aware that Roy Salford would wonder at their odd behavior, Anthony tried once more to establish at least the semblance of friendliness between them. "Your uncle has been most worried about you." He cleared his throat, but his voice remained husky. "Where did they take you?"

"To the Freedom's Arms." She wondered how, if the search for her had lasted a full week, no one had thought to look in that notorious inn. And then she had a thought. "You are sure you did not tell him about . . . everything?"

"Oh, no! I swear it!"

"Yet, he must suspect. A girl alone, abducted by rough men. Uncle Roy is a moral man. He would want nothing to do with me. He must know I at least ran the risk of being—taken . . . by . . ." She could not continue. She felt like crying again, and they were so close to her home. Things were bad enough. She did not want to arrive at her uncle's door with tears streaking down her cheeks.

Anthony flushed. "You cannot believe such nonsense. Your uncle has too big a heart to judge you for something you could not prevent."

She did not bother to reply. If what he said were so, then why had he not told Roy the truth? Suddenly, she stopped. She could not go on.

Anthony caught her arm. "Please! Your uncle will be glad to see you. I swear it." He met her eyes for the first time since their encounter. "I can see that I embarrass you, that you wish I were not so close to your uncle. I regret that I cannot undo what has taken place between us. But I can assure you, I will never mention it again. And I will do all I can to save you from the pain of having to see me. We must not allow this to affect your relationship with your uncle. He is too kind a man and he loves you dearly. Please, let us pretend a friendliness for his sake."

She could not deny the wisdom of his request. "Thank you. You are right. I will do as you ask." She turned and climbed the steps.

The doorman stared in surprise as she entered but this time did not bar her passage. Anthony led the way across the hall to the library door. Virginia paused before she entered. The last time she had been in the house her father had just died and she had carried his body, with the help of David's servant, to the cemetery. She pushed the door open. He had been sitting in his chair. Another figure sat there now.

Anthony paused dramatically just behind her. "Mr. Roy Salford, may I present your *little* niece, Virginia Nelson."

She curtseyed, but Roy would have none of such formality. "Virginia! Oh, my dearest child. You have been through so much." He strode across the room and embraced her. Relieved that he showed no hesitancy about accepting her, she returned his embrace. If she could survive these moments with Anthony beside her, she would be all right. And he had promised she would not see him again, unless it were absolutely necessary.

Roy put her down at last. "My dear, I thank God that

you are safe. What happened to you? Anthony told me of finding you on the road and of your abduction when he was injured. Where were you taken? We've searched everywhere."

"Did you visit Freedom's Arms?"

"I regret that I was not always the one to pursue the hunt, nor could Anthony handle the search by himself for he has only now recovered from his injuries. We have sent men to every inn." His eyes widened. "They did not come to the Arms? The rogues! Anthony! We trusted them. You were right, we should have done it all ourselves."

Anthony did not reply. Virginia cast a sharp glance in his direction.

Roy broke the silence. "Tell me what happened to you. Were you . . . harmed?"

Virginia was certain she understood the meaning of his question. With another glance at Anthony, she replied, "No. I was most fortunate. I was forced to work in the tavern at the Freedom's Arms. David Cavanaugh found me there and planned to return to rescue me."

"Return to rescue you? What fool idea was that?"

"Please, do not blame him. He was on a business trip and could not take me with him, but he said he would return. I just could not wait. I . . . They worked me so hard, and I learned that you were in Philadelphia. And uncle, I overheard some men planning revolution! I felt I had to hurry home, without waiting for David, to warn the Congress of what is taking place in the country."

Roy laughed. "Oh, my sweet little girl! I remember now that your father encouraged you to keep abreast of the politics in which he was involved. But you are mistaken. There is no revolution. There are, if I understand my friend Anthony, some men who oppose the whiskey tax. But they are few, and they are no threat to the safety of the nation." He took her hand. "You are upset. I can understand that. Whoever your friend David Cavanaugh might be, he should be reprimanded for putting his business before your safety. But I cannot even bear a grudge against him, though he has treated you badly, for you are safe. And I have good news for you. Your nurse, Angie, appeared at our door but yesterday. She will be delighted to see that you are home, at last."

"Angie!" For the first time since realizing that Anthony regretted what had happened between them, Virginia felt a glow of pleasure. Angie was here—the nurse who had cared for her from the moment she was born, the one person to whom she dared to be honest. She had felt so alone, but no longer.

"I suspect she is in the hall, waiting for you." Roy laughed. "I imagine she might even have a bath prepared." He squeezed Virginia's hand. "Oh, my dear sweet child. You look so much like my sister. Later you must tell me, if it is not too painful for you, what you can of your mother's last days. I miss her sorely, and your father, too. He was a good, kind man."

Virginia nodded, aware that if she permitted it, she would be crying again. She kissed her uncle on the cheek and ran from the room. As she stepped into the hall, she ran directly into the arms of her nurse.

When they were at last alone in her old room, Virginia knew that she could speak of her unhappiness. Angie was the same as she had always been, full of love, no matter what happened.

As Angie brushed Virginia's hair, a flood of memories swept over them both. Whatever Virginia's problem, somehow Angie had always been able to solve it. And so, now, with a problem far greater than any she had faced as a child, Virginia spilled out her troubles.

As she talked, her fears and anger surfaced. The pain she had felt when she realized that Anthony did not love her grew less sharp, because Angie understood.

When Jonathan entered with the hot water for the tub, Virginia was already feeling better than she had for weeks. Her soul was cleansed through the confession of her shame. Now she would be able to cleanse her body as well.

As the silky smooth liquid closed over her shoulders, she felt a new peace enter her heart. She would be able to face her uncle and yet keep her secret, for she had an ally. If her burdens grew too heavy, she could always lean on her Angie for comfort.

Eleven

"Now let Thy servant depart in peace, for mine eyes . . ."
The singsong voice of the pastor droned on. Virginia
glanced around, thankful that her face was hidden by her
black veil. Hers was not the only graveside gathering. A
small group of worshipers stood somewhat down the hill,
and fresh flowers on other graves spoke of similar religious
services that had taken place throughout the week.

She shuddered as she caught sight of the common grave,
far down the slope. How thankful she was that her parents
had been spared such a fate.

She was reminded of the memory of David Cavanaugh's
kindness. Had she misjudged him, after all? It was possible that she had wrongly blamed him for the behavior of
his underlings. He had been so good to her when they'd
buried her father.

She had long since decided, after much inner struggle,
not to blame him for his behavior that first night at the inn.
He had been overcome with desire. She should have recognized his passion as proof of the intensity of his affection
for her.

Was he searching for her still? She wished there was a
way she could tell him she was well, without letting Bessie and Gregory know her whereabouts. Gregory had
warned her that he would not allow her to leave, and had
not Bessie said that her arm was long?

She slipped her hand over her uncle's arm. He would
protect her.

The prayer seemed endless. Virginia rebuked herself for
her impatience. Surely she should not object to giving this
last hour of devotion to her parents' souls. Yet she felt
drained of strength. Just as she began to wonder if she
might not, after all, faint, the benediction drew to a close.

In the carriage on the road to the city, Roy spoke of
his sister as a girl, of her journey with George to New

York, just at the start of the Revolution. President Washington, who shared the carriage, recalled how helpful George had been as a young soldier and the valuable role he and his father-in-law, Robert Salford, had played in keeping the rebels informed as to the activities of the Tories, during the months before the outbreak of hostilities. Virginia had heard many of those tales from her father. He had never emphasized the importance of his work; he had always shared the honors with others.

When they reached the house, Virginia led the way into the parlor where the servants had draped the walls in black. After seeing to the needs of her guests, she stepped to President Washington's side. "Mr. President?"

He held his cup midway between his saucer and his lips. "Yes, my dear?"

"Please do not think me forward, but I have been worried greatly since my return. My uncle insists I am showing unnecessary concern." She hurried on, aware that a man of the president's stature might have no interest in what a woman had to say about politics.

He interrupted her with a smile and a wave of his hand. "My dear, do not hesitate to speak. It will comfort you, I am sure."

"Sir, I overheard some farmers while I was held captive at the Freedom's Arms. They spoke of rebellion against the government and complained about a tax on the whiskey they brew. They said it was far worse than any tax levied by King George, and they"—she hesitated only a moment—"they threatened to tar and feather the tax collector if he tried to enforce the revenue."

Washington smiled. "You have not heard, then, that they have given up. They did attack one tax collector, but he has been cared for and is well. Now they are back at their farms. Harvest time is near. No farmer can neglect his land when winter approaches."

She felt foolish, but she could not let the matter rest. "But is there not a danger that they will resume their protests when the grain is safe in their barns?"

"Possibly. But then winter will hamper their movements. Believe me, it will take very dedicated men to persist after the first fall of snow."

"You are not concerned, then?"

"My child," the president spoke patiently, "of course I am concerned. I have men studying the situation at this moment. But we face problems far more important than the unrest of a few farmers. We are faced with the need to solidify our government. That is what takes my time and the time of all of Congress."

"Then you feel nothing has to be done about these men?"

He seemed to be growing impatient. "Please, my dear, don't distress yourself. This is a matter that is delicate and cannot be handled thoughtlessly. I assure you, my greatest difficulty lies in holding in check those who would punish the rebels. They seem to forget that these farmers are the same men who fought beside me for liberty. They suffered through Valley Forge. They hold their independence dear."

"Then what can be done?"

"Now? I wait. There will come a moment when I will step in and do what has to be done. But not yet." He smiled. "You must not worry your pretty head over such problems. The men who serve the nation are well qualified. They disagree often enough to act as a check on any impulsive action. Look at the contention that exists between your uncle and Anthony Burke. I value Roy Salford above many men because he dares to include opposition in his own household. Your uncle, as you certainly know, is a strong Federalist and a close friend of Alexander Hamilton. Anthony Burke favors Jefferson and goes even further in his demand for states' rights. I know he opposed the whiskey tax, but he does not threaten the Congress with a sword. He will argue his case, as will others like him. I am certain that he and his friends will do much to pacify the farmers once he understands fully the importance of the government's action."

"Thank you, sir." Virginia felt a vague disquiet. The president had been polite, but he had done little more than tell her that such worries were men's business. Would no one, she wondered, take her information seriously?

"Virginia?" Her uncle approached.

She rose quickly, and the president stood beside her.

"Come along." Roy turned to Washington. "I pray you to excuse my niece. She is impulsive, and her father did allow her to know much of his thoughts regarding the fate of our country. She is not like most young girls."

"That I can clearly see." Washington smiled down at her. "You need have no fear. I have spoken to her before when her father was alive. I find it charming that so lovely a creature should concern herself with such serious subjects."

Roy bowed. Then he held out his arm to Virginia. "Come along now, my dear. The Willings are preparing to depart."

She met Thomas Willing at the door to the parlor. He bent low over her hand. "My dear, forgive me. I must take my wife home, for she seems about to faint. She was, as you well know, most fond of your mother, and she berates herself for departing when you needed her so badly. I fear she does not approve my having taken her and the rest of my household out before the plague overcame the city."

"But there was nothing she could have done. You know how swift the sickness was. I must assure her that I did all that could have been done to help both my parents."

"I am certain that you did. Nevertheless, you know my dear wife. She feels convinced that she deserted your mother in a time of need."

"Then I must speak to her." Virginia approached Willing's wife, who stood patiently waiting for her husband to take his leave. While Thomas Willing moved about the room, saying his farewells, the two women talked.

"Please, Mistress Willing, you must not punish yourself because you were not here when my mother died. I assure you, she understood. My father would have gone, too, had there been time." She wanted to reach up and wipe away the tears that streaked the kindly face.

"But she needed me. We have been so close, she and I—like sisters."

"Yes." Virginia knew her mother had been genuinely fond of this neighbor, and, for Virginia, the Willing household had been like a second home.

Thomas Willing approached. "Come, my dear. We will see much of Virginia, of that I am certain. You can have her over as often as you wish, for I am certain she will need the advice of a woman now that she is grown." He turned to Virginia. "Good evening, my child. I have already spoken to your uncle. Remember, you are welcome at my house at any time. Not only for your mother's sake, but for your own. You are like a niece to us."

Virginia curtseyed. "Thank you, Master Willing. And you, mistress. I will not forget your kindness."

She turned and surveyed the parlor. Others of the guests were taking their leave, and she joined her uncle in their farewells. She could see that the sky was already streaked with red. Soon night would fall, and the streets would be dark. There were few in the city who chose to be out so late. But there were some of the visitors who seemed prepared for a longer stay. In one corner President Washington sat, surrounded by Alexander Hamilton, Thomas Jefferson, and a few other of the leaders of the country. Anthony stood respectfully behind Jefferson. Even across the room, Virginia could hear much of what was being said.

Alexander Hamilton was speaking, and his voice grew loud. ". . . ought to put a stop to such insurrections? How can we possibly maintain the position of a strong nation among other nations of the world, if we cannot control those in our own land who seek to undermine the government?"

"Dammit, man!" Jefferson pounded his fist against the arm of his chair. "Can you not see that we are not the same as those monarchies? What do you want—a repetition of the ills from which we have only recently relieved ourselves? Do you secretly wish, as your opponents contend, that President Washington have a crown on his head?" He waved away Hamilton's protest. "No! Most certainly you do not. Yet, if we are to have a democracy fashioned after the great cities of Greece, we must permit those who disagree with the party in power to have a voice." He half rose. "That is what has made us great—and will continue to set us apart as a leader among nations: We dare to allow those who disagree with established power to have their say. I, for one, do not wish to return to a state where speaking out for liberty is considered a crime."

The last of the other guests departed, and Virginia moved silently to stand beside her uncle. Hamilton had taken up the gauntlet thrown down by his honorable opponent.

He posed dramatically. "There! You seem totally unable to recognize that too much inner dissension can destroy a nation. Do you not see that we face real danger in our relationship with other nations? They are ancient, established. We fight for our very existence. Do you think that England has abandoned the hope that we will return, penitent, to the fold? No! She waits at high sea, her captains ready to abduct and impress every able-bodied male who leaves the safety of shore. I tell you, Tom, if we do not form a forceful federal government, we will be destroyed. It is for that reason that I fight your precious farmers. In their selfish desire for personal gain, they would destroy all we have fought for so gallantly."

Jefferson turned to continue the argument, but then he caught sight of Virginia and paused. "Ah, my dear, I beg your forgiveness. We should not bore you with matters that belong, rightly, within the doors of Congress. I apologize. This is a time for remembering your parents, and we have destroyed the evening with our battling." He turned to Hamilton. "Come, my friend, let us show the lady that we can behave like gentlemen. We owe her an attempt to wipe the tears from her cheeks." He turned again to Virginia. "Believe me, dear Miss Nelson, we make far more of most issues than they deserve. Alex and I are both overly fond of debate."

She looked up into his kindly face. "Is there really danger?" She knew her voice was trembling. "Could King George undo all we have fought to build?"

"Certainly not." Washington rose and stepped toward her. "Gentlemen, I fear you have upset the young lady too much. You should consider the circumstances before you indulge in your penchant for argument." He took Virginia's arm and led her to the settee. "Sit down, my dear. You are the daughter of a man who was himself engaged in just this kind of rhetoric. Did he not speak to you of the importance of debate? These men must decide for many others who cannot speak with such facility. They must weigh each situation before they draw any conclusions. This issue, brought up by farmers here in Pennsylvania, has far-reaching implications. At stake is the form of government we will have generations from now, when all of us here are gone. We dare not act in passion or in self-interest."

Her uncle took a seat beside her. He took her hand in

his. "You must understand, Mr. President, that my niece has been most troubled of late. She has been sorely mistreated. It was at the height of her troubles that she overheard the farmers speak of riots and tar and feathering. It is no wonder it upset her. I am certain she will be fine when the horror fades from her memory." He rose and drew Virginia to her feet. "I trust you will understand if I let the child go to her room. This has been a most trying day for her."

"Of course," Washington said. "Good night, Miss Nelson. You must promise me you will cease your worry. I can assure you, the best minds in the nation are considering the needs of those farmers as well as those of all the other citizens. With God's help, we will make the proper decisions." He took her hand and bowed over it. "Again, good night."

She stood quietly, feeling his lips brush her fingers. "Thank you, Mr. President. I am sorry if I spoke too boldly."

"Not at all. It pleases me to see that your father did not isolate you from the world. Many fathers do not let their daughters learn aught but the skills they will need for raising children."

She felt certain he was trying now to soothe her ruffled feelings. Did he not, like all the other men she knew, prefer a woman who limited her interests to things feminine? She dared not do more than nod in response.

On her way to her room, she mulled over the issue once more. Was she proving an embarrassment to her uncle? Did he wish her to be more feminine? Was his interruption of her talk with the president his way of telling her to confine her interests to domestic matters? She shook her head. No matter what he wanted, she could not do that. She cared what happened to her country.

She was surprised to have heard that Anthony was on the side of the farmers. At the same time, she felt annoyed with herself for being at all concerned with what he thought. He had shown his disinterest in her. Why could she not respond with equal unconcern? Why did she still dream of him at night? And why, at every turn, was she reminded of him, even though he had kept his promise and avoided her as much as possible?

In order to take her thoughts away from Anthony, she brought David to mind. She was still confused by him. He had never been anything but gentle with her, yet she dared not trust him entirely. She acknowledged that most of her distrust of him originated in what others had told her: the things the old hag had said at Amos's inn, the strange conversation David had had with Bessie, only parts of which Virginia had overheard. His open acknowledgment that he owned the Freedom's Arms should have given her confidence in him. He made no attempt to conceal even those things about which he might be ashamed. Why, when he was so honest with her— No. He had not been honest . . . not all the time. He had lied to her about the end of the plague, but perhaps he had had a reason she did not understand.

Angie waited at the top of the stairs. "Did you see me and Jonathan at the grave?"

Virginia nodded. "Mother and father would be pleased to see that you came back."

"I wish I had been here when they needed me. Jonathan and I should not have gone." She led Virginia into her room where a bath waited.

When at last she lay in bed, Virginia tried to remember why she should distrust David, but she was too tired, too heart-weary from all that had happened. And when she fell asleep, it was not David who occupied her dreams. Anthony appeared—and in her nightmare fantasies, he behaved as she had hoped he would in her waking hours. In her dreams he held her close. He dared to admit his love for her.

Twelve

"Good morning!" George Kingsbury greeted her with a smile. "Are you ready for a ride?"

Virginia nodded, a smile lighting her face. George was one of her most charming suitors. Not more than a year older than she, he still seemed more like a boy than a man. He was always well-behaved and scrupulously polite, especially when they were at home. When they went to ride, he would forget to behave with proper decorum, and they would romp across the countryside like two children out to play.

She laughed as he bowed and took her hand. "Silly! I'll bet I can win a race to Braddock's Field."

He frowned. "We'd better not go there, Virginia. I've heard the farmers are congregating again. We might get in trouble."

She stamped her foot impatiently. In the year since her return to Philadelphia, the scars from her mistreatment had faded. She had seen little of Anthony for he had kept his word and had remained distant. David, too, had not appeared to torment her, though she suspected that he had returned to the city and was carrying on his business as before.

She had learned over the months to control her thoughts, so the memories of the night in the inn with David, and the other night, in the woods with Anthony, did not return to haunt her too often. Her uncle, and Thomas and Mother Willing, none of whom knew of her shame, did much to assist her in putting the past behind her. Mother Willing had carefully chosen those young men whom she felt were worthy of Virginia's hand. She reminded Virginia that, as a young lady of seventeen, she should be seriously considering which of her young suitors she wished to marry.

"Really, George, are you going to let a few farmers scare you? They don't frighten me."

George rose to the bait. "Of course they don't frighten me. All right, I'll race you! But we'd better wait to start until we get out of town."

"Of course, silly." She felt very pleased with herself. And delighted that she had had the wisdom to keep her secrets to herself. Once in a while, when she was particularly happy, she could almost forget that she was not what she pretended to be.

Angie seemed troubled at times by the deceit. She even had dared once to speak of the subject. "Miss Virginia, is it right to let the young men court you? Won't you have trouble if you marry one of them?"

Virginia had understood her meaning and had chosen to let it anger her. "How dare you? Angie, you forget your place. I confided in you because I needed a friend. I consider it a betrayal for you to remind me of those terrible things now when I'm happy again."

"But," Angie had persisted, "you cannot ignore it. Your husband will expect you to be—"

"A virgin?" Virginia frowned. "I talked to Mother Willing about . . . what will happen when I marry. She said some girls have no maidenhead, because they break it riding horseback. So how will whoever he is know?"

Angie had shaken her head, and Virginia had grown quiet. She did not actually feel as much bravado as she pretended. Often she felt ashamed because she did not tell the truth to the young men who attended her. She knew she dared not. No man would marry her if her shame was known. And her uncle would feel the disgrace. For his sake, she had to remain silent. She dared not admit that she was concerned for herself, as well.

After that conversation, she had thrown herself with new enthusiasm into riding. If that was to be her excuse for a broken maidenhead, then she had best gain a reputation for being an avid horsewoman.

She held her horse in check as they traversed the streets to the edge of town. George rode beside her, chattering merrily about a new gelding he was to get for his nineteenth birthday. They nodded at acquaintances who passed them by but made no attempt to stop and talk. George loved racing as much as Virginia pretended to.

When they reached the open road, Virginia leaned forward. Her heels dug into her mount's flank, and she held on tightly, aware that she was at a disadvantage riding sidesaddle. George let out a whoop and followed her down the road.

At first he thundered ahead, raising a cloud of dust that choked Virginia when she inhaled. She swerved, pulling her horse to one side of the road away from the dust, and then she urged him on.

George seemed to feel that he had proven his horse's superiority with that one spurt of speed, for he slowed down almost immediately and kept pace with Virginia, riding beside her so neither one was bothered by the dust.

His show of consideration only annoyed her. She hated to be treated as if she was not a worthy opponent. Frowning, she drew hard on her reins. George stopped and waited for her to speak.

"You aren't being fair. I want a race. Why do you act as if I'm not able to hold my own?"

He was clearly distressed. "Please, Virginia. I don't mean to anger you. And I don't think we should go on. Look. You can see the field is full of farmers. What if they started to riot? Your uncle would kill me if you were to get hurt."

Virginia flicked her reins, and her horse began to walk slowly forward. "You don't have to take care of me, George Kingsbury. And I'm going ahead. If you want to go back, don't worry about me. I can take care of myself."

George touched his heels to his horse's flanks and moved up beside her. "I'll stay with you. Do you think I would let you go on alone?" He touched her sleeve when she did not immediately respond. "You must promise you will stay near me. If there is any danger, we might have to leave in a hurry."

She did not bother to answer. The activity at Braddock's Field was too fascinating.

The area was filled with men. Some had rigs that they had lined up along one edge of the field. A few tents were scattered about, with the majority clustered not far from the wagons and carriages. A number of horses were corralled behind a makeshift fence. Most of the men were gathered near the road, listening to a man who stood on the bed of a wagon. She recognized him immediately: Daniel

Mason! He was one of the men who had spoken at Freedom's Arms, the night she ran away. She drew near, curious as to whether he still spoke with as much eloquence as he had that night.

George moved ahead, trying to block her advance. "Please, Virginia, let's go home. My father says these men are not to be trusted. He says they're traitors."

"Oh, George, even if they are traitors, they aren't hurting us. Why, I don't think they even know we're here. Go ahead home, if you insist. I'm staying."

Reluctantly, he fell in beside her. She continued to move closer, stopping only when she was near enough to hear everything Daniel Mason said. He had evidently only started to speak.

"Friends! Let me finish what I have to say before you leave. I have heard the talk this day, and I am shocked. We are congregated here to protest a tax that robs us of our livelihood. Is it possible that you plan to go home unsatisfied?"

The men murmured words that Virginia could not quite hear. Daniel continued. "Do not leave without a fight. We have tried other things, now we must use stronger methods."

He raised his voice above the noise of the men. "You all know that I went to speak to the president, but he would not listen. He does not care how we feel. No one cares."

The mumbling swelled and then subsided. Daniel continued. "What did you expect? Were there any among you who believed that Washington could be dissuaded in his drive for a monarchy?" He paused briefly to emphasize his next words. "What we must do is storm the arsenal. That is the way to make them listen. Take the weapons and powder that will otherwise be used against us. Prepare for the new revolution."

The cry was taken up. "Storm the arsenal! Storm the arsenal!"

Virginia shuddered, but she held her ground. She felt sure she was in no danger, for the men were not concerned with who watched.

She did feel terror at the thought of what would soon take place. There would be fighting and men would die.

Suddenly, a figure detached itself from the crowd. The man moved forward, and as he reached the wagon on which Daniel Mason stood, Virginia gasped. Anthony!

He leaped up beside Daniel and held up his hands. "Wait!" His voice was loud and commanding. "Friends! Wait, before you march to your deaths."

The crowd grew quiet and he continued. "You all know me. I have fought beside you in the skirmishes with the Indians. Seth!" He pointed to a man near the wagon. "It was your wife and child I saved from the redskins when you were too far away to protect them."

Seth nodded, and the men around him seemed to listen as he gave further details of Anthony's heroics.

But Anthony did not relinquish the control he had gained over the crowd. "Richard!" Another man, farther back, lifted his head. He carried a musket he had been brandishing in the air. Now it was at his side, quiet at last. "Have you forgotten who saved your life during the last uprising?"

Richard shook his head. He nudged a neighbor who seemed inclined to interrupt Anthony's exhortation.

Once more, Anthony raised his voice. "You—we—are gathered here to work out a solution to our problems. We face economic disaster if we continue to pay the high tax on our whiskey production. You know it. I know it. But I can assure you on my word as a gentleman, President Washington has not been approached by Mr. Mason or by any of his associates. We are law-abiding citizens, are we not?"

The crowd, led now by Seth and Richard, shouted agreement.

"Will we be able to face our families if we act now like vandals? Will we dare to stand up with our fellows at the next gathering at the town hall if we have rushed now into violence before exhausting every peaceful means available to us for the solution of our difficulty?"

"No!" Richard's voice boomed out, and the cry was picked up by the crowd.

"We are proud citizens of a new nation. This is our country. Think! The men who sit together in Philadelphia and formulate the laws are our servants. Let us not forget that truth. Oh, yes, they serve other men as well, and we must recognize that their decisions are influenced by other demands. Yet, they cannot represent the people unless the people speak out."

Again, the crowd burst into cries of "Aye! Let's tell them what we need!"

Anthony waited until some quiet was reestablished. "And who are the people?"

Richard led the reply. "We are the people! We are!"

"Right! We are the people. We have a right to be heard. But only if we speak in peace. If we take up arms against our elected officials, our servants, we deserve to die. We will have destroyed a dream of a nation. Let us think for a moment. We have a complaint against our representatives. We feel that they are not aware of our problems. We see this tax as destructive to our welfare. Right?"

"Right! Down with the tax!" Daniel led the cry, but Anthony did not permit him to usurp the platform.

"Come, then, let us show the men in Philadelphia how we feel. Let us do more than gather here. Let us enter the city, where they live. If we stop at the arsenal we perform an act of war. But if we enter Philadelphia with banners voicing our dissatisfaction, we will show that our intent is to keep the nation we have helped to establish."

"No! Burn the arsenal!" Daniel's voice had a note of desperation.

Anthony continued before the cry could be repeated. "What happens, friends, if we follow this hothead? We will become outlaws. We will be hunted. Our children and our wives will starve or fall prey to the Indians. And we will deserve the prison to which we will be condemned when we are caught. Is that what you want? Seth? Richard? Frank? Andrew? Are you prepared to abandon your farms? If you do that, you and your families will be worse off than if you paid the tax in silence."

For one moment it had seemed that Daniel might gain control, but now the crowd hung on Anthony's every word. He spoke more quietly, knowing he had caught their attention. "Let us not allow foolish, hot-blooded men to lead us into lawlessness. We have created here a nation unlike any that has existed before. *We* have done it. Are we to abandon our ideals the first time we encounter trouble? We have the means to show our representatives in a peaceful manner that we do not approve of their taxation. And when our voices have been heard, we will be free to return to our farms, for we will have proven that we deserve to live in a democracy."

"Banners! Let us make banners!" Richard began the cry, and it was taken up by many throughout the field.

"What if they don't listen?" Daniel was not ready to give up. "What if they do not care about us or our displeasure?"

"We will return here when the march is ended. We will wait for a response. By beginning our protest peacefully we do not relinquish the right to act more forcefully later! Think, my friends. Never before in the world has such a march taken place. Never before has there been a free country with free men in it who dared to raise their voices in peaceful protest. Let us enter without weapons. Let us display our honest intentions, so that no one can doubt our sincerity. We will be the first free men to give orders to our government. *Our* government!" He raised his arm. "Who will march with me?"

Richard pushed his way forward. "I will. I have materials in my wagon for banners—boards cut this afternoon for my new barn."

Another man lifted a brand from a small fire that had kept some of the protesters warm during the chill night. "Here. We can write our message on Richard's wood with this charcoal." He brandished the burning stick, and others were picked up and held aloft.

Virginia watched the scene in amazement. She had learned, in the year since her return to Philadelphia, to discount Anthony, to ignore him as he ignored her. And she had succeeded in putting him out of her thoughts, if not from her dreams. Now he stood before her, a leader of strength, a man capable of stemming the threat of revolution.

She wondered uneasily whether he had seen her. She could not leave yet. She wanted to find out what he would do, now that he had the crowd in his control. Even when she and George moved closer to the wagon, Anthony seemed not to notice her presence. He was too concerned with his responsibility to the men he addressed.

Daniel Mason held up his hands. "Stop! Don't let him distract you from getting your just due. He lies."

Anthony raised his voice louder. "No, Daniel. It is not I who lie. You are the liar. I know for a fact that you have not approached anyone in Philadelphia with our complaint. You want war. You want revolution. You are not willing to even *try* peaceful means of achieving our goal."

"Of what use are such weak approaches to our problem? The government will ignore us until we prove to them that they can do so no longer. Of what use will your march be? Do you believe it will effect a change in the policy of the government? If you do, you are a fool. And you," he shouted to the crowd, "are fools to believe him!"

Virginia held her breath. Was Daniel going to win after all?

Anthony turned his back on his opponent and held up his hands. "Follow me! Let's show that we're free men. Are you with me?"

The men shouted their assent. The vibrations of their voices sent a thrill up Virginia's spine. What a masterful man Anthony was! How strong—and brave! He alone had taken a crowd of men determined to assault the armory and directed their aggression to more peaceful demonstration.

George touched Virginia's shoulder. "We'd better go." He pulled up on the reins of his horse.

Virginia shook her head. "No. I want to see what happens." She didn't bother to look around at her companion. Her eyes remained focused on Anthony.

He had leaped to the ground and was busy helping the men prepare the signs that would tell the government officials what they demanded. As soon as the preparation was complete, he held one aloft and waved it wildly. "To Philadelphia! Follow me!" His cry was echoed by one after another of the farmers as they swarmed onto the road behind him.

Virginia did not want him to know she was watching. She flicked her reins so that her horse moved to the end of the line of men. George trotted beside her, unwilling to leave her alone among such coarse farmers.

The horses neighed impatiently, for they had to be held back to keep them in place at the end of the parade. Most of the marchers were on foot, but a few farmers rode horseback. Most of the men carried nothing, but from time to time a large banner was raised.

Anthony triumphantly led the marchers. He turned occasionally to urge his followers on, but they did not need his encouragement. He had inspired them with hope. Virginia studied them with interest. She could see now that they did not want to fight unless it were the only way to solve their problem. They were thankful that some other path had been opened to them.

George leaned toward her. "Please, Virginia. When we reach the city, we must go back to your home."

"Go if you wish." She realized that she wanted to be free to watch Anthony without having to concern herself with her companion.

"But you'll be in danger. Don't you see? When this line of men reaches the city, they'll be met by soldiers. Who knows? They might all be shot down. And if we're with them . . ." His voice was filled with foreboding.

Virginia tightened the grip on her reins. "I don't care. I want to see what happens." She had a new reason for remaining. If what George said was true, she wanted to be close by so she could rescue Anthony or bring him to a doctor if he were injured. She refused to consider that Anthony might be killed.

As they moved away from the field, she glanced back. A group of about ten men sat around a campfire. She paused and studied them carefully. One she recognized as Daniel Mason. A chill swept over her. If the march was unsuccessful, those who could would return to Braddock's Field.

And there, waiting, would be Daniel! He'd stir up the bruised feelings and point the way to revolt. The peace of the entire nation hung on the success of Anthony's plan.

Thirteen

The great clock in the church tower struck noon as the men reached the center of town. Virginia was fatigued from the long, rough road, and she wondered at the bravery and strength of the men who walked the entire distance. She could see Anthony clearly, and she felt certain that he stumbled once. But he made no stop to rest, nor did he accept the offer of a horse from one of his men. She realized his motive. Most of the men walked. As their leader, he wanted to show that he was as strong and brave as they.

Virginia breathed a sigh of relief when she realized that no militia stood in the streets waiting to kill the protesters. Still, she watched Anthony with growing uneasiness. What if the soldiers were around the next corner? What if some citizen, angered by the revolting farmers, decided to shoot the man who led them? She clenched her reins tightly, praying quietly to herself for Anthony's safety.

As the first line of marchers approached the meeting hall where the two houses of Congress convened, Virginia could see the men lift their banners, turning the lettered side to face the building. But there seemed to be no one other than the curious townsmen watching the parade. The balcony that lined the building was empty.

A cheer went up when a few men appeared through the doorway and leaned over the banister. One whose tall form and proud bearing was unmistakable was Thomas Jefferson. He did not depart from his usual reserve, but she felt certain that he approved of the restraint shown by the marchers. He was not the only cabinet member to appear. Hamilton, too, stepped onto the balcony, but his expression was sour, and he drew back from the railing, as if desirous of avoiding infection.

Other members of the Senate or the House appeared.

126

They seemed more willing to express their feelings about the demonstration. Some even leaned over the balcony railing and waved to the marchers, shouting words of encouragement.

Virginia guided her horse to a position directly across from the balcony where she would be able to hear what transpired. She could see that the farmers, moments before dropping from exhaustion, were now filled with a new enthusiasm. They called out to townsfolk they knew who lined the street and to the legislators. One man, holding a sign on which was printed the legend ABOLISH THE WHISKEY TAX waved it meaningfully at Hamilton, shouting the words at the same time.

A gasp went up from the onlookers when two men near the center of the mob produced a stuffed cloth figure drawn to resemble Alexander Hamilton. Its neck was secured with a stout rope, and the body hung limply from a long pole.

The effigy swayed over the crowd and then, without warning, it burst into flames. People backed away, seeking shelter from the falling sparks. Threads that had been tied on like hair broke free and floated over the nearest marchers. The figure, identifiable only moments before as that of a scarecrow dressed up to resemble the farmer's most hated opponent, was now a fiery pillar.

Virginia grasped the reins of her horse and held him in close check, for she could feel the panic in the beast. The effigy burned so swiftly that in moments it was only a smoldering heap on the small open area made as the marchers backed away from the fire.

Anthony appeared to do nothing to quiet the outburst. Instead, the panic seemed to subside of itself. A cheer went up from the marchers, and once more they began to move forward. Virginia waited until they were all in motion, and then she fell in behind once more.

City folk who had come from shops and houses followed along on both sides of the farmers. Some jeered the marchers, others seemed to blend in with the parade. This was an issue that roused strong feelings.

Just as the line reached the end of the cobblestone street that passed by the seat of the legislature, a number of men dressed in the uniform of the Pennsylvania militia appeared, blocking the way. Virginia gasped. Was the violence to begin at last? If so, Anthony was doomed.

The ranks at the head of the march stopped, but those in the rear continued to press forward. Virginia shouted for them to halt, and her cry was taken up by women who hung out of windows up and down the steet.

Gradually, the pressure to move decreased. Virginia was relieved to see that the front lines were no longer pushing against the militia.

Would the soldiers fire on the unarmed marchers? Would Anthony be proved wrong in his contention that a peaceful march could bring results that an open assault on the arsenal would not?

An uneasy silence fell over the marchers. Then a command rang out, and as suddenly as the paraders had halted they began once more to move. They continued slowly until they were directly in front of the president's residence.

Their cries rang out as they lifted their banners again. "Repeal the tax!" "Down with the whiskey revenue!" "Government by the people!"

Suddenly a man appeared on the balcony above the street. President Washington! He stood for a moment surveying the scene. Then he raised his hands. Every face turned in his direction. Militia, marchers, citizen observers, all showed their respect for this imposing gentleman.

Washington spoke slowly. "Gentlemen! Friends!" He paused for a moment. "I can read your signs, and I understand the cause of your discontent. I wish to commend you for your restraint. Less responsible men might have tried to storm the city with guns, imposing their will on the legislature with bullets and steel. You have shown that the trust Thomas Jefferson puts in you is justified. He has claimed from the very beginning that the common man is to be trusted with decisions, that he will be able to understand the workings of representative government. He has insisted that, though some laws will favor one group of citizens and some others, all will be capable of realizing that solemn consideration has gone into every regulation. Sometimes one need outweighs another."

There was a murmur, but the crowd remained respect-ful of the man who stood before them. "I cannot say what the effect of your protest will be. It is too early, and there must be many discussions of the issues before a decision is reached." The unrest of the watchers seemed to increase, and he held up his hands. "However, I can assure you that the message you have given us this day will be in our minds."

Virginia watched the farmers. Many had, in Braddock's Field, claimed that Washington was a scoundrel, that he was determined to put a crown on his own head. Yet, faced with the man himself, no one showed anything but total respect. These farmers were, after all, the same men who had fought for freedom. They had known Washington as a general who led them to victory. Daniel Mason and his rabble-rousers were too far away. In the final moment of confrontation, violence did not erupt.

A cheer began at the edges of the crowd, and soon it echoed through the canyon that was formed by the build-ings. Again and again cries of "Huzzah!" "God save the United States!" and "Long live Liberty!" rang out, drown-ing any further words from the president.

With a wave of his hand, Washington stepped back into his room. The door to the balcony closed and curtains were pulled to obscure any view beyond the glass. A cry of triumph rose from the mob. Cheering in victory, the marchers began once more to move.

Darkness was falling when the first men reached the edge of town. Virginia drew back into the shadows, watch-ing the farmers as they broke ranks and headed back to their camp. Anthony stood at the side of the road, exchang-ing greetings with the men as they passed. Despite the wear of the march, everyone was still in good humor. Men called to one another. "It was a good march!" "We showed them what we demand!"

The men had been heard. They had not been turned away. Even the figure of Hamilton was burned in effigy without bringing on a riot, or an attack by the militia.

The disagreement had not been settled, but neither had there been a battle. The farmers had not stormed the arsenal. A second revolution had been avoided—and Anthony was responsible for the peace.

Daniel Mason, who had no concern for the peace of the nation, had been outwitted. Virginia's heart pounded with excitement. How brilliantly Anthony had led his followers! She wanted to rush to his side to tell him how proud he had made her. The wall of reserve she had erected between them restrained her.

George pulled at her reins. "We must go now. I swear, your uncle will never let me take you for a ride again. Do you realize we've been gone since morning?"

She reluctantly turned her horse and headed homeward. George prattled on, first talking of the march, and then turning uneasily to the question of what explanation he should give for her long absence.

No explanation was needed. Roy Salford had not yet returned from the city, and though Angie and Jonathan were obviously worried, they did not dare demand reasons for their mistress's long absence. With open amusement Virginia watched George hurriedly depart. She realized that he would probably have to placate his parents for his day-long absence.

Angie abandoned her quiet as soon as Virginia was alone. "Miss Virginia! You've had us all so upset. Have you heard the news? A band of ruffian farmers invaded the city, waving banners and shouting for freedom and the repeal of the whiskey tax."

Virginia nodded absentmindedly. "Get me some food, would you please? I haven't eaten all day."

"Miss Virginia, you mustn't go off like this again. What would your uncle say? He'd hold me responsible if something happened to you."

"Yes, Angie. I'm sorry. I watched the marchers." She could see that Angie was eager to talk, but she turned away. She wanted desperately to be alone, to have a few moments in which to sort out her emotions.

Anthony was in the habit of ending his day sitting in the library with his employer and discussing the problems that had arisen and their solutions. She fully expected that he might appear any moment at the door. And she had to decide how she should greet him, and if she should greet him at all.

He had filled her dreams often in the year since her return from her adventures but always either as a lover or in a fight for his life. Now she had seen a new part of his nature. He was a born leader—a man who could inspire others to the highest and best within themselves.

She could not deny that she had been filled with admiration as she watched him. Never once in the entire day did he lose his ability to control his followers. Never once did he show fear before adversity.

The emotions she had thought were dead filled her breast. She longed to run into his arms when he entered the house and tell him how wonderful he was. The idea of once again feeling his arms around her sent a shiver of anticipation up her spine. Was it possible?

She still loved him. The realization left her weak with desire, with the need to touch him, to talk to him, to meet his glance and see, reflected in his eyes, the same love that was in her own.

With a sob, she lowered her head onto her arms. What foolish fantasies were these? Why, after so many months of peace, did these dreams come back to haunt her? She did not have the power to make them reality. It was Anthony who had made it clear that he had no wish to associate with her. He was the one who was cold and aloof.

By the time Angie returned with her food, Virginia had regained her calm. She took the tray and sat at a small table in her room.

As she began to eat, she heard a horse approach, heard Jonathan speak to the rider and then move off with the horse behind him. She recognized Anthony's footsteps on the stairs, heard his knock on the front door.

Virginia put down her fork. Nothing tasted good. The meat was dry and the vegetables too salty.

Angie sensed her mistress's mood, and was quiet when she came to take the dish away. She clucked disapprovingly when she saw how little had been eaten but took it anyway, closing the door behind her. She had learned that if Virginia was unhappy, the best treatment was to leave her alone. Later, when she felt better, she might want to talk.

Anthony heard her walk about her room, for it was directly over the library. Many times in the year that had passed he had listened to her footsteps and longed to be beside her. But he dared not intrude upon her privacy. Had she not made it clear that she wanted to forget all that had taken place between them?

And certainly, he could not deny her right to be angry. He had done the unforgivable! He sat quietly, reviewing every move he had made, every word he had spoken. How could he have harmed her so grievously? She was so lovely, so delicate, so beautiful in both body and spirit. He hated every young man who came to court her, for they spoke to her, were permitted to kiss her hand. They could ride with her.

Today he had approached the house with anticipation. He had seen her riding behind the farmers when they left Braddock's Field. He had noticed her watching as the parade reached the center of the city. He had been aware that George wanted to depart and that Virginia had insisted upon remaining.

And what he had seen had brought hope to his troubled heart. Would she at last forgive him? Was her presence a sign that his torment was ended? Would she be waiting for him when he arrived at her home?

He had intended to remain the night with his friends at the field. But the sight of Virginia had caused him to alter his plans.

Virginia paced uneasily between her window and the door of her room. Should she rouse her courage and at least go down to speak to Anthony? He was alone, that she knew, for her uncle had not yet arrived.

With sudden resolve, she crossed the room and opened the door. But then she hesitated. Did she dare? Would he not simply insult her again? Wouldn't he take her attempt at friendliness as a sign that she wanted to return to a relationship which he had already admitted was shameful?

Hoofbeats sounded under her window. The front door was thrown open. Roy Salford dismounted and ran up the steps. Virginia froze.

"Tony!" Roy's voice resounded in the large foyer. "You were magnificent! Washington wants to see you personally to discuss the tax and the revolt. By God, man! I think you've found a solution to the whole problem."

Quietly, so no one would hear her, Virginia stepped back into her room. She closed the door carefully, and then, in a sudden burst of emotion, she threw herself upon her bed and wept.

Fourteen

"But sirs! Surely you can see the inequity of this tax!" Anthony's voice sounded through the hall and Virginia, on her way to the kitchen to discuss an upcoming banquet with the cook and Jonathan, paused to listen. To whom was Anthony speaking? She moved swiftly from the staircase toward the library door.

It stood slightly ajar, and she approached cautiously and peered through the crack. She was afforded a clear view of the room. Her uncle sat in his usual place, the chair which her father had loved so very much. In a circle around the room were many of the most important men in Congress and in the cabinet. Thomas Jefferson, Alexander Hamilton, at least ten of the twenty-six members of the House of Representatives, and seven senators filled the larger-than-average room to capacity. Clearly, this was an important conference, and an unusual one, for it was not often that her uncle entertained so many dignitaries at one time.

Anthony stood in the center of the room. He was speaking to everyone present, yet she could see that his words were directed particularly to the most important guest, the president himself. He had resumed his impassioned plea as she approached.

"Sirs, I beg of you to think of the struggles these men have endured in the past. They served in the lines during the fight for liberty. They deprived themselves and their families of food so as to feed the troops. This country means much to them. Surely you can see that it is not fair to penalize them for their one form of income that comes to them in coin of the realm!"

Hamilton gestured with one hand and in the silence that followed began to speak. "Young man, I recognize the sincerity of your cause, and I am not unaware of the problems this tax presents to your friends. Yet the good of all must

136

supersede the welfare of a few. We must be able to defend
ourselves against the aggression of the British sea captains.
We must present a united front to the nations of Europe,
all of whom are watching us with great interest."

He tapped lightly with his finger on the arm of his chair.
"You surely must be aware that the kings of Europe are all
waiting for us to fail. They send spies to see how close we
are to destruction. They wait, eagerly, to appoint one of
their own to take over the control of our nation. Is that
what you want? Are the rights of a few farmers more important than the freedom of a nation?"

"No! But, sir—"

"Please. Hear me out. We have a responsibility to every
man in every nation of Europe who has ever longed for
freedom. We have begun a great and magnificent experi-
ment to prove that free men can rule themselves in peace.
Do you want to destroy that noble—"

"Enough of this oratory!" Thomas Jefferson rose to his
feet and pounded his fist on the desk. "Please, Alex, we
are not at present speaking for the record before the full
House or the Senate. We have agreed to permit this young
man to speak his mind. We can enter into debates later. I
promise that every word you speak will be preserved for
future admiration by your descendants."

Hamilton glanced angrily at Jefferson. His body tensed.

"Gentlemen, please! I wish to hear what the young man
has to say." Washington rested a hand on Hamilton's
shoulder. The angry Federalist settled back and stared at
Anthony.

Anthony spoke again. "Sirs, Mr. President, I have lived
most of my life on the frontier. I have worked and fought
with farmers who encamp here in Braddock's Field. I know
they are honorable and sincere men who feel as strongly as
any in this country regarding the principles you have enun-
ciated. Yet"—he glanced about him—"they are deeply
concerned for their families. They have farms. They need
tools and clothing for their children. Their sons cannot go
to market in rags nor can we be the ones to say that they
should never enjoy an evening at a tavern in the company
of friends. If they are denied the small pittance they receive
from the sale of their whiskey, they will have nothing."

He cleared his throat. "Sirs, please understand me. I am not fighting the question of strong or weak central government. That is a matter for you and the other representatives of the citizens to decide. What I protest is the unfairness of this tax on whiskey. It penalizes the few. It puts on the farmers' shoulders the burden of federal income. Is that proper? It is in an appeal for equity that the farmers have left their crops."

"Has any among your friends attempted to pay the tax?" Hamilton could not conceal his irritation.

"No, sir. Does that surprise you? They seek to have the tax repealed. They fear that if they pay it while it is still in contention they will not see their money again. They are not unaware that money is short for the payment of government officials."

There was a silence, broken at last by the president. He rose and faced Anthony. "Thank you. Have you anything more to say?"

"No, sir. I am thankful that you permitted me to speak."

"We, too, are thankful. We recognize that you played a vital role in keeping the peace yesterday. Your march was enlightening. I do not believe anything quite like it has ever taken place before."

"Thank you, sir. You are undoubtedly right, certainly not in a free country by free men."

"You have a right to be pleased with your accomplishment. I only pray that the direction you have pointed out to the farmers will continue to be their choice. I understand there are fiery orators among them who advocate violence."

"Yes, sir, and that is what I fear. I do not mean this as a threat, but I worry that if the men in Braddock's Field are rejected, they may turn to rioting."

"Aye, we realize the danger," Washington said quietly, "but we cannot allow that possibility to influence our decision. The weal of the nation must come before the good of the few."

"Yes, sir. Gentlemen, I thank you for your time." Anthony bowed and moved across the room. Virginia backed quickly from the door toward the staircase.

She was starting across the hall to the kitchen when Anthony reached her side. "Good morning. I trust you slept well."

"Yes, thank you."

"Did you hear what went on in the library? Your uncle was kind enough to invite many of the officials for an early meeting. They go now to the floor where the decision will be made." He paused as the distinguished gentlemen filed out. When the hall was empty, he said, "Did you hear what was said?"

She shifted uneasily. To be forced to carry on polite conversation when she wanted so much more from him was a fine form of torture. "Yes. I must confess that I went to the door and eavesdropped. The door was open a bit and—"

He nodded. "Thank you for being honest with me. I believe I was the only one who noticed you."

She paled. "Are you certain? Oh, how humiliating. I didn't think I could be seen."

"Please, Mistress Virginia, don't distress yourself. I'm sure that if you were noticed, no one was upset." He paused, his face twisted with a hidden emotion. For one moment, she met his eyes, and then she turned quickly away.

In that moment, he gained courage. He had to speak to her! But then she closed the small crack that had opened between them. He bowed politely. "I must take my leave. Your uncle has promised to notify me as soon as a decision is reached. God willing, the matter will be ended today."

The sky was dark when Roy Salford returned. He was alone, and he seemed unwilling to meet Virginia's inquiring gaze. He was in good spirits during dinner, and Virginia guessed that the decision had been favorable.

The serving maid was carrying in the tea when Anthony arrived. His face was strained, and he took the seat Roy offered him with only a perfunctory greeting to Virginia. A silence fell on the room. When the maid had poured the last cup of tea and vanished into the kitchen, Anthony spoke. "Please, Roy, I beg of you. Don't keep me in suspense. Even the worst possible answer is better than no information at all."

Roy glanced at Virginia. She met his gaze without wavering. If he attempted to send her from the room, she was prepared to fight.

"I know, of course, of your involvement in the march, Virginia." She looked up in surprise. "Was it your idea, Anthony, to risk my niece's life in that manner?"

"Oh, no, sir! I will confess that I saw her, but she was with one of her suitors."

Roy turned to her. "Virginia, I know you are stubborn. You inherited the characteristic from my sister, your dear mother. But do you realize the risk you took? You might have been killed. Why did you do so foolish a thing?"

For one moment Virginia forgot that she was speaking to Anthony as well as her uncle. "I wanted to see what happened. Oh, uncle, you should have been there in the crowd. It was wonderful." Then she became aware of Anthony looking at her, and she spoke more calmly. "I was curious, that's all. I'm sorry. I will not do such a thing again."

She dared not look at Anthony. Had he moved toward her when she began to speak? Had he smiled in pleasure at her enthusiasm?

Roy turned back to Anthony. "I am afraid I do not carry good news. The men who support Hamilton, and I must remind you that I am one of them, have won the day. I do not understand how you can fail to appreciate the importance of what we are doing. This nation will vanish from the face of the earth if it does not become strong now. A central government with power, real power, is essential to our survival. Can't you see that?"

Anthony rose, his cup of tea untouched. "Sir, I can only see that the faith the farmers and I have placed in the law, the confidence we had in the importance of equitable taxation has been betrayed." He bowed low to Virginia. "Pray, excuse me, for I must go to my friends."

He turned swiftly on his heels and strode from the room. Virginia reached out to stop him, but her fingers closed on thin air. Then she heard his heels click over the stone floor of the hallway and the big front door slammed shut.

Virginia rose, a sob reaching her throat. Clutching her kerchief to her lips, she ran from the room. When she reached the sanctuary of her own quarters, she threw herself on her bed and burst into tears.

Fifteen

Virginia woke abruptly to the sound of hoofbeats pounding below her window. After several months of inactivity on the part of both the farmers and the government, something was about to happen.

The usual morning sounds of farmers and tradesmen hawking their wares reached her ears. She heard Angie and cook bartering with some passing merchant.

Had she dreamed that a rider disturbed the tranquility of the morning ritual? No. She had heard his horse thunder past.

Today Virginia was too impatient to wait for Angie to assist her in her toilette. August seventh! More than a year had passed since the plague had robbed her of both her parents, yet their memory was fresh in her mind. On a day such as this, her mother would have already been in the garden cutting flowers for the breakfast table.

Virginia had not continued that custom, for it pained her too much to recall happier days. She realized, as she pulled on her slippers, that there were few things in which she took pleasure. She rode still with the young men whom Mother Willing approved. She even sat with some in the parlor, under the watchful eye of Angie. But each one, in some way, only reminded her of Anthony.

She had heard little of him. There had been that terrible day in June—the fifth. She would not forget the date as long as she lived. Farmers, still angered by the whiskey tax, had rioted, and in their fury burned the home of General John Neville, the man assigned to collect the unpopular revenue. She had wept that day, and nothing Angie or her uncle had said comforted her.

In the following months, Virginia had longed for news of Anthony, but she had not dared mention his name to her uncle, and though Angie inquired on the street, she could not learn anything more than that the farmers still camped

144

at Braddock's Field and that Anthony Burke remained one of their leaders.

When Virginia entered the kitchen this morning, she was greeted with a babble of excited voices. "Please, one at a time! I can't understand what you're saying."

Angie pushed cook toward the stove. "Can't you see my baby wants breakfast? You prepare the meal and I'll tell her what we know." She sat opposite her mistress. " 'Twas most exciting. Ah, this day will end the trouble!"

"How? What's happened? Tell me, before I die of curiosity."

" 'Twas a messenger from the president himself. He carries a proclamation to the farmers, ordering them to disperse lawfully."

"You think they will obey?"

"Why, they must! Then your Anthony can return to the city in peace."

"Whatever do you mean? Why should the actions of an outlaw like Anthony Burke concern me?"

Angie and the cook exchanged knowing smiles. "Do you think we are blind? I know that each day when you go to ride, you ask to take the road that would lead past the field where Anthony is encamped. I can see your disappointment when your suitors choose other routes. Your uncle may be blind to your feelings, but I have loved you since you were a tiny baby. I know what you want— maybe better than you do yourself."

"Nonsense!" Virginia took the dish cook presented, relieved at having some reason to end the conversation.

After breakfast she said to Jonathan, "You must ride out today to Braddock's Field. Learn what the president's proclamation has meant to the farmers. Please, bring me news, before I die of worry."

Jonathan bowed. "I'm already on my way there, at your uncle's orders. I will bring my report to you as well."

Noon passed without any news. She and Roy Salford ate their meal in silence, each deeply immersed in private worries. Finally, when Virginia heard a horseman riding hard, she leaned out the window. She had expected Jonathan, returning with news. But it was not her servant whom she saw. The man who rode so furiously into town was familiar—too terribly familiar. She felt both fear and surprise. David Cavanaugh!

His black hair seemed a bit longer than it had been a year ago, and his clothes were dusty from the road. He passed swiftly, with only a glance in her direction. But as she drew back from the window, she felt certain he had seen her.

She said nothing of his arrival to her uncle because other matters took precedence. Jonathan arrived shortly thereafter, and his news wiped all other thoughts from her mind. The farmers had howled their defiance when the proclamation was read. Anthony Burke had tried to restore order, but without success.

"I fear they may storm the city, master. They are most incensed."

"I doubt that. There are too many militia here. Nevertheless, they will do some harm before this worry is ended." Roy turned to Virginia. "I was perturbed, in the past, that you seemed so distant with Anthony, for I admired him greatly. Now I am thankful that you found him not to your liking. And, please, ride no more into the country. I will speak to your suitors if you wish."

"I will tell them, uncle. You need not trouble yourself."

When he left for the center of the city, she wandered into the garden where she could be alone.

She had expected to find herself recovering quickly from her parents' death, once the first year was over. But now she longed for her mother's counsel. Mother Willing was of no help, for she was strongly in favor of Virginia's marriage to George Kingsbury. When Virginia tried to speak of her confusion over Anthony or David her words fell on deaf ears.

Angie was more helpful but she, too, had her preference. Anthony was her favorite, for she had learned to respect him during his first weeks in the Nelson home.

Each morning, Virginia listened to the chatter of the cook and the vendors, hoping in vain for news of either David or Anthony, who were so much on her mind. Virginia had heard that David went on business outside the city and returned periodically to his house. But she was reluctant to inquire directly about him, because she was not at all sure as to the part he had played in her misfortunes.

One night she finally mustered the courage to speak.

"Uncle, I have heard that David Cavanaugh is in town."

"Yes, so he is. He has visited me in the city. And he has requested that he be permitted to court you."

She hesitated, waiting for him to continue. When he did not, she spoke. "It is true that he was kind to me when my father died."

"Is there something you have not told me about that time?"

He took her silence as a sign that all had been proper between them. "Good. I have given my consent. However, he informed me that he would be gone on another business trip for a while."

Virginia nodded. Should she have insisted that he stay away from her? Time had done nothing to simplify her choice or help her understand the real meaning behind all that had happened to her.

On the seventh day after the president's proclamation to the farmers, Anthony rode into town. Virginia was sitting at the window, watching the horsemen pass, and her heart leaped when she recognized his face. He glanced up as he reached her window but made no move to stop.

Roy did not return home from Congress until after dark. Virginia, hoping to learn what had transpired, waited until he arrived to eat. Virginia watched her uncle in silence, waiting for him to speak.

After the maid cleared the dishes away, Roy looked across the table at his niece. Before he could announce his intention of retiring to the library for a smoke, she began to speak.

"Uncle? I saw Anthony Burke ride by this morning. Did you encounter him in town?"

"Anthony? What concern to you are his actions?" She blushed. What concern, indeed? Yet, she had to know what happened to him. Roy frowned. "I told you once that I was pleased that you found him not to your liking. Was I wrong? Well, if you harbor any thoughts of him, put them aside. His name is not to be mentioned again in this house. Do you understand?"

"No, uncle. He was your friend. What has happened?"

"He was my friend, or I thought he was. Now I have seen his true colors."

"What has he done? Please, don't keep me in suspense."

"I believed that he was sincere in his love of our country. But today Anthony Burke delivered a message to the president from the farmers. They have had the gall to issue a declaration of their own. They refuse to obey the law of the land. They are determined not to disperse. I am certain Burke had a hand in framing the paper, for it was well-written. But what it says is infamous. They are agreed that they will fight the whiskey tax. They have declared war on the nation!"

Virginia felt dizzy. She grasped the table and held on, afraid that if she let go, she might fall.

Roy hurried to her side. "Virginia! Are you ill?"

"I'm fine, uncle. It's just . . ." She could not continue. She felt the darkness close in around her.

When next she became aware of her surroundings, Angie was sponging her body with a soft, damp cloth. Virginia wished desperately that she could return to blessed unconsciousness, for the reality of her life had suddenly grown unbearable. She had been so impressed with Anthony's leadership of the farmers, so convinced that he was noble. "I never want to see him again! Never!" She was not aware that she spoke aloud.

"Who, little missy?" Angie's voice was gentle, like it used to be when she sang lullabies to a tired child.

Virginia did not answer. Her throat was too choked with tears.

Sixteen

"Miss Virginia, are you awake?" Angie stood over the bed.

Virginia reluctantly opened her eyes. "Yes, Angie," she answered dully.

"Angie leaned over and touched Virginia's cheek with her fingertips. "Oh, my sweet, you have been sick for so long. Master Roy was afraid it might be the plague come back to torture you. But the doctor has told him it is just female vapors, brought on by not eating. It is my fault that you are sick, for I saw that you played with your food, but I said nothing. Oh, my baby! We must not lose you again, now that you are awake."

Virginia forced a smile. "Oh, Angie, don't blame yourself." She closed her eyes.

Angie touched her arm. "Please, Miss Virginia, don't let yourself drop off again. I have kept you alive with broth. Now you must eat something more solid. Please, for my sake."

Virginia realized that a bowl of broth rested nearby on a table. She frowned. How could she eat, when she was so troubled?

Angie saw her glance. "You must tell me what bothers you. Why have you refused food until you made yourself ill?"

Slowly, Virginia began to speak of her dilemma, all that had happened between her and Anthony, of her confusion when she compared him with David. She reminded Angie of all that Carolyn Nelson had said about recognizing one's true love. "Angie, I don't know what I feel. I am too confused. Anthony was so wonderful when he led the farmers on the march. I thought for sure that I loved him—but is it true that he delivered that terrible message to the president?"

"Yes, mistress. And in the week since you first fell ill,

150

the declaration from the farmers, coupled with Anthony's plea for consideration, has been rejected by Congress."

"Then he'll be killed!"

The cook entered, carrying a steaming bowl of stew. The delicious smell aroused Virginia's appetite although her thoughts were far from food. Angie approached with the bowl. "Please try to eat something. You need the strength. Your uncle is so worried about you."

Virginia sat up weakly. How selfish of her to think only of her own sadness, and not of her uncle. She took the bowl and began to eat. Each spoonful increased her appetite a bit more, until, to her surprise, she had reached the bottom of the bowl. Angie was smiling when she carried the empty dish from the room.

By the next day, Virginia's strength was restored enough so that she was able to leave her bed. She spent much of the day near the window, gazing out on the crowded street. She felt like an observer, removed from life, yet still concerned with its affairs.

Her uncle tried to draw her out of her depression. "Virginia, my dear, you have had me so worried. I cannot endure the thought of losing you, for you are all the family I have left." She could see the pain in his eyes "Your suitors have called every day. I had difficulty concealing the extent of my concern. Thank God you are better, at last."

"Thank you, uncle. You are so good to me."

"I love you, my dear. We all do." He paused, as if to consider his next words. "You have had another visitor."

She felt herself flush. Anthony? The hope died in birth. Never! Roy had made it clear he would not permit him in the house, now that he had chosen to lead the farmers.

"David Cavanaugh." Roy paused. "He was most polite and sincere. He seemed honestly perturbed that you had not waited for him at the Freedom's Arms, and when I explained that you had been mistreated by the tavern-keeper, he was enraged. He has begged to be permitted to call on you and right the misimpressions you might have had regarding him. My dear, he is an honest man and a good businessman. You could do no better than to accept him as a suitor if he were so inclined."

Virginia wondered whether she should now tell her uncle

the truth about what had happened between her and David. Would he be outraged if he knew David had taken her?

She chewed uneasily on her upper lip. She could not speak of that time. Only Angie knew her secret, and Angie could be trusted to remain silent.

"Think on it, my dear. David is a good man, as I say, and he would have my full approval were he to choose to court you. I have told him I would give him an answer tomorrow."

David had been very kind to her when her father died. True, he had taken her when they reached the inn. But he had been so gentle. She could not recall those moments with David without a stirring of her emotions.

If it were only his caresses that came to mind, she knew what her response now would be. She would accept his suit, and even agree to be his bride. But she could not forget the strange things he had said as he played upon her passion. Nor could she ignore the words of the old woman who had come to clean the room.

David owned the Freedom's Arms. He made no attempt to hide that information from her. That meant that he at least consented to the use Bessie made of the old inn. What Virginia was not sure of was his involvement in procuring the girls who occupied the upstairs rooms. Geraldine had claimed that she had been delivered to the inn by David. Had she told the truth? *Was that what David had had in mind for me?* The thought sent a shiver up Virginia's spine. Had he been successful, she might never have escaped Bessie's control. Now David was saying that he wished to marry her.

Why, with so many eligible young men interested in her, was she thinking about David Cavanaugh? Why could she see nothing in George or Richard?

Her memory continued to replay her escape from Amos's inn. And the image of Anthony loomed before her.

That night with him had been so strange. Had he actually been asleep when he first took her? There had been something unreal about their encounter, but her responses to his touch had been terribly real. She felt the same weakness that had possessed her that night. If only he had not been so formal with her when she arrived in Philadelphia! If only he had shown that their shared love had meant as much to him as it had to her.

What else was there about Anthony that drew her to him? Her uncle thought her foolish because she was concerned with the politics of her country. But Anthony had appreciated her involvement. Would any of her suitors treat her with such similar courtesy? She shook her head. If they knew of her interest, they would turn their attention elsewhere. As Angie said, a woman who concerned herself with man's business was unnatural.

Now she knew she had to see Anthony once more. Before she accepted David as a suitor she had to know what Anthony's true feelings were. She knew her plan was foolish but she also knew that she would go through with it, no matter who objected.

"Angie!" Virginia said suddenly, hurrying to the wardrobe. "I wish to go for a ride. Help me dress, and have Jonathan prepare the curricle!"

"A ride might be good for you, but not in an open shay. Let me order the landau, instead."

Virginia stamped her foot. "Do as I say! You may bundle me to your heart's content, but I will not be shut up any longer."

Virginia had her way. The warm summer air raised her spirits as they drove. She did not at first tell Jonathan in which direction to drive. Only when they had traversed most of the city streets did she say, "Go to Braddock's Field."

Angie gasped. "Oh, no, Miss Virginia! Master Roy will be furious."

"Do we have to tell him everything we do?"

Angie pursed her lips. "Miss Virginia, I know I seemed to favor your interest in Mister Burke before all these things happened. But your uncle is right. He is no good. He is out to destroy all your father worked for."

"Nonsense! In the past, you urged me to hear all sides before I made a judgment. Have you changed now? Is Anthony not to be permitted to speak for himself?"

"But why does he need to speak at all? What do you need to do with him that has not already been done? You have told me how he shamed you. Would you give him a chance to repeat his inconsiderate behavior?"

"Enough! I will be with you and Jonathan. Certainly I will be in no danger. Anthony cannot harm me if I remain in the carriage." She leaned forward. "Now, tell Jonathan —or I will tell him, myself!"

Angie did as she was told. As the carriage moved into the countryside, Virginia said, "You worry too much. Angie. I am curious as to what is happening at the field. If I see no reason to stop, we will pass by and turn home at the first possible opportunity."

"You wish to see Anthony Burke, and I cannot understand why. But rest assured, if you behave foolishly, I will speak to your uncle."

Virginia did not bother to respond. Sometimes, she thought, Angie was much too officious.

Her heart began to pound as they approached the field. Anthony was there, somewhere. Much as she had tried to pretend that she cared not a whit for his safety, she knew that she wanted desperately to see that he was well.

As her carriage drew near, men began to move toward the road. Perhaps the passengers were emissaries from the president. When they saw two women inside and an old man at the reins, they returned to their campfires. Virginia leaned forward. "Jonathan, stop!"

She beckoned to a young boy. "Yes, mistress?"

"I am looking for Anthony Burke. Is he here?"

"Aye, mistress."

"Would you get him, please? I must see him."

"Aye, mistress!" The lad turned and ran toward the tents. It was then Virginia realized that there were women in the field. She thought at first that they were the wives of the farmers, but she quickly realized that was not true. These women were most open in their behavior. They walked arm in arm with the men, and they shouted to one another in loud, raucous voices. These were camp followers, the loose women who made their living satisfying the wants of strange men.

Virginia blushed. Did the lad think she was such a woman? She leaned forward, ready to direct Jonathan to drive on, when Anthony appeared at the entrance to one of the tents. He moved slowly across the field, and then, when he recognized her, increased his pace.

"Virginia! I never expected to see you here. Is something wrong? Your uncle is not ill, is he?"

"No." Now that he stood there before her, she was suddenly speechless. "I came to . . . I wondered what has happened. Uncle Roy tells me only that you've rejected the president's order."

He took a clue from her stiff language. "That's true. It seems that the president does not necessarily live up to his word. He had said he would consider our reply."

"I saw you ride into town."

"Yes, and I had difficulty escaping after I delivered our declaration. Hamilton had men searching the streets for me. However, I managed to get past them. And now we wait. It is our hope to avoid open conflict, if that be possible."

"You still want peace?"

"Certainly, though I fear we are being forced into violence." He turned toward the field with a broad gesture. "Our ranks are thinning, for it is nearly time for the harvest. Rumor from Philadelphia is that Hamilton is urging that we all be arrested as insurrectionists."

"Oh, no! Then you would go to jail?" She regretted her response immediately. He was being as formal as ever, maintaining a distance from her. Why did she let her fear for him show?

He did not seem aware of her emotion. "At present, no, for Hamilton's motion has been defeated. It seems that the general opinion is that there are too few of us to matter."

"Then it will soon be over?" She was beginning to feel uncomfortable. Why had she come? Not, certainly, to discuss politics, though that mattered to her. What she wanted to ask Anthony was too private to speak of, even before Angie who loved her. "Uncle Roy misses you, though he is loathe to admit it. You provided him with excellent assistance." She stopped speaking. She was only building a higher wall between them. If he knew how Roy felt toward him, he would know she was lying.

"I doubt that he cares what happens to me. Why did you come, Virginia? Did he send you to learn of our plans?"

She met his eyes. How dare he? He was as much as telling her he thought she was a spy.

He seemed suddenly abashed. "Please, forgive me, I did not mean to suggest that you would take on such an assignment." He waited for her reply, and when it did not come, he continued. "Besides, Hamilton has spies enough among us. I am sure that we do not speak but our words are repeated in his ear. And not, certainly, by you." He gestured toward Angie and Jonathan, who were both sitting patiently in their places pretending that they were not listening. "Why did you come?"

"I—I feel an involvement in what happens here. After all, I watched the march. I came only to see what has taken place since then."

His gaze was steady, and she could not tear her eyes away. "This is all? There was no other reason?"

"None. I have been ill, and—"

"Ill?" His concern was obvious. "Are you well, now?"

"Yes, thank you. I'm fine." She wanted suddenly to leave. She had seen him—and she had accomplished nothing. Much as her heart cried out to him, much as she longed to return once more to the closeness of his embrace as she had felt it that night in the woods, she could not move toward him.

She leaned back against the cushions. "Jonathan, drive on!"

Anthony watched as Jonathan turned the carriage around and headed back toward town.

Why, he wondered, had Virginia made this journey? Was it only to learn news she could easily get in the marketplace? And what was it her eyes said when they met his? Did she still feel the magic of the night they had spent together?

He had not dared to speak of it to her even once in the time after her return to her uncle's house. Each day he had searched her eyes for some sign that she cared, that she felt something other than shame when she recalled his embrace. And now here was this unexpected, unexplained ride of hers from town to Braddock's Field. Why? Was it possible that he had been too reserved? Was she asking him to make the first move?

But what if she rejected him, as she had that day on the street when she escaped from Freedom's Arms?

He watched in silence as the carriage disappeared. He would have to take the risk. Better that he bear another rejection than that he live the rest of his life not knowing. Next time I'll force her to talk to me, he decided. He did not permit himself to admit that he might never have another chance.

Seventeen

Roy Salford stood in front of the fireplace with his legs braced apart, looking at Virginia in amazement. "You are not delighted at the thought of travel? What strange sort of girl are you? There is no other in the whole state of Pennsylvania who would consider refusing such an opportunity."

Virginia did not meet his angry eyes. "Please, uncle, don't be annoyed with me. It is only that I never expected to visit England."

"Would I conceal the knowledge of such an important journey if I knew it? Certainly not! This appointment is as much a surprise to me as it is to you. Such a mission is certainly needed. Far too many American citizens have been pulled from American ships and impressed into the British navy. The king does not yet realize we are no longer a colony, but an independent nation. We must change that."

"I realize that, uncle. But must you go? And must I travel with you?"

"Virginia, it is an enormous honor to receive such an appointment. I dare not refuse, nor have I any desire to do so. President Washington has appointed the Honorable John Jay as his personal representative to negotiate for a new treaty between our country and England. I am proud to be associated with such a noble endeavor."

"Yes, uncle, but must I accompany you?" she persisted.

Roy stared at his niece. "Sometimes, my dear, you show little common sense. You do, indeed, resemble your mother. Of course you must come with me. The last time you were alone, you found yourself in serious trouble. Do you think that I will leave you alone again?"

"I could stay at the Willings'."

"No, you could not. Thomas is leaving for another trade commission and will not return for almost a year. I do not consider his wife, gentle as she is, to be the kind of protector you need. Besides, my dear, you have had little experience. All of your life you have remained within the limits of this city."

"Oh, no, uncle! Remember my family lived in New York when I was a small child."

"This, however, is quite different. Have you any concept of the distance from here to England? We will be at sea for a month. You will see the land from which your grandmother came, and the estate she abandoned when she married your grandfather. You'll attend balls the likes of which have never been seen on these shores. Enough! You are going. The matter is closed."

Virginia gazed at the dancing flames after her uncle left the room. How could she speak of her confusion? The journey was one she had longed to take ever since she was a small child. Now she was reluctant to leave America.

Why did she feel that her departure would be a betrayal of Anthony's trust? Did he need her presence? Of course not! He had no use for her at all. Yet, ever since her visit to the field with Angie and Jonathan, she had worried about him. Why had he stared at her so intently?

At first she had concluded that he had expected her to join the other loose women in the field. But that thought she had dismissed quickly. He was, generally speaking, a very direct man. He spoke his mind without fear, even when he stood before the president. Why would he be other than direct with her?

She had sensed an underlying emotion in his glance, as if he was waiting for something. Waiting for what?

With sudden determination, she sat down and drew a sheet of stationery from the desk drawer. She would let him know she was leaving. If he had something to say to her that he had been holding back, he would find the opportunity to speak.

Dear Anthony . . .

No, that would never do. He would misinterpret such a heading. She began again.

Dear Mr. Burke:

I regret that I must leave for England. My uncle demands my presence with him. May this time of unrest soon come to a close.

She sat with her pen poised and considered her closing. Did she dare use any friendly words? What would he think of it? At last she signed her name.

She studied the letter in silence, then abruptly tore it up and threw it in the fire. What foolishness! He had done nothing to indicate concern for, except to show mild upset when he heard she had been sick.

Carefully, she gathered all the pieces of paper and tossed them after the letter. She had almost made a terrible mistake. No self-respecting girl would allow herself to show interest in a man who cared nothing for her!

If only she did not feel so disturbed. If only she could control her thoughts and put all consideration of Anthony behind her.

Resolutely, she headed up the stairs. How could she allow her feelings for Anthony to interfere with her pleasure at going to England? How foolish! She was going, at last. And maybe, while she was gone, her dilemma would somehow be solved.

The next morning, when Angie knocked on her door, she found Virginia in tears. Virginia gestured at the piles of dresses that were spread over the bed. "Oh, Angie, look. I've tried every one of them on, and they're all terrible. I can't wear any of them. I'll be the laughingstock of England."

Angie chuckled. She had been worried about her mistress ever since that visit to Braddock's Field. But evidently she no longer had cause for concern. "Have you considered speaking to your uncle? He might have some solution to this problem."

Virginia had no desire to face her uncle so soon after their disagreement, but at last she took Angie's advice. She knocked softly on the door of his study.

She paused just inside the door. "Uncle Roy?"

"Have you come to argue? If you have more reasons for your remaining here, do not waste my time."

She sat in a chair beside him. "No. Please forgive me for my behavior. I can see now that you are right. But, uncle, I have nothing to wear. All of my clothes are so outdated!"

Roy threw his head back and roared with laughter. He seemed unable to control his amusement, even when tears came to his eyes. Virginia forced herself to remain in her chair, but she wished, fervently, that he would not make fun of her predicament.

He gasped for air. "Ah, woman, how fickle thou art!" He brushed the tears from his cheeks. "Oh, my dear little girl, that is the least of my problems. If I promise that we will take a seamstress aboard, and any material you choose, will that please you? And if I also assure you that as soon as we reach England we will locate a woman, the queen's own, if necessary, who knows the latest styles to make, will that satisfy you?"

"Oh, uncle, thank you! That will be wonderful." She bent and kissed his cheek.

Roy chuckled. "You need not thank me. Your inheritance would pay for such frills many times over. And the gowns you buy in England will serve you well when you return here. You seem not to realize, my child, that you are a wealthy woman."

"Yes, uncle, I do. But papa always took care of such matters."

"Yes, I know, as I care for it now. And as your husband will when you marry. I can see that it is just as well, for there would be no logic in wasting it all on frivolities." He smiled. "If this is what it takes for you to look forward to the journey, it is a small price to pay. Now that you no longer object, you will find that each day of the voyage will bring you new experiences that you will remember for a lifetime."

"Yes, uncle. Thank you." She suddenly wanted to end the conversation. The thought that she would be too far away to see Anthony again, that he might be arrested and maybe even killed while she was gone, made her feel like crying again.

Jonathan returned that afternoon from a trip into the country to buy fresh eggs from a nearby farm. Virginia listened as he reported on his trip to Angie.

"I went past Braddock's Field. They're back again. From all over they come. It isn't over, Angie. Not a bit."

Virginia shuddered. Anthony had been right. The farmers had not given up the crusade. Now that the harvest was over, they were returning. Someone in authority had to be warned. If someone, an official of the government, perhaps, spoke to them, the danger would pass. Once more, she hurried to her uncle's study.

"Yes?" Roy sounded impatient with this new interruption.

"Uncle, forgive me for intruding again. But I have just heard that the farmers are gathering again at Braddock's Field."

He raised his eyebrows. "You are in contact with the rebels? Virginia, I cannot believe that you would disobey me and contact Anthony Burke. The one aspect of your upbringing I cannot understand is the indulgence with which your father approached your intrusion into political matters. Your woman's lack of logic shows at times like this. Do you honestly believe that you are the only one concerned with the rebellious farmers? Do you think Congress is not watching Braddock's Field? Well, disabuse yourself. We have men stationed there who bring us daily reports."

Her shoulders sagged, and he softened his tone. "Dear, do not think me unkind. It is for your own good that I speak. No man wants a wife who tries to outthink him in matters that do not concern her. You must develop your femininity. I fear your father did not consider your welfare, but only his wish for a son. He should not have tried to change you from what you are, a most charming young woman, who, if she behaves modestly, will grow into a beautiful lady."

Virginia did not answer. Clearly, Roy put no credence in what she had to say. She wondered whether Thomas Willing might turn a more receptive ear.

The following morning, while her uncle attended a final meeting with President Washington, Virginia went to see her friends. Thomas Willing was home, but he was about to depart on his own travels. Nevertheless, he listened patiently as she described what Jonathan had seen at Braddock's Field.

When she paused, Thomas Willing said, "Virginia, thank you for confiding in me. I thoroughly understand your perturbation." He took her hand. "I never completely approved your father's insistence that you be permitted to learn politics, for too much thinking spoils the beauty of a woman. Yet you do not lack in comeliness, so maybe I have been wrong. I can, fortunately, assure you that you have no cause to worry. The situation is not being ignored."

He lowered his voice. "I can tell you little of the strategy. However, since you are departing shortly . . . President Washington and Alexander Hamilton have already alerted the militia in New York, in Maryland, and in New Jersey. I can assure you that the matter will not be allowed to get out of hand."

Virginia paled. The militia! Not only of Pennsylvania, but of other states as well. If they were called to alert, Anthony would surely be killed.

Thomas Willing lifted her hand to his lips. "I beg you to forgive me, but I must be on my way. Stay as long as you wish, for my wife loves you dearly, and she will be alone until I return. God be with you on your journey. May every day be filled with pleasure."

"God speed your journey, too, Mr. Willing. Thank you." Virginia prayed that her concern for Anthony was not too evident.

Thomas Willing gave his wife a final farewell kiss and departed. When the sound of his horses could no longer be heard, Mother Willing turned to Virginia. "You were fortunate to arrive before my husband departed. Did he solve your problem?"

"There will be another war. Oh, Mother Willing, what shall I do?" Virginia said.

"Is there anything a woman can do? I do not understand."

"Mr. Willing says the militia has been alerted. If there is a confrontation between the soldiers and the farmers, many men will be killed."

"Aha!" The plump little woman held out her arms, and Virginia crept into their shelter. "So that is your worry. I had the feeling that my husband did not understand." She rocked her gently back and forth, like a mother comforting a sorrowing child. "Do not let his words upset you. Things cannot be as bad as he says. You know how men love to exaggerate."

Virginia fought in vain to control her tears.

"Now, now. You mustn't let your eyes get puffy. And do not take my husband's words too seriously. Consider, my dear, that every state is jealous of its militia. What reason have we to believe that these four states will cooperate to enforce a law passed by the central government? And even if the governors of the states comply with the governmental requests, will men go to kill their brothers? I cannot believe they are that stupid."

"Oh, Mother Willing, why do men think we do not know what is happening? Do they truly believe that we cannot understand?"

"I do not think so, my child. I suspect that they fear we might be capable of much more thought than they allow us. You must not judge them harshly. They cannot be unaware that it is women who keep them fed, manage their homes, and provide them with the freedom to play at the games of politics. Like little boys, they do not wish to acknowledge their dependency. I suspect that they sense our strength, and they are frightened by it."

"Our strength? Are we not smaller, weaker?"

"Think, my dear. Could a man endure the pain of child-birth? Could a man rise above hardship and carry on for the sake of others, as so many women have? Perhaps. But they are too accustomed to our presence and to our support. They guard politics from us, because they want something that is their own. Do not be angry with them."

"Thank you," Virginia said. "You make me wonder why I allowed myself to become upset."

"Now, my dear, do not belittle yourself. You cannot help but worry for a man who is intent upon playing the game of power. You must learn to accept your place, to learn to wait and pray."

"I do not know if I can ever do that. I feel such a need to do more." Virginia forced herself to put her worry aside. "Tell me, Mother Willing, is there anything I can buy for you while I am in London?"

When she departed, Virginia had a list of gifts that would be welcome at the Willing home. She vowed that at least one of them would be delivered without charge, a sign of her appreciation for all that kind family had done for her.

Everyone in Virginia's household bustled about for the remainder of the day so that Roy and Virginia would be ready to board the ship that very evening. As the sky turned red, the last of the cases was loaded on the wagon. Roy assisted Virginia into the carriage. Angie and Jonathan sat together atop the luggage. Jonathan was to be in charge of the house during Roy's absence.

At the docks, Virginia watched the parcels being carried

on strong shoulders to the ship. Was this, she wondered, how her grandmother had departed from England? She knew there had been many differences. Elizabeth had been fleeing her home, and she had taken refuge with a boatload of doxies on the way to the Colonies to work as indentured servants. She had slept in the hold next to pickpockets and whores.

Virginia had a cabin of her own, small but well appointed. Angie's room was below Virginia's, but she offered to move her mattress onto the floor of Virginia's cabin if that were necessary. Virginia refused to accept such generosity. "Stay where you are. I will need little attention on the trip that cannot be provided during the day." She clapped her hands. "Oh, Angie, how exciting this is!"

Angie seemed unimpressed. She tended to the chore of preparing Virginia for sleep, and then, grumbling, departed for the smaller cabin she was to share with the seamstress.

Virginia woke to the noises of departure. The rumbling of the anchor chain was the first thing she heard, followed by the rhythmic singing of the seamen. The gentle rocking of the ship at harbor that had lulled her so quickly to sleep seemed almost natural now, and she remembered her uncle's remark that it might take her some time to get her sea legs.

She pushed open the window that faced the stern of the ship and gazed into the harbor. The sky was still dark, but the call of a bird told her that dawn was near. Then, suddenly, a beam of sunlight lit the crest of the ripples, and a flock of gulls shrieked skyward. The light reflected on the buildings that lined the shore, turning their windows to gold.

She inhaled the fresh salt air. How good it felt to be at sea! The odor of salt water and fish had always delighted Virginia; it spoke of mysterious journeys into the unknown. Her excitement made her forget her worries.

She dressed quickly and hurried to the deck. She joined her uncle who stood talking with John Jay. Both men greeted her with a smile. "Did you sleep well, Miss Virginia?" John bowed slightly at her approach.

"Very well, thank you." She turned to watch the retreating land. How much like a dream this all seemed. Already the docks were small, and the men who moved about seemed like dolls. "Uncle, I am thankful that you wanted me to come with you. This is all so beautiful. And see, I have no difficulty walking on the deck."

"Be prepared, my dear, things may not always be so calm. We are not yet in the open sea. The Delaware Bay still shelters us from the full roll of the ocean swell. We may also encounter a storm, though I pray we may be spared that."

Virginia pointed toward the sides of the bay, still visible in the morning light. "Will we see the land all the way down the bay?"

"No, my dear, it falls away quickly. We will seem to be in open water long before we reach the ocean. Do not fear, I will tell you when we pass out of the bay—if you are not able to sense it yourself. The water becomes more choppy, and the swells are deeper."

Virginia stepped to the railing. Behind her, the sailors raced about, raising sails, calling to one another. She watched the shore until it vanished from sight. When they reached the sea, she glanced back at her uncle and smiled. The journey had begun.

Eighteen

Virginia endured the rough passage far better than her uncle had expected. For him, the journey across the ocean was invariably one of discomfort, with much of his time spent in bed. But she seemed almost a born sailor, walking with ease across the deck as it rolled and thriving on the constant rocking of the waves.

John Jay remained shut in his cabin. The envoy to the royal court had much to prepare before he arrived in England. When Roy felt well enough, the two men consulted. Otherwise, John Jay worked alone.

Other than to sympathize with her uncle's malaise, Virginia had little to do with either man during the journey. Nor did she concern herself with the purpose of the mission until the *Jolly Freeman* reached a point in its voyage five days from the coast of England. A shout from the lookout brought her running to the bow of the ship. She strained to see what she expected to be the first sign of land but instead observed a British man-of-war sailing into view.

The sailors hurried to raise additional sails and trim them for speed. The helmsman spun the wheel wildly, and the little *Jolly Freeman* began to widen the distance between the two vessels. Virginia watched the furious action with astonishment. Why, if they were headed for England, did they flee from a British ship?

Roy appeared on deck as the man-of-war began the chase. He stood beside Virginia, holding his discomfort in check, and only when the gap between the two ships grew wide did he return to his cabin. Virginia trailed behind him.

"Why, uncle? What have we to fear from a British man-of-war? We have treaties between us, don't we?"

"Aye, but not enough! Were that ship to reach us, they would board and remove all able-bodied men they wanted. We would have no defense, for we carry no arms aboard. And we would have no recourse nor any way to rescue our

170

citizens from years of labor behind the mast of some British vessel. Our formal complaint to the government would stir no response."

"How terrible! Would they even take gentlemen like you and Mr. Jay?"

"I think not, for we are influential. Their target is experienced sailors. They have been known to leave only enough men on shipboard to bring the vessel safely into port." He lay back in his bed. "How thankful I will be to reach land again."

"Yes, uncle." Virginia stared through the large window at the rear of her uncle's cabin. "Will they catch us?"

"It appears not. The *Freeman* behaves as one so named should. It knows when retreat is the better part of valor."

Virginia sat with her uncle for the remainder of the day, watching the sails of the pursuer grow smaller with each passing hour until, at last, it dropped from view.

The *Jolly Freeman* arrived at the port of London a day earlier than expected. Virginia was thrilled by the journey up the Thames and the rumble of the anchor as it was dropped. This was her grandmother's home! From these very docks the young Elizabeth had fled—and from the king's own palace.

Virginia stood to one side as the roustabouts hauled the baggage from the hold. The ship had carried cargo which had to be loaded on dories and rowed ashore.

The very air itself was different from any she had smelled before. There were exotic spices and fine woods, smelling of shadowy forests. Bales of cotton and raw silk were stacked, each with its own distinctive aroma. The odor of burning coal and smoke from a thousand chimneys hung heavy over the city. As Virginia stepped onto the dock, she began to cough violently.

She soon forgot her discomfort. There was too much to see. Englishmen in bright uniforms moved among the newcomers, checking shipments, recording arrivals, watching everything with sharp eyes. Soldiers! Were the sailors on the *Jolly Freeman* still in jeopardy? She whispered to her uncle, and he smiled. "No, my dear. This is part of the problem we face. What goes on on the high seas is not recognized by the land authority. When we claim to have been stopped, when we state that our sailors have been removed from our ships, they deny any possibility of such a thing. It is a conspiracy. We must break through that wall of silence here at the court and force the British to declare such behavior on the part of their sea captains as illegal."

"Will you succeed?"

"I do not know. But we will try." Roy took her arm. "Right now, I am only thankful that we have reached dry land safely. I swear, I would never set foot on a ship were it not for the orders of the president!"

He led the way to a carriage on which much of their luggage was already stacked. As Virginia climbed in, she noted that the large case containing her new gown was tied safely in place. She would be dressed well when she was presented at court.

On the ride to the inn, she was torn between observing the crowded streets and thinking of her new dress. Never before had she owned anything quite so lovely. She had chosen a pale blue for the skirt and bodice, and the seamstress, Gladys, had found a fine silver braid for trim. When she put the dress on, Virginia looked both innocent and grown up.

The inn was well furnished and was the favorite residence of many dignitaries. Now many rooms were empty, for the war with France limited travel between England and the Continent. As a result, Virginia was given a large suite of her own, instead of only a small room, and she was able to keep Angie and Gladys in an alcove, available whenever she might need them. The furnishings of both Virginia's and the servants' quarters were elegant but of a basic simplicity that spoke of good quality.

When the luggage was put away and her new gown hung up to remove the wrinkles, she opened the window. Men of every class hurried along the narrow passageway between the buildings. She caught sight of a small boy in the act of removing a watch from a gentleman's pocket, but before she could cry out, the child had vanished.

Soldiers marched past, and she wondered if they were on the way to battle. Did they leave wives and mothers behind? One man looked up and called to her, and she drew back, blushing.

When Virginia joined her uncle and John Jay for supper, she was full of questions. She learned that England had declared war on the revolutionary government of France in 1793, and that the citizens of England considered the fight to be for their lives. Feelings ran high. Old animosities between England and the other nations that fought the French were forgotten. Few people in the government would have time to discuss what the British considered a nonexistent problem with representatives from the colonies they had so recently lost.

Nevertheless, as the meal ended, a messenger arrived from Mr. William Pitt, inviting the Americans to attend the king the following afternoon at three. Roy and Mr. Jay took the promptness of the greeting as a good omen.

Virginia slept poorly that night. Her mind was buzzing with speculations. Would the king show signs of the madness that had almost lost him the throne in 1789? Rumors of his illness had reached Philadelphia, and her father had shown sympathy for the old man. Virginia had not shared his pity. She had been outraged that the crown prince had been denied his rightful place during that year of difficulty.

Would the crown prince attend the king on the morrow? If he did, would he notice her in her lovely gown? She was well aware that the king's sons were notorious for their appreciation of beautiful women.

Angie spent the entire morning combing Virginia's hair into many small curls which she gathered in the back and crowned with a crest of fine feathers taken from exotic birds found only in Africa. At two o'clock, the seamstress helped Virginia into her gown and cheked her for any final seams that might need reinforcing. Then, her feet in a pair of dainty slippers, Virginia took her uncle's arm and departed for the palace.

She dared not lift her eyes when first she entered the large room where the king received his official guests. She moved forward slowly, keeping a distance behind her uncle and John Jay, who approached the throne with their heads bowed. Suddenly, a titter drew her attention to one side of the room. She glimpsed a broad, pale face with gentle eyes and a wide mouth. Then, abruptly, it was gone.

The king's age and delicate health were evident. His face was wrinkled, his eyes tired, and his cheeks sagged into heavy jowls. He wore a dark coat, much like a military uniform, with gold braid up the front that closed just above his large, protruding belly. A bright blue garter graced his left leg just below his knee. His feet seemed small, too small to hold so large a man.

He rose as Jay and Roy Salford approached, his hand extended. "Welcome, gentlemen. I recall that once a leftenant of mine bore the name of Salford. Are you by any chance related to him?"

Roy bowed. "Yes, Your Majesty. He was my father. My mother was Elizabeth Bartlett, who also came from your court."

"Ah, yes," George's eyes grew misty. "I remember her well—a lovely child, much like this young lady." He turned toward Virginia.

"She is Elizabeth's granddaughter. May I present my niece, Virginia Nelson."

Virginia curtseyed as low as she dared without losing her balance.

"My daughter Catherine was particularly fond of your grandmother. I regretted her decision to remain in America." He turned back to Roy. "Are your parents well?"

"No, Your Majesty. They have been dead for some time."

"A pity. The war?" Roy shook his head. "Well, I regret their passing." The king nodded once more to Roy and turned again to Virginia. "Virginia Salford Nelson. A lovely name for a lovely child. You might have heard of my daughter Charlotte. I am sure she would love to visit with you."

As he spoke the princess emerged from behind her screen and approached Virginia. She smiled nervously at her father, curtseyed to the two gentleman visitors, and then took Virginia's hand and led the way into the corridor. When the door closed behind her, she sighed with obvious relief. "I was afraid papa would give me instructions for entertaining you. What I'd like to do is take you for a ride into the country. Would you like that?"

Virginia nodded her assent. As the two girls moved toward the exit, Mr. William Pitt arrived. It was with him, Virginia realized, that the greatest part of the negotiations would take place.

While they waited for their carriage, the girls began to get acquainted. "Where do you wish to go? I want only to be as far from the palace as I can. It is seldom that I get

such an opportunity as this to be away from my father."
Charlotte grimaced.

Virginia could not conceal her shock at such lack of
filial respect. She dared not question the princess. Instead,
she reviewed those places in and near London which had
once been important to her grandmother. "My great-grand-
father owned the Bartlett estates not far from the city.
Could we drive there?"

"Oh, yes!" Charlotte's face brightened. "It's a lovely
drive." She gave an order to the coachman and settled
back in her seat. Virginia remained erect, excitedly watching the passing scenery.

The ride was a bit longer than Virginia had anticipated,
but it passed quickly, for she found Charlotte a charming
companion. They spoke of dresses and the latest styles.
Charlotte bemoaned the fact that the clothes from France
were not available, though she remarked that many of the
masters of design had moved from Paris at the beginning
of the unpleasantness and were building new factories in
and around London. "Papa is very pleased. England will
soon be the center of culture. And all because the king of
France could not control his subjects!"

Virginia hesitated to become involved in a discussion of
politics with the princess, so she simply smiled. There was
little need for her to speak, for the princess had warmed
to her duty and was busily describing every new scene.

When they reached the village just outside what had once
been the Bartlett estates, Virginia leaned forward. Her
grandmother had spoken of a small borough, with clean
cottages enclosing a large green commons. Now the grassy
square, which had once held cattle, was gone. In its place
stood a large, ugly building. The tiny houses were covered
with soot, and even the light covering of snow was black.
There were no children on the streets. Virginia could not
restrain her curiosity.

"Oh, the children are at work." The princess gestured
toward the factory. "It's just as well. When they are left to
roam the streets, they turn to crime."

Virginia thought of the children playing happily near
her home. "Who owns this factory?"

"Oh, the new baron. It was built by his father. Only recently, he hired a new overseer from France. Some of the best cloth in the country is woven here."

Virginia could not speak. She was too outraged. Her grandmother, Elizabeth, had described the fight to keep the factories from this land. It had been a bitter battle, and it had been lost. She was thankful that her grandmother had not lived to see this destruction of beauty.

"Do you wish to meet the baron?" Charlotte seemed unaffected by the ugliness around her. She did not wait for Virginia's answer. The gates of the estate were in sight. Virginia wondered if the children at work in the factory had time to look at the serene landscape that surrounded the manor house.

The coach paused at the gate, and a command rang out. Then they were on their way once more. Virginia gasped. An exquisite landscape lay before them. Even the bare trees reached skyward with grace and pride. Evergreens shielded the residents of the manor from the squalor that surrounded them.

The carriage passed through a small woods into an open meadow. Deer started and ran from their approach. The manor was in full view.

It seemed unimpaired by age. Its great stones were half-hidden by vines which, in early summer, were covered with thick leaves. A rose garden had been protected by mulch against the coming cold of the winter. Near the entrance bright green holly bushes lent a touch of color to the reddish gray of the walls.

As the carriage approached the entryway, a young gentleman emerged. He was tall, with curly dark hair that refused to stay tied in back. He wore a red hunting habit with black boots glistening with polish.

He leaned into the carriage. "Charlotte! How delightful! I had no idea that I would have the pleasure of your company!" His smile was broad and friendly, and his eyes twinkled merrily. He glanced toward Virginia, and his expression changed. "Zounds! She's come to life!"

Virginia frowned. Before she could speak, the princess interrupted. "Percy, this is Virginia Nelson. Her uncle is a guest of my father's. Her grandmother was born in the manor here."

Percy took Virginia's hand and brought it to his lips. "I

would have guessed. There is a portrait of your ancestor in the great hall. It could be of you, my lady."

Virginia blushed. Percy sensed her discomfort and addressed himself to the princess. "Tell me, Your Highness, are you coming to my midwinter ball?"

Charlotte shook her head. "You know papa would never permit me to attend a party to which the crown prince was invited. However, it might be possible for me to slip out, at least for a brief period. It is so trying. I wish, at times, that I were a man."

"Oh, never do that, Your Highness. You would deprive the world of much charm and beauty."

"Charm, maybe." Charlotte smiled at Percy. "Beauty, never. But I am content with charm. It is a kindly word."

Percy turned back to Virginia. "I still cannot recover from seeing the girl I have loved since I was a child come suddenly to life. There were many wet days when I whiled the time away gazing at your grandmother's portrait and longing to have been born when she was young. To think now that my wish has been granted." He leaned close to her ear. "You are truly beautiful, my lady."

Virginia blushed again. "Please, do not address me with such a title. I am an American."

"Ah, yes. I recall being told once that the lovely Elizabeth fled to the Colonies. Well, if your countrymen do not know how to properly honor a lady, it is their loss. For me, I take great pleasure in acknowledging your superiority over all other women."

Virginia glanced at Charlotte. The princess seemed not at all perturbed that such flattery should go to another. Her round face and wide-set eyes showed good nature. Rumor had it that all the children of the king were more German than British except for the crown prince, whose features, unlike his habits, were sharp and clean. He had a reputation as a lecher and a man too fond of drink.

Percy glanced at the sky. " 'Tis growing late. I suppose I cannot persuade you to come in for a sip of wine and a bit of warmth? No? Well, tomorrow, then. I have a hunt scheduled for five in the morning. Princess Charlotte, would you honor me with your presence?"

Charlotte pouted. "I am sorry. I cannot." Her face brightened. "But mayhap Virginia could take my place?"

Percy met Virginia's eyes. "You would give me much pleasure if you agreed."

"I will speak to my uncle. If he does not object . . ."

"Good, then, it is decided. I will expect you." He took her hand once more. "I will not live again until I see your face once more."

Charlotte broke into a laugh as the carriage approached the gate. "Percy is such a droll man. He is a kind gentleman and an honorable one. Even my father does not object to his occasional presence at the court. You will have a most pleasant day tomorrow."

"I just remembered. I can't go. I have no riding dress."

"Then you must take one of mine. I will be confined to the palace all day tomorrow. Papa has planned a party for my niece's birthday, and he would be most upset were any of us to be absent."

Uncle Roy looked annoyed as the carriage approached him. He controlled his temper until they were back at the inn. "Virginia, you must not again vanish without telling me where you are going. Had it not been that you were with the princess Charlotte, I would have worried. The king urged me to move you into the palace, into the quarters your grandmother once occupied, but I refused. I feel it important that I supervise your activities."

"I'm sorry, uncle. I will not be so thoughtless again." Virginia could not conceal her disappointment. "The princess has plans to send a carriage for me this evening. She has invited me to dine in her quarters, and she has offered to lend me her riding habit."

Roy raised his eyebrows.

Virginia continued quickly. "I have been invited to ride the hunt tomorrow with the baron Percy Hancroft, the new owner of my grandmother's estate."

Roy did not seem as displeased as Virginia had expected him to be. He saw her into the carriage the princess sent, urging her only to watch her manners and not to forget to curtsey if the king appeared. But he insisted that he would accompany her to the hunt.

When Virginia returned to her rooms, Angie helped her prepare for bed. She seemed amused at her mistress's high spirits. "You are not sorry, then, to have come to London?"

"Sorry? Never. Everything is so exciting." Even as she

responded, however, she thought of Anthony, who would perhaps have to spend the winter in discomfort in Braddock's Field.

"Indeed!" Angie pulled the covers up over Virginia's shoulders and picked up the candle. "If you need me, I will be near."

Virginia stared into the darkness. The days ahead gave promise of many experiences. There would be parties and more hunts. And Percy Hancroft was such a gentleman.

Nineteen

"You would deny your niece a glass of brandy? Why, Mr. Salford, it is the only thing that will protect her from the winds when we begin the hunt." Percy's polite smile did nothing to soften the arrogance of his tone.

Roy Salford met his host's eyes. "My niece is young, too young for strong liquors. She is dressed warmly, and she needs no alcohol to lift her spirits."

"Please, uncle!" Virginia glanced from one man to the other. "I'm sure he means no disrespect. Papa let me have a glass once in a while."

Roy saw that her face was flushed with excitement. For the first time since leaving Philadelphia, he regretted his insistence that she accompany him. "One glass, then."

Percy winked at Virginia as he handed her a goblet. His words were directed to her uncle. "Mr. Salford, I beg you to honor me with your presence in the great hall. Did Miss Virginia tell you I have a portrait hanging there that would be of interest to you?" All the hauteur that had been evident when he sought to persuade Roy to permit Virginia some brandy was gone. He spoke now with what Roy considered oily politeness. But Virginia seemed too charmed by the man's good looks to note such subtleties.

Roy contained his irritation. This man was insufferable. However, he had something Roy dearly wanted. He assumed his most diplomatic voice. "No, but I have been hoping you would permit me to see it. My father spoke of it often and was greatly sorry that he could not bring it with him to America. No artist in America equaled Gainsborough."

The painting was large, the figure of her grandmother life size. Although the hair was styled differently than Virginia's and the gown was not the same style, the features could have been her own reflection. The rendition was so

182

perfect, that it seemed as if Elizabeth might step out at any moment and greet her son and granddaughter.

"How beautiful!" Roy's voice was filled with awe. "I see why my father regretted leaving this behind."

"You do not intend, do you, to take my golden princess from me?" Percy sounded truly distressed, and Roy's annoyance with him faded. "I would be devastated."

"I don't know. I have considered it, of course." Roy could see that his host was sincere, and he suddenly felt more friendly. "We will meet again, I am sure. And it appears that I will remain in England for some time. I am certain we can work out a compromise."

"Thank you. From the bottom of my heart." He gazed up at the portrait. "This painting means a great deal to me. It would pain me to let it go unless . . ." He glanced swiftly at Virginia.

An awkward silence was interrupted by the sound of a horn. Percy tilted his head. "Ah! The leader of the hunt is calling. We must hurry."

The yard was filled with horses. The chatter of voices, the neighing of the mounts, and the baying of the dogs threatened to overwhelm Virginia. She glanced up at Percy. He met her eyes and smiled. "It is a bit overpowering, isn't it?" She nodded. "Well, don't let it bother you. Enjoy the excitement."

She smiled and followed him to where a stableboy held three reins. After Percy lifted her into the saddle, he and Roy mounted their horses. A man in a bright red coat who held a curled horn in his hand lifted the instrument to his lips and brought forth a haunting note.

The horses were suddenly running toward the open field in pursuit of the dogs. Virginia found herself riding near the head of the column, next to Percy. Her uncle seemed caught between two very talkative ladies.

"I hope you will forgive me my little subterfuge," Percy shouted. "When I learned you were a practiced rider, I could not resist having you to myself."

Virginia smiled. It flattered her that so handsome and important a man should consider her desirable. She glanced back again at her uncle. He was frowning. "I fear my uncle will be angry if I do not remain in his sight." She was ashamed to admit that she was so closely super-

vised, but felt oddly nervous at the thought of being alone
with Percy.

Percy had been steering his horse away from the crowd.
Now he relaxed his hands. The two horses resumed their
positions close to the leader. "Well, then, we will do nothing to get you into trouble." His smile assured Virginia
that he was not annoyed.

She felt a flood of thankfulness. How gentlemanly he
was, how considerate—not like David, whose politeness hid
cruelty, nor even like Anthony, who showed signs of blunt-
ness and who treated her more like a younger sister than
a lady. She forgot, for the moment, that it was her wish to
have her opinions respected.

Percy leaned toward her. "How wonderful that you will
be in England for some time. I am thankful to William
Pitt for any delays in the negotiations. It permits me to
enjoy your company."

She blushed. The wind was chill, and her cheeks were
already red, but in Percy's presence, she felt warm. "Uncle
tells me we are sure to be here at least through Christmas."

"How wonderful. Then you can attend my midwinter
ball."

Virginia frowned. "I do not know. My uncle—"

"Watches you closely. Well, never fear, he will have an
invitation, too. He may find it interesting to meet the crown
prince."

The pitch of the dog's baying changed. Percy raised up
in his saddle. "The fox has been treed. Come, we mustn't
miss the kill!"

The body of the fox lay still, covered with blood, when
they reached it. Virginia's stomach rolled uneasily. "My
dear!" said Percy. "You are pale. Have you never been on
a hunt before?"

"No. I grew up mostly in the city. In my country, men
hunt for food, not entertainment."

"You disapprove of this, then?" He appeared ready to
sweep it all aside to please her.

"I don't know. It seems so cruel. The poor fox had no
chance to escape."

"Of course not! What good would a hunt be, if the fox
outwitted the dogs?"

Virginia kept her head averted from the sight of the dead animal. "Please, can we go back? I don't feel well."

Percy rode close beside her on their return to the manor. Inside, he led her to the great hall and sat her before the portrait. He glanced quickly from the painted face to hers. "My dear Miss Virginia. There is only one condition under which I would permit your uncle to have this painting. If in Elizabeth's place I were permitted to keep the live version of my dream."

Virginia blushed. She had barely met Percy Hancroft, and he was already proposing marriage. Were all Britishers so impulsive?

He drew her to her feet. "Please do not think me impudent. You must understand. I was not teasing when I said I had fallen in love with the portrait when I was still a child. It is true. You are my dream woman come to life. I cannot believe you are real. I live in fear that you will vanish if I close my eyes."

She drew free of his arms. "Please, Baron. We hardly know each other."

"Then you must promise me you will allow me to see you often."

At that moment Roy stepped into the room. "Sir! I find it difficult to understand your behavior. Is it proper for a gentleman in England to be alone with a young lady? If you care not at all, let me make it clear that I am concerned for my niece's reputation."

"Please, Mr. Salford, I beg your indulgence. I freely admit to the crime of which I am accused. But you can see that I have done nothing to soil the young lady's honor. She was feeling ill, and I chose this place for her to rest. I cannot deny that it gives me great pleasure to see her so close to the portrait." He lowered his voice. "I realize that my reputation is not the highest. But there will never be any hint of dishonor cast upon this lovely lady. I am sincere when I say she has been in my dreams since I was a child. She belongs here as lady of this manor. I beg permission to court her. And I promise I will never compromise her in this way again."

Roy glanced toward Virginia. There was something he did not like about the man but he could not put his finger on it. Still, there was no reason to deny Virginia some pleasure. He would make sure he had her properly supervised. He met Virginia's eyes. She was begging him silently to say yes.

"I will give my consent, but you must understand this is only for the privilege of courting her. Let me warn you, sir, that the first hint that you are leading her into the wild ways for which the prince and his companions are noted, and she will be sent packing back to America."

Percy seemed more than willing to accept Roy's conditions. Whenever she came to the manor, either Roy or Angie accompanied her. Percy treated her with the utmost respect. And as the days passed into weeks and the weeks into months, Virginia found it increasingly difficult to remember why it was she had been reluctant to leave Philadelphia.

The midwinter ball was every bit as exciting as Percy had said it would be. The guests wore costumes and masks. Even the crown prince came, dressed as a devil.

Virginia wore an all-white gown with a small white cap that covered her hair. Pointed ears and whiskers sewn to the front edge of the cap identified her as a kitten. Her white mask had big eyes painted on it, and Angie painted lines over her cheeks to bring the whiskers close to her mouth.

Percy was charmed by her ingenuity. "You have seen Mozart's *Magic Flute*! I did not realize you were in town when it was last performed."

"*The Magic Flute*? What is that?"

"Oh, my sweet, you are truly an innocent. It is an opera composed by the great Wolfgang Amadeus Mozart. If there is another performance this winter, I beg the honor of escorting you to it, so you can see why I thought of it now."

The Magic Flute was performed in January. True to his word, Percy bought four tickets for opening night and invited John Jay, Roy Salford, and Virginia. This was one of the king's favorite operas, and the royal box was filled. Virginia waved at Charlotte when she entered and visited with her briefly during one intermission.

For Virginia, the evening was appropriately described by the opera's name. It was a night of magic, filled with sparkling songs and colorful costumes. She fell in love with the man who was dressed as an exotic bird, and she wept when it appeared that the heroine would not be allowed to marry the hero. When the final curtain fell, she cheered with the rest of the audience.

The singers appeared for many curtain calls before the king rose and left his box. Percy leaned toward Virginia. "He's going backstage to reward the performers. Do you wish to attend him?"

She glanced at her uncle. "Oh, may we?"

Roy agreed that it would be all right. As they followed the royal party to the backstage area, Virginia took Percy's arm. She was still bubbling with enthusiasm. He smiled with pleasure. "The king will be pleased at your appreciation. You've been introduced to him, haven't you?"

"Yes, and I have seen him since. He visits his daughters often in their quarters. He is a very devoted father."

"True. There is no one in England who would dispute that." Percy's voice had an odd note to it.

Virginia did not attempt to pursue his meaning. The king and his daughters were just ahead, and the actors were lined up, waiting to be presented to their monarch. . . .

By the time the snows began to melt, Virginia was growing tired of London. Even with fresh breezes blowing up the Thames, the odor of the city was unbearable. The stench of the sewers and soot from the factories, combined with the smell of dead fish and rubbage from the river, created an unbearable atmosphere.

Most of the other fashionable people shared her distaste. The court was moved out of town. Parliament closed its meetings until fall. Social activities came to an end. Virginia was delighted when Percy suggested that she and her uncle stay at his manor until Pitt and the king decided to resume the negotiations.

John Jay and her uncle spent most of their days deep in talk. Percy was busy with his overseers and the directors of his factory. Virginia rode every day to the fields, to watch the first signs that winter was past.

One day she realized she had deliberately avoided riding close to the village. At last, unable to ignore the poverty any longer, she spoke to Percy. "Is it good for the children to work so hard? I have seen them enter the factory before dawn, and they do not leave until darkness has fallen."

He smiled indulgently. "You worry overly much. In London many children run free, and they are in constant mischief. Most of the pickpockets in London are children. Besides, who would support the families if the children did not work? The machines cannot be operated by coarse hands."

"But shouldn't children have time to play? I'm sure you did, and so did I, when we were young."

"Ah, but you forget. These are lower-class people. They cannot expect the same privileges as their betters."

Virginia did not answer. She reproached herself for ignoring so long the conditions that surrounded her.

On Sunday, the one day when the children were not at work, she went to the town. She was immediately surrounded by a crowd of youngsters. Their faces were sooty, and they smelled of sweat, but she forced herself to conceal her reaction to their filth. She sat on a step of one of the less dirty cottages and began to recite the stories she had learned as a child. The chattering ceased, and all ears seemed tuned to her words.

Suddenly, a door opened behind her and a stout woman pushed her to her feet. "Wat ya doin' 'ere? Ain't no place fer a laidy!"

The children scattered. Virginia turned to face her accuser. "Where I come from children are sent to school."

"Aye, 'n their parents starve! Mind yer own business, ef ya please, yer laidyship. We got 'nuf trouble 'thout havin' someone fill our brats' 'eads with learnin'."

Virginia glanced about. The children were gone. She felt certain they would not return, no matter how long she waited. She turned without answering and walked to the manor gate, where she had insisted that Angie wait. "What happened? Did they attack you?" asked Angie.

"Oh!" Virginia shook her fists. "It makes me so angry. They treat their children like animals."

"Maybe that's all they are. I'm only thankful that you were not harmed."

"No one threatened me except a grown woman who resented my kindness to the children. Oh, Angie, how can Percy permit this to go on?"

"What can he do? If he closed the factory, everyone in the town would starve."

Virginia led the way back to the manor. "I must speak

to him again. Surely something can be done to relieve the burden the little ones have to bear."

She found Percy totally lacking in sympathy. "Virginia, my dear, you trouble yourself unnecessarily. You have been alone far too much lately. The king is moving his court to Bath. Your uncle and Mr. Jay might have an opportunity to speak with him there."

Roy and John Jay leaped at the opportunity to confer again with William Pitt, who would also be at Bath. In the days that followed, Virginia found her concern for the children lessening. Perhaps Percy had been right, she thought. She did not, after all, know everything involved in the situation. What right had she to interfere in the lives of others?

Virginia spent much of her time with Princess Charlotte. Percy attended her every day, and she was aware that he was pressing his suit with greater persistence. The day came when he managed to find her alone.

He led her into a garden, out of sight of the town. "Virginia," he said, "I have been patient. Surely you cannot deny that. I have loved you since first I saw that picture in my father's house. We are alone for the moment. Let me hold you now. And promise me you will marry me as soon as the banns can be posted."

She pulled away, startled by the daring of his words. Let him hold her now? David had assumed that he had a right to her body because he offered her his name. Was Percy of the same mind?

She turned and stumbled against a bush. Immediately, Percy was at her side. "Forgive me, please, Virginia. You must understand. I am not accustomed to dealing with so virginal a female. The women who share the prince's companionship are not generally so proper. I am, after all, a man, with a man's appetites."

Virginia backed away. He caught her arm. "Please! I will not make so rude a suggestion again. But consider my proposal. I am sincere in my desire to have you for my wife. Will you not take pity on me?"

She stared up at the clouds, fighting to sort through the confusion of her thoughts. Would she be able to endure living in the manor, so close to a factory where children labored without hope? Could she accept being sheltered, as the princesses were sheltered, totally removed from the rest of society and its cares? Would she be willing to give up the freedom which her grandmother, Elizabeth, had desired so much, even if it meant living in the house that had once belonged to her family?

In a rush, memories of Anthony and David flooded back. How long had it been since she thought of either one? She realized that she still was uncertain about her feelings for them. "Please, Percy, I can't answer you now. I must have more time to think."

Percy couldn't conceal his impatience. "I've never pretended that I didn't want you for my wife. You've had all winter to think about my proposal." Seeing her displeasure, he stopped sputtering. "I'll wait. But I will want an answer soon. My desire for you is great."

Virginia was withdrawn for the rest of the day. By evening she had made up her mind. She would speak to her uncle. Suddenly, she wanted desperately to sleep in her own bed in the room she had had since she was a child. But most of all, she knew she had to see Anthony once more. Anthony—and David. She had a decision to make. David had asked permission to court her. Anthony seemed to have no desire to see her again. Somehow, she knew she had to face what each had meant to her. She could no longer avoid the problem.

Twenty

"Miss Virginia, come quickly. I see land." Angie tapped on the door of Virginia's cabin. She waited until her mistress appeared and accompanied her to the railing of the *Suzannah*. "There!" She pointed toward the horizon. "We're home."

In the mist that hung between water and sky, she could discern a dark shadow. The darkness spread until it lined the horizon. The lookout had seen it much earlier, but now it was visible even to deck-bound passengers. Home! Until she stepped onto the deck of the *Suzannah* after the ride from Bath, Virginia had not realized how homesick she really was.

Not that her visit had been unpleasant. Other than her pain over seeing young children at hard labor and her inability to ease their fate, she had enjoyed her visit. But she could not forget the children.

At first, she had envied Princess Charlotte's ability to ignore all the suffering around her. But Virginia's parents had raised her to be sensitive to the needs of others. She could not ignore the conditioning of a lifetime just so she could more completely savor a few hours of entertainment.

She remembered her British friends fondly. The princess had come with her to the docks, surrounded by many of her companions. Even Percy, still smarting from Virginia's rejection, could not let her depart without a farewell visit.

Virginia and her uncle were standing on deck when the boat carrying the royal party appeared. Roy, who was not happy at the thought of his niece leaving without him, was in the middle of a lecture on how she should behave while she stayed at the Willings'. "Thomas should have already received my letter regarding your arrival. He will meet you at the dock. Virginia, do as he tells you. Do not, please, indulge yourself in your whimsical habit of roaming alone. And try, if you can, to limit your intrusion into men's

192

affairs. Politics are not for female minds, no matter what your father said."

Virginia was aware that she resented her uncle's criticism of her father but she knew better than to argue. She watched the longboat approach and was thankful that the opportunity for such an exchange would soon be over. She had listened to this exact same lecture at least five times since Roy had agreed to her departure and could have recited it from memory.

"Virginia!" She could see now that Percy was at the prow of the boat, directing its passage through the crowded water of the harbor. "We're coming aboard!"

The captain had hesitated to drop the ladder, but when he saw the princess, he issued the order, and the men obeyed quickly. Percy was the first to reach the deck, and he guided Princess Charlotte over the railing. Together, they approached Virginia.

Charlotte extended one arm. "Virginia, I will miss you. Are you certain you must go?"

"Yes, Your Highness." She made no attempt to explain her decision. "I will miss you, too. You have been a good friend."

Most of the well-wishers retreated to the main deck where a keg of ale had been opened. Then Charlotte took Roy's arm. "Come, Mr. Salford. Will you escort me to the festivities? Our farewell is for your niece, but you also are a favored friend."

Roy could not refuse the invitation, reluctant though he was to leave Virginia with Percy. He watched them carefully as he moved away.

Percy turned to Virginia. "I wish you were not going. I will miss you sorely. What is it that I did to cause you to turn down my proposal? Surely you do not doubt my sincerity."

"Oh, no." Virginia felt regret that her leaving should hurt so kind a host. "You have been generosity itself. And I am sure you meant everything you said. But though I may look like my grandmother, I cannot take her place, for I have my own, in my own world."

"And with your own lover, I suspect. You have no room for me in your heart, because another already rules there. Tell me, is that not true?"

"I— I do not know." How, if Anthony ruled her heart, could she have forgotten him for so long?

Percy seemed to sense her uncertainty. "Oh, my innocent little friend, do not think that because you were momentarily distracted your love is less sincere. I saw his shadow in your eyes more than once. Even when you were most filled with the pleasure of the moment, you seemed to look for another face, another pair of eyes, another mind that matched yours more closely than mine did. No, my sweet, he is there"—he touched her bosom lightly with one finger, and drew it back swiftly—"so well entrenched that nothing can dislodge him. God knows, I did my best."

Virginia did not reply. Percy seemed so sure. In her heart a war raged. Anthony versus David. Each had his peculiar charm, each his place in her memory. Yet both men, for different reasons, seemed unsatisfactory: Anthony because of his obvious rejection of her affection, given freely as they lay together in the woods; David because she dared not quite trust him since he had lied to her. And, though he had indicated a desire to court her, he had not yet visited her or written to her.

"Enough of such talk." Percy held out his arm. "Now is a time for well-wishing and bon voyage. Come, I am sure your uncle is worried enough about you."

At midnight, alone, Virginia had realized she was too excited to sleep. She'd sat on deck, out of the way of the sailors, watching the sky turn from black velvet to golden silk. She felt the pounding of the anchor chain as it was drawn up, and she watched as the ship began to drift slowly toward the sea.

The sails billowed as the *Suzannah* reached the mouth of the Thames, and the vessel picked up speed. Only when England was no longer in view had Virginia retired to her cabin.

And now, after almost a month, the journey was over. Virginia searched the shoreline for the first sign of the inlet that led to the Philadelphia docks. The *Suzannah* moved unerringly forward, maneuvering the passage with ease, coming to rest, at last, in the harbor.

Thomas Willing and his wife waved eagerly when they saw Virginia. She was the first on the plank. She ran swiftly, throwing herself into Mother Willing's arms.

"Thank God you have returned safely!" The kindly woman was close to tears. "I have worried so. What if you had been drowned in a storm?"

"My dear, that is enough. You have bothered me for weeks with your needless fussing. See, Virginia is safe, as I said she would be. Speak no more of watery graves." Thomas softened his rebuke with a smile. He, too, embraced Virginia, and the strength of his arms told her he had been concerned for her safety.

During the ride home Virginia described the journey, the race with the British ship on the way into the London harbor, her meeting with the princess Charlotte. When she spoke of the children working in the factories, Mother Willing wept, and Virginia compared her reaction to that of the heartless woman who had chased her from the village when she tried to teach the children.

During supper Thomas sat listening to Virginia's stories. He was amused by King George. "Aye, he's a good father, so they say—if one does not consider the behavior of his sons. I approve his caution when it comes to liberty for his daughters. They are, I understand, exemplary young ladies."

"Oh, yes. Princess Charlotte was so kind to me."

"Did you meet the crown prince?"

"I met him once, at a party given by Percy Hancroft."

"Is he the dissolute rogue rumor has him out to be?"

"He is a most charming man, and a gentleman. I heard the rumors, too, but I saw no evidence of his bad behavior."

"Thank God for that!" Mother Willing said. "He has a reputation as quite a ladies' man."

"How goes your uncle's work with John Jay?" asked Thomas.

She relayed what information she knew, aware that Thomas Willing expected Virginia to speak of politics with understanding. She wondered whether she would continue to enjoy such a liberty during her stay in his home.

When Virginia finished speaking, Thomas poured himself a brandy and sat studying her in silence. "You are a good observer, and you tell a story well. I might, in the near future, ask that you speak of some of these things to the people most concerned. Will you find it difficult to appear before the president and possibly Hamilton and Jefferson?"

"Oh, no, sir. As you know, my father encouraged me to be at ease in the company of his friends."

"Good. Then that is settled. Now, we have other things to discuss. You know, of course, that your uncle has put you in my charge until his return?"

"Yes. He has told me to do as you tell me and to cause you no trouble. I will do my best to comply."

"Fine. I must confess I have been concerned regarding that matter. You have been accustomed to greater independence than I gave my daughter.

"I am aware that you were deeply concerned with the whiskey tax matter before your departure for England. I trust that you will show the common sense to let that subject rest, at least until your uncle returns. I have no time to chase after a girl who wanders into danger."

She knew he was speaking of her ride to Braddock's Field, and of her presence during the protest march. "If that is your wish, Mr. Willing. I will cause you no trouble."

"Good. Then we understand each other. You will be busy enough, that I am sure. Your suitors will no doubt keep you occupied. Then there is the preparation for the celebration." He rose. "I will leave you two now. I am sure there are many things females wish to speak of that hold little interest or meaning for a man."

When she heard the library door close, Virginia turned to Mother Willing. "Tell me, please. Are the farmers still in revolt? Do they still camp at Braddock's Field?"

"They still cause some trouble, that I know. I can tell you little else. They have burned the houses of several tax collectors and one man was tarred and feathered. But there have been no clashes between protesters and the government."

"My uncle was concerned for the safety of Anthony Burke." Virginia did not meet Mother Willing's gaze, for she knew she was not speaking the truth.

"Well, I can give you no information about him. I have not heard of his death, so he must still be living, and as much a troublemaker as ever." She watched Virginia sharply. "Are you sure it is your uncle who is concerned for him?"

Virginia remembered Percy's remarks and decided, suddenly, that it was time for another subject. "Tell me about the celebration. When does it start? Who will be there? Is there a dance?"

"Yes, to the last question. At noon of the Fourth of July to the first question, and everyone, to the second." Mother Willing beamed with pleasure. "Let's get busy on your dress. This celebration can serve as your reintroduction into Philadelphia society." She led the way into the sewing room. "Have I told you? Mr. Willing has procured magnificent fireworks from China made especially for the occasion. It will be a spectacular display."

The morning of the fourth dawned clear despite a rain that had dampened the ground the day before. Virginia dressed in a gown she had chosen for the daytime festivities, a white linen with red streamers draped over the skirt and a blue bodice capped with white sleeves. Although Anthony and David were both on her mind, she knew there was little she could do until the picnic was over and the city returned to normal.

Mother Willing escorted Virginia, carefully selecting those young men of whom she approved. Virginia was polite and pleasant, but she could not keep her eyes from wandering. Would Anthony dare to attend the celebration? If he came, would she find a moment when she could escape Mother Willing's watchful eyes and meet him?

They spread their picnic lunch on a blanket under a shade tree and ate while the band played spirited marches. Then, exhausted from the days of preparation and relaxed by the balmy breezes and the warm sun, Mother Willing leaned against the tree. Thomas Willing saw Hamilton across the park and hurried over for some conversation.

"Mother Willing?" Virginia stood before her guardian. "Will you object if I walk about?"

"Go ahead, my child. I'll just rest here a while."

Relieved of her close supervision, Virginia walked toward the stage where the band continued to hold forth. She could not but compare the performance with others she had heard in London. She realized she preferred the spontaneity of the band to the practiced control evidenced by most of the performers she had heard in the great halls of London. She stood half-dreaming, enjoying the familiarity of her surroundings.

"Virginia!"

She turned, her heart pounding. "Anthony!"

"Shh!" He held his finger to his lips. "Come with me. I wish to speak to you."

He led the way through the crowd to the town hall and drew her into an alcove, hidden from Willing's view. She stood close to him, aware of his manliness, of the musky fragrance of his body. Would he kiss her now, as he had kissed her on the road that first day after her escape?

He held her shoulders. "Tell me, how goes your uncle's project? Has a treaty been signed?"

She felt a wave of disappointment. "No. He and John Jay will likely remain in England for many months. The entire affair has grown so difficult. They seldom have an opportunity to speak with Pitt or the king."

"Damn!" Anthony's jaw grew tense. "I warned him. I told him it was more important to solve domestic problems than to worry about the few men who are impressed by the British. Yet money and time are being spent there, while here important matters remain unsolved."

"The protest is not over? You are not remaining in town?"

"I fear not. I am sick over the plight of my friends. No one cares for our problems. They have forgotten us."

"But Washington said the entire question would be reconsidered."

"Yes, a year ago. But nothing has been done. Only more men have been appointed to enforce the revenue. It is a battle. Farmers against their own government."

"But Washington and Jefferson, all of them, are reasonable men. How can they ignore so sore an issue?"

"They consider other matters more important than the wishes of a few unhappy farmers. Oh, Virginia! How I long for the freedom of the frontier. I am sick of politics, sick of the dealing and compromise. I am a farmer, after all. I do not belong here among men who talk of freedom but who have never lived it."

"You are wrong." She pulled away. "These men have fought hard for liberty. Do you not see that for each man, freedom has a different meaning? I learned that in England. There, men of wealth consider themselves and their country free, even though many of their less fortunate neighbors suffer terribly, working long hours without ever experiencing the pleasures available to their 'betters.' It was there I learned that I cannot be content with freedom for myself when others are in bondage."

"Nor can I. Here come Mr. Willing and Mr. Hamilton. I do not wish to be seen by either."

She clutched his sleeve. "How did you know I was back, if you still remain at Braddock's Field?"

"Oh, I get into town, though I do not seek out many of my old friends. I would not have spoken to you, but I am sure I can trust you."

"Oh, Anthony, of course you can." She felt him slip from her grasp. She wondered whether she would see him again, but he was gone before she could ask.

Cautiously, she stepped from the shelter of the building. Mother Willing sat propped against the tree, sound asleep. Angie and Gladys appeared as Virginia approached.

" 'Tis good he departed before Master Willing saw him." Angie looked stern. "Your Master Anthony is not in favor. Surely you understand that."

"Angie, I am not a child. You will not speak so to me again." Virginia assumed her most severe expression. Then her voice broke. "Besides, he just wanted to tell me something and say he was pleased that I had returned safely." She stumbled over her lie. Anthony had made no mention of her return, except to inquire after her uncle. She wished she had not seen him at all.

Why, when every encounter she had with him was so unsatisfactory, did she find it impossible to put him from her mind? Because of that one night, which he had obviously misinterpreted? Because he had seemed pleased to see her the day she returned from the Freedom's Arms? Because he had spoken to her when she visited the field? Because he had appeared brave and strong when he had led the farmers in the peaceful march?

Why had she not realized it before? He was using her as a source of information. As Roy Salford's niece and a guest in the Willing household, she was privy to important decisions. All Anthony wanted was to learn what she overheard!

She reached the green where Mother Willing was resting. "Angie, when Mother Willing wakens—"

"I'm awake, child." Mother Willing struggled to her feet. "Come along. The band is starting to play again. And there's Richard. Do you know he has refused to call on any young lady since you went away? He'll be delighted that you're back!"

Virginia pushed her angry thoughts out of her mind. She could blame her flushed cheeks on her excitement. Certainly, she wanted no one to suspect the true cause of her upset.

Twenty-one

Virginia stood quietly while Angie and Gladys fussed about, pulling her gown over her head and applying themselves to the task of securing the buttons that ran up the back. The day had been far from satisfactory, and yet there had been some pleasant moments. Richard was delighted to see her. George Kingsbury and Donald Greenville had made it clear that Philadelphia was exciting again, now that she had returned.

She had been, she admitted, far from an ideal companion, for she had been preoccupied with sorting through her dilemma. Had she been right in ascribing Anthony's interest in her to his need for information? And David—did he wish to court her so he could get her back in his power? Or was she being overly suspicious of them both?

She remembered how concerned for her welfare Anthony had appeared to be. Was it all pretense? She had told him how she had been treated by David, and she had spoken of her fears that he meant to deliver her, eventually, to a brothel. The thought had outraged Anthony but it had not disgusted him. Or had he taken her that night because he already thought of her as a whore?

She pressed her hands against her brow. If only she could stop this endless questioning! If only she could know which of the two men spoke the truth. If only she could know what was in her own heart.

By the time her preparation for the ball was completed, she had gained control of her runaway emotions. She was determined to enjoy the ball and her suitors. The questions could be faced again later. She gazed at herself in the mirror, very pleased with her appearance.

The gown had been designed by the princess's dressmaker. A deep, rich blue, it was decorated with white lace made in Ireland. The crown prince had informed her that this gown brought out the brilliance of her eyes and gave her dignity and charm equal to that of the most attractive woman in England. She knew he spoke of Mrs. Fitzherbert, his true love, and the woman who usurped his wife's place in his life. The memory of that comment gave her a feeling of wickedness that brought color to her cheeks and an extra brightness to her eyes. Were she truly such a woman, she would know how to deal with Anthony and David.

As she entered the great hall between Thomas Willing and his wife, she glanced swiftly about the room. Were they here, after all? She tried to decide which face she wished most to see, Anthony's or David's, but she could not tell. All she knew was that neither man was present. Repressing her disappointment, she descended the stairs and was immediately surrounded by gentlemen seeking a place on her dance card. Mother Willing, as her guardian, took charge, leaving her free to flirt and chatter merrily with her admirers.

The evening was filled with bright music, delightful conversation, and lighthearted flirtation. She noticed that Mother Willing was not completely pleased with her behavior, but Virginia was unable to control her frantic spirit. She teased each suitor in turn, her laughter high and brittle. She felt compelled to exhibit a gaiety that didn't feel altogether sincere.

She continued to search the room for the two men. At one point, she decided that she would choose whichever one appeared. When neither appeared, she wondered why she was distressing herself over men who cared not a whit for her.

Her anger grew, and, with it, her exhilaration. She flitted about, aware of the admiring eyes of her suitors, playing to them, flirting outrageously. And, although she was aware of the admiration in her partners' eyes, she was barely aware which man held her in his arms.

Samuel Holden took her hand as his dance finished. "Have we a moment, Virginia? I wish so to speak to you."

"But we have been speaking, Samuel." She tapped him lightly with her fan. "If you wish to hear more of my journey to England, you must come to dinner sometime." She turned away, impatient to be finished with him.

She felt another pair of arms catch her, and she looked

up. David Cavanaugh! His eyes at the same time admired and mocked her. "I believe this is our dance."

She felt a sharp stab of disappointment. Must she choose David and forget Anthony forever?

David took her into his arms and led her into the dance. He moved smoothly, with a grace she could not but admire. Would Anthony be so at ease on the dance floor? She did not know.

Nor did it matter. She had promised herself whichever one of them appeared that evening. The matter was settled. She need no longer contend with the endless questions. She smiled up into David's face. "I wondered when you would call. My uncle said you asked permission to court me before we left for England."

His smile widened. "I trust you will forgive my negligence. I was off on a business trip."

They danced for a time without talking. Then, suddenly, she spoke. "I forgive you for frightening me so."

"Frightening you? How did I do that?" The tone of his voice seemed to mock her, but when she looked up into his face, he was smiling politely.

"When you left me at Amos's inn, and at the Freedom's Arms. I thought you . . ." She paused, embarrassed now at what she was trying to say.

"You thought I wanted you to join Miss Bessie's girls? Come now, my dear, surely you cannot mistrust me to that extent. What did I do to deserve your lack of faith except leave you in as safe a place as I could find when I had to go off and tend to my livelihood." His smile seemed slightly forced. "Didn't we settle all that when I saw you at the Arms?"

She did not reply immediately, and he continued. "No, obviously not, or you would have remained there, as I requested. I should put you from my mind, for it promises no good when a bride mistrusts her affianced, but I cannot. You have won my heart, and there is nothing to be done."

She was flattered by his words. Here she had been playing at courting with lads whose chins were barely covered with down, while grown men sought her favors: Percy, who begged for her hand only a few months after their meeting; and Anthony. Quickly, she sought to push his name from her consciousness. He had never spoken of marriage. He had just taken her, when she was helpless.

Still, David had made his intentions clear, if not that first night, certainly now. And David was her choice. She gathered her courage. This was the time to settle all of her uncertainties, now, when she could still back away. "David?"

He seemed so patient. "Yes, my sweet?"

"Do you still own the Freedom's Arms?"

He raised his eyebrows. "Generally, my dear, it is the duty of a woman's guardian to concern himself with the matter of her future economics. It should be enough for you to know that you will suffer no lowering of your style of life when you become my bride."

"Please, David. I am certain uncle would not have approved of your courting me had he thought you were not worthy. Can you not humor me?"

"Ah, well, I suppose so, if you do not expect me to do so too often. Yes, I do. And will continue to, for that matter. The Freedom's Arms is located at a very excellent place on the road to New York. It is busy all year 'round."

"Is it proper for a gentleman to own a brothel?"

"Have you acquired such strange ideas from your British friends? Surely, my dear, there is less dishonor in owning a house where grown women ply a necessary trade than in owning a factory where children work while their parents wander the streets in idleness." She tensed, and he smiled. "Ah, yes, my dear, I have heard you speak about the factories in London. Now I ask only that you consider my question, and if your answer favors me, not bring up the subject again. I will admit, I am an old-fashioned man who approves of tradition. I feel it improper that a woman involve herself in man's business."

David felt her obvious disappointment, and he pulled her closer. "My dear, please do not be unhappy. I am sure we can find plenty that will interest you, for even I can see the importance of keeping a clever woman occupied with valuable activities."

She smiled. David had proven that he could give her pleasure in a most intimate way. Surely he would be considerate of her other concerns. And then, of course, there would be children. She blushed. She would have no need for outside interests when she had a child to nurse.

He shifted her hand in his, and she became aware, suddenly, that he was missing a finger. She gasped and touched the stump. "Oh, David. You have been hurt. What happened?"

"Nothing." He seemed annoyed at her concern. "It was of little consequence. I was injured during a battle with a British warship, when it waylaid us to impress the sailors on our vessel."

"Oh! How terrible!" She visualized him fighting for the poor sailors, defending them when other, lesser men might stand aside and let them fight their own battles. "Uncle told me the British seldom take passengers. How brave you were to fight them!"

He smiled. " 'Twas nothing. We were, in fact, most fortunate. We fought them off and escaped without losing a man to them." He paused, for the music was coming to an end. "My dear, I know you have other partners for the night, but I must have my say before they take you away. I am aware of how much you and I have shared. I was the one who helped you bury your father, when you were alone. And I am the one who has shared your love. Those other suitors would reject you were they to know how much we have meant to each other. For me, that night was a confirmation of our love. I come now to claim my own. I trust that henceforth you will dance with me alone."

Virginia nodded. This was, after all, what she wanted—wasn't it—a man, not a child? A man who knew what he wanted and knew how to claim his rights?

He misinterpreted her hesitancy. "Think, my love. I love you. I have said it before. I repeat it now. I loved you before we shared passion. I love you the more for knowing that you are capable of matching my desire." His voice grew low. "Oh, my darling, how I long to once more drown myself in your charms."

She knew she was blushing, and she wondered if he knew how his words stirred her emotions. But before she could respond, he bowed, brought her fingers to his lips and was gone. Richard appeared for the next dance.

She glanced about the room during the gavotte and blushed when she realized that it was not David for whom she searched. Even now, when she had made her choice, she still hoped to see Anthony.

It was wrong for a woman who had given her promise to one man to think of another. Well, she would just have to control her waywardness.

The dance came to an end, and Richard whispered his thanks. She looked at him in surprise. She had not heard him talk to her, though she had murmured some sort of answers. Never before had she felt that time passed more quickly. She smiled as Richard departed. It must be because she felt so happy.

She frowned. Yes, that had to be the reason. She was so delighted that she had made up her mind.

Twenty-two

The remainder of the night passed quickly. Virginia struggled to pay attention to her young partners, but she could not pull her thoughts away from David's words. He had wanted her, searched for her, loved her, ever since that night. And she had misjudged him so terribly.

The thought of his embrace brought a rush of other memories. There was the old hag, who had insisted that David intended to deliver every girl he brought to Amos's inn to some brothel. But David had denied the truth of that statement.

Her greatest problem was coping with the ghost of Anthony Burke. It seemed to hover around the edges of her dreams, reminding her of the ecstasy she had shared with him. And no matter how forcefully she tried to push his image away, he continued to haunt her.

At last, she faced his memory squarely and rejected the hold it had upon her. She belonged to David, as she had all along. What had happened between her and Anthony had been a mistake. She was thankful that he had not made an attempt to hold her to the promise that had been concealed in their embrace.

Free at last, she returned to the dance with renewed gusto. When President Washington approached her, she blushed with pleasure. She was aware that her friends were watching her with unconcealed envy. And she thought of her wedding to come and glowed with even greater pride. How wonderful it would all be. She left the hall, wondering how long it would be before David declared himself to her guardian, Mr. Willing.

She did not know how a young girl should feel when looking forward to her wedding, so she was not surprised at her own lack of ebullience. It was enough that she accepted her future, and that she put the thoughts of any other man behind her.

When she reached home, she stepped from her gown and into the hot bath Angie had waiting. As usual, the water refreshed her. But she did not immediately start prattling about the evening's entertainment, as she usually did.

Angie soaped her mistress in silence. Eventually, she broke the silence. "Well, Miss Virginia, were you the most popular girl at the ball?"

Virginia spoke quickly, as if a cork had been removed from her bottled-up emotions. "Oh, yes, Angie. It was so . . ." She paused. Why didn't *wonderful* seem to be the right word to use? ". . . great! I danced with the president!"

"So I hear. But Mistress Willing told me you also danced with David Cavanaugh. Did he apologize for his treatment of you? I'm surprised you would choose to speak to him at all."

"Oh, Angie. I'm not a child anymore. It was because he loves me. He wants to marry me! He said he'll talk to Thomas Willing."

Angie frowned. "Marry you?"

Virginia felt her anger rising. "Angie! How dare you act dismayed? He's an honorable man. He never had any intentions of hurting me. He's wanted to marry me all along."

"Yes. I'm sure he has." There was a coldness in Angie's voice that startled Virginia.

"What do you mean? Out with it, Angie. You should not keep secrets from me. And, since I have full intentions of taking you with me when I go to live in my new home, I expect you to develop a respect for your new master. So say it, whatever it is. Now. I command you!"

Angie was more amused than offended by Virginia's bossiness. But she was reluctant to continue. Virginia scowled. "Angie, tell me now. You can be so exasperating."

"Yes, Miss Virginia." Angie began to wash Virginia's hair. "It's Jonathan. He went to a tavern near the docks today."

"So? What has that to do with Mr. Cavanaugh—or me?"

"He heard things about Mr. Cavanaugh. He has lost a great deal of money lately."

"Oh, Angie! What is so surprising about a man losing money on a shipment of merchandise?"

"He was injured by one of his own men."

"No, you're wrong. He lost a finger while fighting for his freedom against British raiders aboard his ship. He told me himself. He saved his companions from indenture."

"Jonathan heard otherwise. Jonathan has a cousin, Loren Jacobson, who has a son who is a sailor. His name is Francis, after the famous Francis Drake."

"Get on with it, Angie. I have no interest in Jonathan's family tree."

"Yes, Miss Virginia." Angie seemed reluctant to continue. She sighed deeply and then resumed her story. "Well, Francis Jacobson was on the ship David Cavanaugh took to Santo Domingo. He has quite another story."

Virginia fumed. "Stop all that foolishness. Tell me what you know, or I'll throw you out in the street."

It was an idle threat, but it served to loosen Angie's tongue. "He says David Cavanaugh was working for the British, for they seemed to know just where was the best place to intercept the ship, and they knew just which seamen were to be removed."

"Do you know what you're saying? If David Cavanaugh is responsible for even one man being taken by the British, then he is a traitor."

"Yes, Miss Virginia. It is God's truth. Francis says Mr. Cavanaugh shouted orders to the British men and fought alongside them when they seemed to be losing. He says he saw Cavanaugh battling Harry Greenflow and that Harry cut off Cavanaugh's finger before he, himself, was killed."

"That's enough. Father dealt with David before he died, and Uncle Roy is sure he is an honorable man. What you are saying is outrageous." She paused, too angry to continue. Then she took a deep breath. "What other proof has this Francis?"

Angie did not immediately reply. She rinsed Virginia's hair and wrapped it in a towel. Finally she spoke in a low voice. "No one else saw it happen. The fighting was too fierce. But our men sent the British packing, and in the commotion, Mr. Cavanaugh managed to make it seem he had fought to defend his companions. Francis swears that what he saw was true. David Cavanaugh is a traitor. Oh, Miss Virginia, you must not marry a man like him."

"If Francis is so certain, why doesn't he go to the authorities? There are ways of dealing with traitors."

"He is a poor man, and his skin is black. No one would believe him. I have no wish to bring David Cavanaugh to justice. I only want to save you from him."

"Well, you will not succeed by bringing false accusations against him." She pulled on her robe. "You have no right to upset me in this manner. I have made up my mind. Now, that is the end of it. Do you understand?"

Angie watched Virginia in silence. At last, she lowered her head. "Yes, Miss Virginia, I understand. I will not speak of it again"—she turned away, so Virginia could not hear her words—"until I can prove what I know."

Twenty-three

"Virginia, do hurry! David Cavanaugh has come to ride with you this morning." Mother Willing's cheeks were flushed with excitement. "Wait till you see his new stallion —and his clothes, fresh from England! I doubt any of the men you met in London were better dressed." She bustled down the stairs, tugging at Virginia's dress to make certain it was smooth. "He's waiting in the garden."

Virginia sat down at the table. A serving girl put a platter of food before her. Mother Willing had already eaten. "He is such a handsome man." She chattered on without waiting for a response. "And so wealthy. He's the catch of the year. You're a very lucky girl."

Virginia ate quickly. Although she had felt little regret at dismissing her other suitors, she did miss the wild rides she used to have with George Kingsbury. David was far too proper a man to race with her.

In the days since the Fourth of July ball, she had tried to forget Angie's accusation of David. And she had succeeded well enough so that when the thought did arise, she could easily brush it aside. She dwelt most of the time on his good looks, his fine figure, his envious position in Philadelphia society, and her memory of his passion. Though she did not admit it to him, even when he pressed her for more intimate favors, she anticipated their wedding night with pleasure.

Angie had not mentioned Francis's accusations again, but Virginia was certain that her nurse still distrusted David and that annoyed her. The easy communication that had existed between them since Virginia was a child was shut off. Virginia had no one to whom she could speak intimately regarding her emotions—no one except Mother Willing, and she seemed too aloof for such female talk . . . and too set in her opinions.

Mother Willing bustled about the kitchen, peering into

216

pots, making comments to the cook, who pretended to listen. At last Mother Willing settled beside Virginia. "Are you ready?"

"Yes. I must not keep him waiting too long."

Mother Willing nodded in agreement. "A woman who learns early her duty to her husband will be a happy wife." She was reciting a platitude, the sort of thing young girls embroidered on samplers.

"Is David truly wealthy?" Virginia asked. The doubt planted by Angie's information would not go away.

"Oh, yes! And that makes your uncle most happy. Only yesterday we received a letter from him, approving of your choice, and urging you to wait for his return before you wed. Mr. Willing will be speaking to David regarding the delay this evening. But, Virginia, you must know that we are all glad to see you wed to a man who has a fortune of his own, who is not dependent on your dowry. This way, you can be certain his affection is for you alone."

Virginia impatiently tugged on her gloves. Her riding dress was of the latest style, and she knew she and David would make a pretty picture as they rode out through the town. She leaned over and kissed Mother Willing's cheek. "Good-bye."

"Enjoy your morning. Shall I have cook make lunch for you?"

"No. I'm not sure when we'll return. Thank you." She had a fleeting thought, as she responded. What if David should direct their horses to an inn? Maybe to Amos's place. Would she be ready to accept his attentions again? Her body said yes. But some contrary part of her nature rejected the idea. They had shared love once before marriage. Now, she had a stubborn, unreasonable wish to delay any further show of affection until they were properly wed.

David greeted her with a restrained kiss. Certainly, she admitted, he behaved in a very correct manner. She blushed as she considered her earlier thought. Maybe he did not realize what a passionate person she was.

He helped her mount and turned their horses toward the harbor. She felt both relief and disappointment. The docks were safe—and yet . . . did she really *want* safety?

She smelled the water long before it came into view and was aware of the wonderful lift the ocean brought to her spirits. Good things came from the sea. Ships traveled across it with cargos from many exotic countries. As a child, she had spent many days on the docks, visiting with Thomas Willing and playing with his daughter. Angie had watched as they sat on the wharf, studying the ships that docked in the bay. She had dreamed, then, of faraway countries. Now she had been to one of them. But the fascination of the sea had not diminished.

David drew rein beside her and stared out over the harbor. There had been piracies lately that had ruined more than one merchant, and Virginia wondered if he feared for his own ships. He stirred restlessly. "I have need to speak with Thomas Willing. Do you wish to ride over to his warehouse with me?"

Virginia smiled up into his face. "Oh, yes. I love that place. It's so exciting. Have you visited him before?"

"Oh, yes, many times. And you are right. He has a prosperous business. He has shown great hospitality to me since we announced our engagement, and I wish to seek his advice. I am not the worldly-merchant he is, and I could learn much from seeing how he deals with certain problems of storage."

"You no longer limit your trading to fine liquors?"

"I am expanding." He fell in beside her. "A man with a family must consider his future. The day will come when we produce as fine liquors here in America as come now from Spain. I must have other fields in which to trade."

Virginia did not respond. Despite her anticipation of the coming wedding, she had a difficult time thinking of David as the head of a household. He was too much the independent man—the bachelor. His reputation as a man-about-town was well-known, even to women who were supposed to know nothing of such things.

Thomas Willing was delighted to see his guests. He took David's arm and led the way to the new warehouse. Virginia trailed behind, aware of how little attention was paid to her by either of the men. It did not perturb her. She listened idly to their conversation, concentrating her attention on the magnificent wares that waited shipment to cities all over the country.

Thomas was obviously pleased at the opportunity to show off his efficient method of cargo disposal to a man with similar interests. "The ship *Katherine Ann* will sail tomorrow morning with the material that is now being moved aboard. She is heading for Canton, where she will trade for silk, teakwood, and fine china dishes. She is the first of the season, for the Horn will be navigable only during our most inclement weather." He pulled open a crate of furs. "The Chinese pay great prices for these, and their products, brought back here, will make me a fortune."

David stroked the fur. "Is the *Katherine Ann* your first ship to bring cargo from China?"

"Oh, no! The *Rebecca Sue* sailed the Horn at the end of the season last year. She's already on the high seas, laden with produce from the East. She should dock within a week. My captains are brave men who dare the roughest weather to extend our trading period. And they are well protected against pirates, as well. Each ship carries a cannon in the helm. I expect the *Rebecca Sue* to carry furniture, carved by the best artisans of China, and fine jade pieces that will sell for small fortunes here and in New York."

David seemed unusually quiet when they left the warehouse. He returned directly to the Willing house, explaining that he felt ill and wished to rest. "I'll come for my regular visit this evening. Please forgive me. I have no wish to be apart from you any more than is necessary."

"If you feel ill, come in here. Mother Willing can give you a tonic that will cure your malaise."

He smiled. "Thank you, my sweet. No. It is best that I go home. Please forgive me. I will see you tonight."

Virginia did not dismount immediately. She watched him ride away with a feeling that she had left something undone. He would be alone at home, feeling ill and she had not offered to accompany him.

He was out of sight by the time she decided to remedy her mistake, but she did not allow that fact to deter her. She covered the distance between their two houses easily. But when she reached his door, she paused. The street was busy, and she found herself blocked behind a carriage.

As she struggled to extricate herself, David appeared on the front steps. He had changed his clothes and now was garbed in a nondescript outfit that blended with the merchants who filled the road. His horse, too, was different. The boy led it around from the barn and held the reins as David mounted. Virginia drew back. For some reason she could not understand, David wished to be as little noticed as possible. And he did not appear to be sick at all.

She let him move ahead, and then, carefully, she followed. Was he going to visit some female he had used during the year they were apart? The thought made Virginia burn with jealousy. So that was why he had not pressed his cause, why he had made no attempt to enjoy before their wedding the favors he had taken pleasure in after her father's death.

Determined to find out who he had to see and for what reason, she followed him as closely as she dared. He did not look back, even when he left the town and entered the open country along the bay. She found it more difficult to follow him now, for the road was empty, and she pulled back, making certain that she stayed hidden in the woods that bordered the road.

They had been riding for almost an hour when he paused and turned around, studying the road behind him. Virginia held her horse still, praying that he would not notice her in the darkness of the forest. Only when he turned again and went on his way did she breathe easy.

She had second thoughts regarding her pursuit. He would, she was certain, be furious if he learned that she had followed him. He had made it clear that women should not involve themselves in men's affairs. Now that she had gone this far, she hesitated to go back without accomplishing her mission. She knew there was nothing she could do, even if she did surprise him in an intimacy with some other woman, but she had to know.

So immersed was she in her thoughts that she almost lost her cover. David had stopped on the road ahead, and she saw that he was speaking to another man who had approached him on foot.

Cautiously, Virginia slid from her horse and tied him to a tree. She crept carefully forward, keeping well into the woods, until she was close enough to hear what David was saying. She felt reasonably certain that her suspicion had been wrong. Her curiosity was enough to give her the courage she needed to risk being caught as she drew nearer.

She stopped behind a bush, still well out of sight, yet

close enough to hear most of what was being said. There was still a risk. Her horse might nicker, or David might see it as he returned up the road. But she was committed now to her eavesdropping, and she ran as great a risk going back as remaining.

The stranger was speaking as Virginia approached. ". . . all waiting. You got the news?"

David glanced about, as if fearful of being overheard, but when he spoke, he did not try to be quiet. "I do. The *Rebecca Sue* will be off Florida by the time you reach the islands. 'Tis a good cargo, containing much delicate jade. Be careful with the crates when you take them."

Virginia gasped. Angie had been right. David was in league with men who robbed ships. If he was capable of such perfidy, he might also have been working with the British to impress sailors. Was it possible that the two activities were related—that the same men who robbed the ship stole the men and delivered them to British merchant ships?

Virginia felt momentarily breathless. And then, all of the doubts that had beset her in the past flooded back to lend credence to this new discovery. He had whispered something to Bessie, that day when he had arrived so unexpectedly at the Freedom's Arms. And there had been so many delicate Chinese objects at the brothel. She clutched at the bush, afraid her trembling might draw David's attention.

And then, unexpectedly, her horse whinnied! She froze in horror. Would David and this coarse stranger search for her now?

David looked up at the sound. Then he bent low from his saddle and whispered something to his companion. The man nodded and vanished up the road. David turned his horse and headed back toward the town. As he passed the place in the woods where her horse was tethered, he dismounted. Virginia watched in horror as he continued down the highway. He had released her horse's reins, and the beast was trotting peacefully behind him.

She considered, for one wild moment, rushing onto the road and crying out for him to stop. Certainly he knew her mount! And if he did not, all he needed to do was give it its head when they reached the city, and it would lead him directly to the Willing stables. But if he knew it was she who had followed him, why did he not at least call out, so she would not have to walk home?

As she watched, he slowed his mount until her horse was beside him, and then, with a sharp cry and a slap on the beast's rump, he sent it racing ahead. He did not look back, nor did he slow down. As she watched, he vanished from sight. She was alone. And she was miles from home.

Now she scolded herself for hesitating. Better that she face David and endure his anger than that she be stranded on the road. She tried to understand why David had sent her horse ahead, and she could think of no reason. Would he return, after he had frightened her by leaving her alone?

She waited for a while, but his hoofbeats faded in the distance. No, he had no intentions of coming back. She stepped onto the road. Did she want him to return? Was it possible that he had not recognized her mount, that he had assumed it belonged to some wayward boy out for a romp? She shook her head. That was not possible. No lad would ride sidesaddle. Perhaps he assumed it belonged to some farmgirl out for a ride who had dismounted to relieve herself in the woods. He might have chased the animal away to teach her a lesson—or just to be unkind.

Aside from her worries about her own safety, Virginia felt deep concern over what she had learned. David had spoken to some strange man and given him information about the arrival of Thomas Willing's next ship. He had spoken of taking care with the crates for they contained jade. She could not deny what she herself had heard. David was in some way part of a band of pirates!

She gazed toward the bay. Far in the distance, a man could be seen walking along the road. Was it the same man who had spoken to David? As she watched, he reached the shore. He waved his arms above his head, then repeated the signal, as if he was waiting for someone at sea to notice.

Was there a ship, hiding far out near the horizon? She could not tell. As she stared out over the water, the man began to descend the slope to the shore.

And then she saw it. A longboat pushed away from the beach. The man scrambled in, took a seat at one oar, and the boat pulled out into the bay. She watched until it was out of sight, lost in the blue of the water and the distance.

Then, with a sigh of resignation, she turned and began the long walk home.

Anger gave her strength to endure the roughness of the road beneath her feet. Anger at herself, for being careless about where she had tethered her horse, anger at David, for she knew now that she could not trust him. But there was fear mixed with her fury. She was alone. Even though she had traveled only a little more than an hour to reach the spot where David spoke to the stranger, she had covered the distance on horseback. It would take her far more than an hour to reach home.

She was thankful that the day was still young. They had left for the wharf early, and now it was scarcely noon. At least she would be home well before dinner. She would cause no worry in the Willing household. Unless David alerted them to her absence, they would assume she was still with him at the docks or riding in the country.

As she plodded along, Virginia considered what she should do with her discovery of David's planned crime. Her inclination was to rush directly to the harbor and warn Mr. Willing. It was his ship that they were planning to attack. But she realized the futility of such a warning. There would be nothing Willing could do to alert his captain to the danger. The *Rebecca Sue* was already on its way to an encounter with the pirate ship, if that was who David had provided with the information. And a week would pass before news of her could arrive—or she would arrive safely in the harbor.

She formed a plan at last, aware that it might have to be altered if, when she arrived home, she learned that David had been aware of her absence. For the rest of the long walk, she concerned herself mostly with avoiding the roughest places on the road and with looking for some way to shorten her journey.

She was close to the edge of the town when she encountered a farmer, heading into town to deliver a pig to the market. He showed little sympathy when she informed him that her horse had run away, but he nevertheless gave her a ride to the end of her street.

She was immediately surrounded by frantic activity. Jonathan had been in the stable when her horse arrived, and he had quickly ridden to the wharfs to see what had happened. Angie embraced Virginia as if she had been missing for a week.

Virginia drew back. "Did Jonathan go to David's house?"

"Oh, no, miss! We assumed that if your horse was the only one to return, you both must have been injured. We feared you might have been attacked by highwaymen."

"In the city? You know better than that."

Angie looked abashed. "You're right, Miss Virginia. I didn't let Jonathan go to Mr. Cavanaugh's. I thought he might have done you some harm."

Virginia sighed with relief. Of course! Angie had no love for David Cavanaugh. She mistrusted him. No matter how worried she might be, she would not go to him for help.

"Thank you, Angie. Does Mother Willing know I've been missing?"

"No. I felt there was plenty of time to tell her if we didn't find you ourselves. Jonathan and I have the responsibility of caring for you—no matter who your uncle appoints as your guardian."

Virginia appreciated, for the first time since returning from England, the jealousy Angie and Jonathan felt toward the Willings. And she was thankful that her nurse felt so strongly. Maybe she could keep this excursion a secret, at least until her plans were complete.

That night, when Mr. Willing returned from the docks, Virginia handed him a sealed packet. Inside was a letter in which she detailed all she had overheard on the road. The note was dated. Thomas Willing was amused at her secrecy. "What's the conspiracy, my dear? What game are we playing now?"

Virginia frowned. "Please, Mr. Willing, don't make light of this. And please say nothing of it to anyone, not even to David. In a week, when the *Rebecca Sue* is in harbor, I'll either ask you to return the letter unopened, or I'll expect you to read it aloud in the presence of the other merchants who have suffered losses at sea."

Thomas Willing chuckled, but he did as she requested. He tucked it into his pocket and promised to put it in the back of his vault at the office in the morning.

David arrived as he had promised. Virginia watched him carefully, looking for some indication that he knew she had seen him on the road. But he was as polite and proper as ever. By the end of the evening, she was completely reassured. She was safe for the time being—until the *Rebecca Sue* was pirated. And then her note would serve as evidence to put him in jail.

She could not sleep that night. She understood now that David was using her in an even more nefarious way than Anthony ever had. She tried, unsuccessfully, to match other piracies with times when she and David had talked to Mr. Willing or to other merchants in the town. Had she been an unwitting accomplice before? She decided that she had not, but only because David had his own contacts with the traders in the city.

David used her to get information on shipping. Anthony had used her to learn of the activities of his enemies. Was there no one who loved her for herself?

She reached a decision before she fell into a fitful sleep. She would visit Anthony at Braddock's Field. Maybe she had judged him too harshly. Certainly, of the two, he was the less dangerous. And though he seemed not to think as well of her because of what had taken place between them, still he had shown himself to be, in other matters, an honorable man. He had offered a sort of friendship which up until now she had rejected.

She would accept his friendship now—if he still was willing to give it. She suspected that he would be far more ready to help her solve her present problems than any other person she knew.

The thought brought her some comfort. She would ride out alone tomorrow. She would talk to Anthony. She tried to pretend that the happiness she felt on reaching that resolution had no roots in her emotions, that she was only relieved to have something to do. She tried—but she did not completely succeed.

Twenty-four

Braddock's Field resembled an army encampment. Tents were clustered close to a stand of birches and sheltered partly from the heat of the August sun by a line of wagons. Horses were corralled nearby, with a stack of hay for their feed. Sentries were posted close to the road, and though they were unarmed, it was clear they had munitions close by, in case of an attack.

Virginia was depressed by the sight. Was this the way for Americans to live now, when the war was over and the time had come for the victors to enjoy the peace? Why did Anthony and his friends persist in defying the law of the land? Why did they not go home, as they ought, to their families? Soon it would be harvest time again. Would they never give up the fight?

She halted when the sentry challenged her approach. "I've come to see Anthony Burke. Is he here?" She held her reins tight, prepared to turn swiftly and depart. She already felt foolish for traveling to see a man who had proven his disinterest in her.

"Wait here. I'll send for him." The sentry signaled to another man to call Anthony. The second man headed for the tents, and when he appeared again, Anthony was behind him.

Virginia rose in her saddle when she saw him. "Anthony!"

He turned abruptly. "Virginia?" Then he saw her, and his face lit with pleasure. "Virginia!" He ran across the field and stood beside her. As he approached, she slid to the ground. They stood, close enough for him to embrace her, yet his arms remained at his sides. "You should not ride out so far alone. The roads are not safe for a woman."

"Are they safe for you or your friends? You seem determined to protect yourselves from some enemy. Who is it— the government of your own country?"

228

He ignored her irony. "I did not think I would see you again. What brings you this far?"

She was not ready to speak of her inner dilemma. "Is this all there is left of your friends? Can you not see that your cause is lost?"

"Don't be deceived." He drew up proudly. "There are more ready to come to our aid. The battle lines are still drawn. Our demands must be satisfied."

She wished, suddenly, that she had stayed home. What good did it do to tear open old wounds? What value lay in recalling emotions that had never had the chance to bloom? "You can't win, Anthony, don't you see that? If you and your friends don't die of hunger, or exposure, you'll be thrown into prison as traitors."

"But we aren't traitors. We are honest American citizens who don't approve of the taxes levied upon us by our government." His expression was haughty, and she thought for a moment that he would leave her without further conversation. Then his expression softened. "Please, we must not fight . . . not now, not when you have appeared so unexpectedly. I never thought you would care to come visit me."

She hesitated for a moment. For some reason she could not comprehend, he seemed pleased to see her, as if he had actually missed her! He took her arm, and she was aware that he was prepared to back away if she protested. "Virginia, I had hoped you would come out here again, as you did on the day of the march."

"I don't ride with George anymore. I am engaged to be married."

A shadow covered his eyes. "Married? I hear nothing but news of politics. Have you then found the man you love?"

She thought of David. She knew now she could never love him, that she never really had loved him. She just had not known her own feelings. She had been so confused.

When she did not reply, his frown deepened. "You do not love him, and yet you have agreed to be his wife? Who is this man who has such power over you?" As he asked the question, his eyes lit. "David Cavanaugh? Has he returned to torment you more?"

She spoke then of her fears and of what she had learned when she followed David along the bay. "Oh, Anthony, you were my friend once. Please, if you can, forget your disgust of what I am—forget that you consider me no more than a—" she hesitated, and then, bravely, she continued, "whore. I need your advice. I know that if I accuse David of piracy, he will find some way to prove me a liar. And if I do not find some way to show him for what he is, I will be forced to marry him."

Anthony watched her with growing amazement. "Virginia, how can you say that I think poorly of you? I adore you. I worship the ground you walk on. You have made it clear that you cannot forgive me for what I did that night—and I understand. I had no right to force myself upon you in such a manner. But consider you a whore? God! I could never conceive of such a thing. What have you done that would demean you in any man's eyes? You have been harmed by Cavanaugh—and then, when you asked for help, by me! I am the one who must beg forgiveness. I am the one who does not deserve to ever have you speak to him again."

"Do you mean what you have just said?" Virginia asked in amazement. "Oh, Anthony! You do not consider me worthless because I responded to your embrace?" She was blushing now, and she spoke quietly, as if she were afraid to be heard.

He took both her hands in his. "Oh, my dearest! God knows I have cursed myself a thousand times for harming you. Is it possible that you can forgive me? Can I hope that you do not hate me because of my importunities?"

Their eyes met, and she stood immobile, staring into his face. How could she have been so wrong? How could she have thought he hated her? "I thought"—she lowered her head—"I thought you wished to speak to me only to get information about the actions of my uncle and the other members of Congress. Did you? Was I right?" Her eyes begged him to say no.

He grasped her shoulders. "Oh, my dear! No, you are so very wrong. I longed to see you, just to know that you were well. I missed the brightness of your laugh, the cheerfulness of your smile. I do not, and I never did, need you as a source of information. Many of the farmers enter the city every day. There are no barricades to impede our entry. I learn all I need to know from my own men. You have never served as my informant. That is not why I have missed you."

Her heart wanted to believe, but she still hesitated. He continued, a new passion in his voice. "Please, my dearest. I have restrained myself whenever I was with you, because I did not wish to remind you of my cruelty. I have punished myself many times for taking advantage of you that night in the woods. If I could wipe that night from your memory, I would be the most thankful man in the world."

Her voice was low, and he had to bend down to hear her. "I find it good to remember. I do not wish to forget it ever." She was shaking with emotion. She knew her face was pale, for she felt the blood rush from her head. It left her lightheaded, almost dizzy with a new, unbelievable joy.

He caught her to him and led her across the field. "I must find a place where we can speak without others hearing us. Will you come with me to the grove?"

She nodded, letting herself be led over the damp grass to the stand of brush and timber. When they reached the shelter, he took her cape and spread it over the ground. Then he drew her down beside him. "Please, sit with me. I must look at you once more. I must have time to understand that you do not dislike me."

She sat where he asked her to, but she still did not meet his gaze. "I do not dislike you, Anthony. I have never disliked you."

She was blushing now, and her hands were trembling. He slid his arm around her shoulder. "Is it possible that you dwell on that night with the same fondness? Oh, Virginia . . ." He moved suddenly, pulling her into his arms. His lips closed over hers. When he drew back, his eyes were gentle. "Virginia, strike me if I dare too much, but I must say it. I love you. I have loved you from the first moment I saw you outside the inn, cowering and frightened and stripped of your clothing. What you have taken for disinterest has been my concern for your sensibilities. I have had no wish to frighten you with the force of my passion."

She dared not move. This was a dream, and she would wake to find herself alone again. "You love me?" Her tone expressed her uncertainty.

His face was close to hers. "Can you believe otherwise?

Oh, Virginia, I love you so very much! You are the only woman I have ever met who cares for those things that matter to me. You are the only woman I have ever seen who shows evidence of a mind as well as a body. You have a love of freedom equal to mine. You love our country—as I do. But all of those reasons do not explain why I love you." His eyes were alight. "I love you because of your sweet self. I love you because you are so beautiful, because you are pure of soul. Because you are so honest to yourself. Because you are not afraid to face what you believe is the truth. Oh, Virginia!" He buried his head in her shoulder. "I cannot say why it is that I love you. There are too many reasons." He threw back his head, a smile on his face. "I love you. Lord, how wonderful it is to say those words at last."

She still did not speak. She watched him, instead, with growing wonder. How handsome he was, even now, with his face and beard covered with dirt from the dusty field. How beautiful were his eyes when they met hers in an open acknowledgment of affection. Had she mistrusted him? She had been wrong. Had she thought he cared only for the news she brought him? She had been deceived.

But she was confused no longer. A conviction was growing in her breast. This was what she had been seeking all along. She had heard her mother describe love—and she had never understood. It could not be one-sided. Until he spoke, she was alone, uncertain. Now, at last, the circle was complete. He loved her, and so her love for him could blossom. Her lips parted slightly. "You truly love me?"

"Oh, yes, my dearest! Do you think I would have missed you so otherwise? That day when you appeared in Philadelphia, bruised and exhausted from the flight away from the Freedom's Arms, I wanted to hold you close and never let you go. But I dared not. I released you quickly, for fear you would learn to distrust me as you had learned to distrust David Cavanaugh and his lackeys. I knew you had endured too much. And I had caused you much distress myself." He paused for a moment before continuing. "I knew you had to have time to learn to trust again, and I feared you would never feel safe with me, that you would find another."

"But we have seen each other often since I returned.

Why did you remain silent? If you had spoken—even once . . ."

"I dared not. Oh, Virginia, you were so trusting, and I violated your trust. I was thankful that you did not decide to speak to your uncle, for I was sure he would have sent me away had he known." He paused again. "And when should I have spoken—in Roy's presence? When you were attended by the young fops from the city? When it became clear my path would lead here? Should I have dared to claim you, and then take you here, away from all the comforts that made your life good? Virginia, I love you so much I can hardly breathe when I think of you. I have no wish to trap you into a life you do not want. I cannot take you against your will. I want you only if you want me, and I thought I saw, in your reticence, a rejection of me and what I had done to you. But I have spoken at last. Is there any hope for me? Can it be that you love me a little?"

"No, Anthony." She was smiling at last. "I do not love you a little. I love you with all my heart. I think now that I was upset because I feared you did not feel as I do. But I know now. I love you, Anthony Burke."

Suddenly, they were clasped together. She felt her lips press against his, felt herself rise from the ground and push against him. She had thought she had no ability to feel desire ever again. She had feared that her worry at being taken for a whore would forever hold her back, that she could never again give herself as she had that night.

Now she knew she spoke without shame. Her words came from the depth of her heart.

He brought her fingers to his lips. "Oh, how I have longed to hear you say that. I have dreamed that someday you would . . ." He shook his head. "My darling, I had almost lost the power to dream." He lay back and pulled her close against him. She knew, as her body pressed against his, that she wanted him. She tore restlessly at her clothing. He felt her move, and he gently pushed her hands away. "Let me, my dearest. Let me show you the love I have held within me so very long."

She relinquished her control to him with a feeling of elation. She felt his hands slide under the cotton of her gown and pull it down from her shoulders. The air felt fresh against her breasts, and she pressed toward him, begging him to caress her.

He bent down and kissed each breast, loving it gently with his tongue. And then he unbuttoned the rest of her gown and drew it from her body.

She lay exposed before him, covered only with a light summer chemise. Her firm breasts pushed up under the fine cotton, her nipples erect. He released them from their cover and took them into his lips. At the touch of his tongue on her body, she moaned softly and sank into his arms. This was what she had missed for so long—this gentle strength, this demanding passion!

She touched his arm. "I want to touch you, too."

He smiled and sat up beside her. When his clothes lay in a pile on the ground, he took her again in his arms. Now she felt the force of his desire. She felt him push against her most private parts, and she knew that she had missed him far more than she had known. Far more than she had dared to acknowledge.

He thrust himself between her thighs, and she opened up to receive him. Their embrace was close. She clung to him with all of her strength, loving every sensation he stirred within her body. This was what she had been missing—this feeling of power, of surrender, this merging of her body with his, of her emotions with his.

Their first union had come upon her unawares. This one she sought, and she reveled in the knowledge that his desire equaled her own. She felt him move within her, and she pressed her body against his, wanting him to thrust deeper, to take every part of her, to own her completely.

She felt his pulsations begin, and her body responded. She lost all awareness of where she was, of whether she was dressed or nude, of whether the sun was out or it was the moon that lit her forehead. A tingling sensation started at her abdomen and spread over her body, reaching to her fingertips and to her toes. She cried out and wondered who it was who spoke. She pulled him close and was amazed at the power of his embrace. She felt her mind drifting, lost in ecstasy. And she knew at last that thought only matters when it can be abandoned to passion.

Her consciousness returned slowly. This, she knew, was what her mother had described. This was the ultimate union. This was the full expression of love, the blending of male and female into one inseparable whole. All she had ever dreamed of in the past was realized in Anthony's embrace. He was her man, her lover. Her husband!

They lay together at last, drained of emotion, their energies spent. Then he lifted himself up on one elbow. His bare chest brushed against her uncovered breast, and she shivered with a sudden return of passion. He leaned over her and kissed her lips once more. "We will marry, my dearest. Right now, if you wish. I will leave this place and take you home with me. Oh, Virginia, nothing matters to me except your love."

Gradually, she became aware of her surroundings. A bird was singing overhead. Had it been there before? She did not know. She had been blind to everything but Anthony's closeness. Now she let herself consider his words. Should they marry now? "No, my dearest. Not yet. You have a responsibility to these men. You joined them once to keep them from violence. It is still your duty. What would they do without you? Turn to Daniel Mason? He will start a revolution."

He drew himself up and began to pull on his clothes. She sat beside him, fumbling for her dress, slipping into her chemise. Yet, as her clothes touched her body, she felt again the heat of his skin against hers—the fulfillment of his love.

He spoke as they dressed. "You're right, of course. Oh, my darling! Can you see why I love you? You understand me better than I understand myself." He rose and stood above her. "Yet, I cannot let you go. I want you beside me forever."

"I will be—always." She rose and lifted her cape from the ground. From this day forward, it would be special to her. "But not yet. We both have duties. Still, I am yours. I have been since first we met. I will miss you until we can be together forever." She rested in his arms, and as she felt his love, she remembered her worries. "You have to complete your commitment to these men. I must break free of mine to David. I fear him, Anthony, for he is a dangerous man. He lies without conscience. He associates with brothel-keepers and pirates. I fear what he has planned for me, if we marry. In my foolishness, I permitted my uncle to pledge me to him."

Anthony's arms crept protectively around her. "Then I must take you with me now. I cannot leave you at David's mercy."

For one moment she considered the thought: to go with him, freed of the responsibilities that saddled her, to be content, safe. And then she drew herself up. "No, my love, I cannot. You would not want a woman who did not dare to face her self-made troubles and put them to rest. David is not only a threat to me, he is also a threat to every merchant in Philadelphia. I am sure he has been the cause of many piracies and of many lost cargos. I must find a way to stop him. And when I do, he will no longer cause me any distress."

Anthony turned her and looked into her eyes. "Oh, my wonderful darling! What other woman would care for anything but her own comfort? What other woman would think so responsibly of others? I ask only one thing. Take care! You are so precious to me. Do not risk our happiness, even for the safety of all Philadelphia's shipping."

"I will take care. But you must, also. Oh, dearest, I will miss you so."

"I will miss you, too." He embraced her once more. "Do not forget that I love you. I know you are right. I cannot leave these men, nor can you run away from your troubles like a guilty child, even if it is to live with me. We must be married in style, in the church in the center of town. Then, with the full acceptance of our friends, we will begin our life together." He took her hand and led her toward her horse. "You must not come back again until this matter is resolved. Here, you are in danger. I don't want the militia to think of you as one of us." He lifted her onto her saddle, and handed her the reins. "Wait for me, no matter how long I am gone. And take care of yourself. We must never again forget our love."

"I will never forget." She held the reins tight. "Please, come for me soon. And keep a channel open, so I can contact you. Oh, Anthony, I am so weak, so fearful."

He touched her arm with his hand, and his fingers put courage in her heart. "Take strength, my love. Nothing is impossible for us, if we keep our love fresh in our minds."

He released her, then, and she turned the horse's head to the road. At the bend, she drew reins and glanced back. Anthony stood where she had left him. She raised her arm in a farewell salute. He waved back. Then she turned and continued on her way.

Had she considered, even in the secretmost depth of her heart, that this would be the outcome of her ride? She knew she had not. All she had dared hope for was an opening of communication between them, a return to a civil tolerance that would permit her to ask his advice. She had wanted his help in solving her problem regarding David's association with the pirates.

She had come for advice, and she had received the gift of love instead. Her life had been changed forever. As for her troubles with David, they, too, had been settled in an unexpected manner. She knew now that it was her responsibility to expose him for what he truly was. She could not depend on Anthony for help. He had work of his own to do. All he could give her was the knowledge that she was not committed to David, now that he had shown his true colors.

The understanding that she was no longer at David's mercy brought a smile of satisfaction to Virginia's face. Her life would never be the same again. Anthony's love had set her free.

Twenty-five

"Good morning, Miss Virginia. I trust you had a satisfactory visit—and a pleasant ride."

Virginia turned in alarm. David Cavanaugh drew beside her and slowed his horse to a trot. She had not been aware of anyone approaching, so deeply had she been lost in the thought of her love for Anthony. She was immediately conscious of the mocking tone in David's voice, and the implications of his remark. She did not look at him as she replied. "Yes, thank you."

They rode for a time in silence. When he spoke again, he did not conceal his anger. "So! You have been pretending all along! Never before have I seen a woman assume such innocence when she has already accepted her natural profession."

"My natural profession? What are you talking about?"

"Come now. No more coyness. Surely this is not the first time you have ridden out to care for the needs of the farmers. Truly it is most generous of you, but most unwise. They are men without women, and they possibly pay you well. But are you aware that they are also traitors? No, I suppose not. You have no cause to interest yourself in politics. You should know that President Washington has declared them outlaws and has ordered them to return to their homes. Why do you think girls like Geraldine stay at Bessie's brothel? It is because Bessie sees to it that the men she accepts are respectable. You have been foolish to try to work alone, especially out of the city. Can you not imagine how shocked the Willings would be were your avocation to be known?"

She was too startled to respond. He was calling her a whore! His lips were turned up in a sneer. As she watched him, his expression changed. His voice deepened. "Let me make this clear, my sweet. I, and I alone, truly understand you. I was the man who lit your passion, who awakened you to the pleasure of carnal acts. I have a responsibility to keep your lust in check. I cannot allow you to disgrace your uncle or the memory of your father and mother."

"Do not speak of my parents!"

"Ah, but you must think of them. I can control your venal desires, for my needs are as great as yours. You're a lusty wench, Virginia. I saw how you responded to that rough farmer. Such a man could never control you. You need me, my sweet, to lead you back to respectability. I am the only one who can fill you so totally that you will have no desire for other stags in your garden." He smiled, and she found his smile more infuriating than any of his previous expressions.

He seemed to sense her anger. "No, my dear, the time for self-deceit is past. You cannot afford to run such risks again. I am the man who has been chosen for you. I will make you forget all other men, even the roughnecks you have enjoyed lately. I can be whatever you desire. I can subjugate your body to my will, and your heart will be content at last."

She felt ravaged. He had seen her with Anthony! How long had he watched her? And from what vantage point? What had been sacred and beautiful suddenly became ugly and tarnished. "What right have you to spy on me?" She knew what his answer would be before he spoke.

"You ask such a question? Come, now. We are affianced. The day your uncle returns to Philadelphia, we are to be married." He glanced back at the field, almost out of sight behind them. "Under the circumstances, however, maybe I should write for permission to move the date up. You are sorely in need of a firm hand to control you."

Her heart was beating wildly. Marry David sooner than arranged? Now, at least, she had time to work out a solution to her problem, but if he were to gain permission to hurry their wedding . . . "Please, David, Uncle Roy is my only living relative. He must be present at my wedding." David seemed in no way placated. He frowned angrily, and she wondered if he were thinking of how she'd followed him and overheard his conversation with the stranger on the road. Did he knew it was her horse he had released just yesterday and sent trotting back to town?

She continued hurriedly. "Please. I will make no more journeys to this field or to any other. I will do as you ask.

I want only to have my uncle at my wedding." Another thought came to her, and she added it without thinking. "And I would love to have my gown made by the princess's own dressmaker. Oh, David, you may do whatever you wish with me after we are wed, but give me these two requests, I beg of you!"

She wondered at her own bravery. It was one thing to feel free of his power when they were apart. It was something entirely different to realize her courage when he rode beside her.

He hesitated, and she felt certain he was considering the consequences of giving in to her requests. Would her uncle approve and therefore be more friendly? Would Willing admire his indulgence, and so take him more closely into the brotherhood of traders? "You are a feisty slut—bartering with me, when you are so clearly at a disadvantage. I admire a woman with spirit. She makes a far better partner in bed than a weak, fainting, unsure female ever can." He smiled grimly. "You never told your uncle of our meeting. I was surprised to find him only thankful that I had assisted you in burying your father."

"I was too ashamed. I could not speak of it to anyone." She knew she lied, for she had told Angie—and Anthony.

"Ah, you were so lovely, a virgin, not yet awakened to the joy of love."

"I knew nothing of love then."

"You are right. Yet you came with me eagerly because you sensed my sincerity. Your uncle understands that I am a man worthy of a woman such as you." He drew rein. They had entered the city, and were already at the entrance to the Willing stables. She dismounted and handed her reins to Jonathan. David sat high above her on his stallion. She looked up at him. "You need not visit me tonight, for I will not receive you."

"Ah, but you will. What explanation will you give your host? How long do you think you would stay in his home were he to learn of your lusty appetite?" He leaned down. "You need not fear me, my sweet. Never have I found a woman more attractive. I will not rebuke you for your little pleasure trips, as long as you journey with men of my choice. I find such evidences of your passionate nature exciting." He leaned even closer. "Oh, my sweet, the nights we will share. My passions rise just contemplating them."

She blushed. Had Jonathan heard David's words? No, they were alone. Jonathan was already at the stable, tending to her horse. She turned and ran into the house.

She had reached no solution to her dilemma when David arrived that night. He still had power over her. Anthony had asked her to wait. He did not want her to stay with him in the field. Though she might no longer care what the townspeople thought of her, she could not let David speak until she had some other place to go.

Then she remembered her letter, and the plans David had made to waylay one of Willing's ships. Her problem would be over soon—a week, two at the most. All she needed was to delay.

That evening, David spoke, for the first time, of the need to set a definite date. They had to wait, of course, at least long enough for Roy Salford to return from England. But when Virginia spoke again of the gown, and her desire to have it made especially for the occasion by the princess Charlotte's dressmaker, Thomas Willing was at first opposed to the idea.

"God knows how long that might take. You are beset by enough delays already. Do not add another."

"But, Master Willing." Virginia said, putting on her most persuasive manner. "It is an occasion that will happen only once in my lifetime. Please, I am sure she will work with speed, and the princess will give her the time she needs to get immediately on my dress. It will mean so much to me."

Mother Willing was her immediate ally. "Oh, yes, husband, you must permit it. I am certain Mr. Salford would have no objection. Think how he has catered to Virginia since his arrival here from Pittsburgh. She will be the only girl in Philadelphia to have so great an honor or to have so lovely a gown for her wedding. It will be an auspicious beginning for their life together."

Virginia had not dared to look at David, and when he spoke, she trembled with fright. For he was obviously opposed to any delay, even the initial one of waiting for her uncle. "She has been pledged to me. Now I find obstacles thrown in my path. I am in favor of our marriage taking place now. Why must I wait to claim my own until one man returns from a journey of indefinite length?" He glanced up, and saw that Thomas Willing was frowning. "However, much as I am impatient to take Virginia as my bride, I will not rush her if it would perturb her uncle, or if in my haste, I caused her grief." He looked straight into her eyes. "I will defer to her wishes. She is, after all, a virgin, and unaware of the pleasures of wedded bliss. . . ."

Again Thomas Willing frowned, and cleared his throat. David stopped speaking. "Sir!" Willing's voice was harsh. "Consider that there are ladies present. You speak of things too private for another man's ears. Just give me your answer. Are you willing to wait for a special gown? Yes, or no."

David chewed on his upper lip. "Yes, sir. And please, forgive me. I am young, and impulsive—and I find your ward most desirable."

"Hrmph!" Willing was not to be easily placated. "Then the matter is settled. Do you ask that we set a definite date now, as well?" Again, he met David's eyes, and his glance was kindly once more.

David nodded. "It would give me great comfort if we did." He glanced from Virginia to Mother Willing. "And it will also give the women a limit by which to confine their preparations."

Virginia returned his smile with a small nod. She had succeeded in her first aim. With the wedding set, she would have time to explore ways of stopping David, if the letter Willing had in his safe was not sufficient for the job. "Shall we say June? Somewhat past midmonth, the twentieth, maybe? That will give us a bit more than nine months for my uncle and my gown to arrive."

David frowned. She guessed that he hoped her assessment of the time it would take might be more faulty. Then he forced a smile. "Nine months it will be. I will attend you eagerly during the long delay."

"Nine months!" Mother Willing beamed. "It seems enough time for all the preparations. We must begin at once. There will be a wedding party to choose."

"Please, Mother. Spare us all that foolishness." Thomas Willing turned to David. "I will see to the publishing of the banns, when the proper time arrives. In the meantime, you will continue to be welcome here any time." He took

David's arm and led the way toward the library. "Nine months is not too long for an engagement. Why, Mother and I were pledged to each other for over two years before we wed."

Virginia watched them depart. The months ahead would be filled with plans for a wedding that would never take place. This strategy was necessary to keep David from growing restless. When Willing's ship arrived, having been attacked by pirates, or if it did not arrive at all, David would be disgraced. He would be put on trial, condemned, perhaps even imprisoned —and she would be free to marry Anthony. She took Mother Willing's arm. "Come to my room. I need to have you help me decide what we shall write to Princess Charlotte's seamstress."

Twenty-six

Thomas Willing saw the sails of the *Rebecca Sue* as he approached the docks on the morning of September third. He waited impatiently through the morning for her to reach the harbor, and he was the first to rise from his desk and lead the way to the wharf to greet her.

The dockworkers began to unload immediately. Each box and bale was carried past Willing's clerk, who checked it off the ship's docket. Nothing was missing. The captain reported that the journey had been uneventful, except for a heavy gale around the Horn.

Virginia was disappointed. She had anticipated a moment of triumph when, after the report that the ship had been waylaid by pirates, she could produce the letter she had entrusted into Willing's care and prove that the perpetrator of the crime was the man she hated the most—David Cavanaugh.

While Willing continued to oversee the unloading of his cargo, Virginia returned to the office and retrieved the letter from the safekeeping of her guardian's head bookkeeper. She dared not allow her unhappiness to show, especially when David appeared at the dock, a smug smile on his face. He caught her eyes and nodded his head knowingly. Then he took her hand and brought it to his lips. "Good morning, my dear. You seem uncommonly sad for such a lovely day. Surely you are not sorry to see that your guardian's trade is successful?"

"Oh, no. I'm delighted! The seas can be dangerous."

"Well, don't despair. I will far outdistance him once I concentrate my efforts on shipping. I still have some unfinished business I must tend to." He turned to Willing. "Congratulations on the arrival of your ship. You have excellent crews aboard your vessels. I must speak to you when I begin outfitting my own fleet."

"Aye." Thomas Willing nodded toward the deck. "Captain Hanson is a good man, as are the others who work my fleet. How goes your acquisition of ships? Be sure to come to me when you need help. I will gladly assist the man who marries my friend's only daughter."

"Thank you, sir." David watched Virginia as he spoke. "I have decided to wait until after the wedding to invest time in locating ships and crews. Now it is important that I woo my affianced in the proper manner. After we are wed —ah, a new life, a new business! I see only good fortune coming to me from this union."

When Virginia was alone, she tore up the letter and threw it into the Franklin stove. She could think of no explanation for the failure of her trap. She was sure she had heard correctly. But nothing had happened. What was more upsetting was the fact that David seemed actually pleased to see the ship arrive safely.

She reviewed again and again what she had overheard. She had crept close, and then her horse had whinnied. Had that changed David's plans? She realized at last how devious he was. She was certain, now, that he knew she was the one who followed him. He had known, and he had allowed her to trap herself. She would have looked a fool had she spoken of what she had heard to anyone.

For the first time since she wrote the letter she realized the wisdom of her action. She had kept her peace and recorded what transpired so that later if need be it could be proven.

She recognized how great a risk she had taken. David did not care if he discredited her, if he made her out to be a fragile-minded female, capable of wild flights of fancy. He was aware of her suspicions. And somehow, he would make certain that if ever she spoke out against him, she would be shown up as a fool.

She understood suddenly that David planned to delay any more attempts at piracy until after they were wed. And then his fortune would grow. She knew, too, that it would be at the expense of every other merchant in town.

She stared at the flickering flames as they ate into the paper. How cunning! After they were married, it would not matter if she suspected him. He would be able to control her, and if she threatened his plans, he could even arrange for her to be killed. She shivered with fear. She was playing

with fire, for if her plans went awry, if Anthony did not
return in time to save her, she would be bound to David—
and at his mercy. She had dreaded the thought of marrying
him before because of his cruelty toward her after her
father's death. Now she had even more reason to delay any
plans for an early marriage. Only one way remained open
to her.

She could escape to Braddock's Field and speak to Anthony. If she begged him, he would certainly be willing to
desert his friends and take her with him to Pittsburgh.

In the weeks that followed, she tried more than once to
find a free moment when she might ride for help. David,
however, seemed determined to thwart her plans. He arrived
early every morning to take her for a short ride. When he
could not attend her because of pressing business, he sent a
messenger who remained near the stables, ostensibly so that
he would be ready to carry any message she might wish to
send his master, but actually to keep her from going out
alone.

There were other matters that interfered with her plans
to escape. Mother Willing had taken up the idea of a large
wedding with tremendous gusto. She and Thomas Willing
had had only one daughter, and so for her this was the
second chance to enjoy all of the intricacies of a wedding.
Every day there were new problems to be solved. What sort
of gown should she wear? After all, she was not the bride's
mother, though she felt that Virginia was her own child.
What wine would be best to serve at the reception? How
many attendants did Virginia want? Where would Virginia
prefer that the ceremony be held—at the church or in her
uncle's home? Every decision was, for Mother Willing, a
reliving of her own joyous days of preparation. She could
not understand that for Virginia, the days of activity served
only to lock her more tightly into a trap.

October passed, increasing Virginia's feeling of desperation. She did, finally, toward the middle of the month, succeed in sending Jonathan to Braddock's Field with a note
for Anthony, but he returned to her with the news that the
farmers were gone. Rumor had it they were reassembling
at Parkinson's Ferry. When he had gone there, no one was
around. They appeared to have vanished completely.

One other problem distressed Virginia greatly. She woke

many mornings with a nervous stomach which refused to be quieted until Angie brought her some small bite of food. This discomfiture was accompanied by a delay in her usual time of bleeding. She blamed both disturbances on her worry. Now, when she needed him the most, Anthony could not be found. And David was closing the trap around her.

November started bleak and cold with a flurry of snow that turned, by nightfall of that first day, into a full-grown blizzard. Now David had no need to supervise her, for she could not travel far. She spent her time at the windows, staring out at the blowing snow and praying that by the time the storm was over, her problems would be ended as well.

On the thirteenth, Virginia woke to see sun shining through her window. She rose carefully, as was her habit during these trying days and sat in a chair watching the bright light reflect on the hardened snow. Time was still on her side. Seven full months remained before the ceremony would take place. Certainly by then Anthony would come to rescue her.

Was it not odd that she had received no message in all the time he was gone? She tried to imagine Anthony departing without considering her concern, and she could not. He had to have tried, at least, to communicate with her.

Angie came in carrying a tray of food. Virginia nibbled at a few crusts of bread. Then, suddenly, she sat forward, her eyes alight. Of course! Anthony had sent her a message. But Mother Willing had been persuaded by David to keep her from receiving any communication from her former suitors.

"Angie, bring me a dress. I wish to go downstairs!"

"So soon, miss? Are you sure you feel well enough?"

Virginia answered by walking to the wardrobe and selecting a gown. She pulled the dress over her shoulders, tapping her foot impatiently while Angie buttoned the back. Convinced that she had guessed correctly, she hurried down the steps to confront her guardian.

She was greeted by bedlam. Jonathan, who generally accompanied the cook on his shopping, had returned with important news. He was busy explaining the details when Virginia entered the kitchen.

"Two hundred of them! That ought to put an end to the insurrection."

Virginia froze. "Two hundred of whom? Tell me, Jonathan! What has happened?"

"The farmers, Miss Virginia. They were preparing for an assault, and President Washington put out a call to the militia of Maryland, Virginia, New York, and New Jersey. They all responded. It's a great victory for the Federalists. Mr. Hamilton is certain now that the central government has proven its power. The fighting is over!"

Angie stepped close to Virginia. "Don't worry, dear. Your Anthony may not be among those captured."

Virginia met Angie's sympathetic gaze. Her own eyes were filled with hurt and worry. "Oh, Angie, what will I do?"

"Wait and pray. There is nothing more a woman can do. But don't worry until you know. I'll send Jonathan back later, when things have quieted down, to get a list of the men who have been captured. Surely Anthony won't be among them. He s too clever. And didn't you say that he opposed violence?"

Virginia tried to recall what Anthony had said about such matters the last time they were together. He had shown the same dislike of fighting, but hadn't he said he would remain with his friends, no matter what developed?

She kept to her room throughout the morning, sending word to David, when he arrived for his usual visit, that she was ill. He nevertheless insisted upon being admitted to her chamber. Mother Willing accompanied him, her sincere concern obvious as soon as she entered. Virginia felt guilty for pretending an illness, yet, she had no wish to speak to anyone for long. She smiled as they entered, but then she lay quietly. When she was once more alone with Angie, she breathed a sigh of relief.

Jonathan returned late in the afternoon. Virginia waited impatiently while Angie descended to speak with him, and when her maid returned, pulled her onto the bed. "Tell me! Is he all right?"

Angie's voice broke. "He is among them. Oh, my baby! They are all locked in prison, under constant guard. Feelings run high in the city. There are many who are calling for the execution of every one of the prisoners."

Virginia buried her face in her hands. She tried to speak, but all she could do was sob. Angie pulled her close. "Now, now. Maybe it isn't so bad, after all. Anthony is known in the city. People remember that he was responsible for the peaceful beginning of the protest. Maybe he will be tried separately and given his freedom."

"But if he isn't?" Virginia dried her eyes. "I cannot lie here and weep. I must speak to Mr. Willing. He knows how close Anthony was to my uncle. Surely, if I try, he can be persuaded to intercede on Anthony's behalf." She rose. "Get my clothes. I can indulge myself no longer."

Thomas Willing listened to Virginia with obvious displeasure. When she ended her plea, he rose from his chair. "My dear, I hope you have at least had the wisdom to conceal your unnatural concern for a traitor from your affianced. David is too fine a young man to be deceived in this manner. Do you think I cannot see that your concern for Anthony Burke's life rises from an unreasonable affection you have for him?"

"No, Mr. Willing. Please! You misinterpret my interest. Anthony Burke was a trusted employee of my uncle. I have, of course, spoken with him often. He is my friend. I cannot desert him now when he needs friendship the most." She could see that she was having no influence on Willing, but she had to continue. "My uncle is a man who remains loyal to those who have been close to him even when they do not agree with all of his beliefs. He may not wish to associate with Anthony Burke again or wish me to see him, but he would not want the man to die for a treason he did not commit!"

"Ah, but it appears that he did. I strongly advise you to put this man from your thoughts. Remember that your heart and hand are pledged to David. Be sure that you do nothing that will bring disgrace to you—or to him."

"I swear I will not! Only, please, tell me you will try to help Anthony. He is not a traitor. I am sure of it. He loves our country—for it is his, too."

Willing walked to the door of his study and pulled it open. "Our conversation is ended. You will not speak of this matter with me again. Return to your room until you have regained your senses. I do not know how well you have known this Anthony Burke, nor do I wish to be enlightened on the matter. However, I want this perfectly clear. You are to do nothing that will bring disgrace on your uncle or on the memory of your father. Put this traitor from your thoughts. He deserves nothing from a law-abiding citizen except condemnation. Do you understand? I wish to hear no more of him—nothing—until we are notified that he has been properly punished for his crime."

Virginia was dry-eyed as she ascended the stairs to her room. Her nausea had returned. When she recovered, she was too weak to make any further moves to save her lover.

For the remainder of the week, Virginia remained in bed. She woke each day to face nausea, loneliness, and the realization that no day was worthwhile if Anthony was in prison. Each day, Jonathan traveled into town to learn the news. Nothing seemed to be happening. Virginia took comfort in the knowledge that the prison walls, though they separated Anthony from freedom, also protected him from the anger of the mob.

On the sixth day, Jonathan returned with news. "They are to be tried next week."

"Is there no other information? Will they be tried one by one?"

"I do not know, mistress. The crowd is angry."

Virginia dismissed Jonathan and turned her face to the wall. A trial! How could she save him now?

When she recovered her calm, she felt a new resolve. She had to try. In spite of Mr. Willing's warning, she had to make an attempt to rescue Anthony.

Her spirits rose as she formulated a plan. She knew now she had been foolish to abandon herself to her grief. She had to act before it was too late.

Twenty-seven

The day of the trial was clear and cold. A dusting of snow remained on the ground, blackened by soot from the many fires that threw smoke up the chimneys of the city. Virginia rose early and dressed in her warmest clothing. She had not yet decided how she would get away to watch the trial, but she was determined to do so.

Thomas Willing was seated at breakfast when she entered the dining room. He looked up in surprise. "Well! So you are feeling better, are you?"

Virginia nodded. She still felt weak, but she was sure he had no interest in hearing of her continued distress.

"Good. I regretted that you were too ill to come with us. We are going to watch the trials. I feel it is important for all loyal citizens to witness the prosecution of those who try to overthrow the government."

Virginia refused to respond to his taunt. She ate silently, struggling to control her elation. She would see Anthony! There would be no problem, as she had anticipated. Maybe she would even have an opportunity to speak with him. She decided she would at least make an attempt to do so, for she had a plan that might lead to his freedom.

David arrived as they were preparing to depart. He eyed her sharply as he entered the hallway. "Virginia, my sweet. How wonderful that you feel better again. You have had us all most worried."

She would not meet his gaze. Now, more than ever before, she had no wish to speak to him. He turned his attention to Thomas Willing. "So you are going to the trials, after all?"

"Yes. One of the men involved worked, for a time, for Virginia's uncle. I feel it is important for Virginia to see exactly how untrustworthy he is, for she showed some sympathy for him at the time of his capture."

"Yes. I believe I know the man. Anthony Burke, is that

not his name?" He looked again at Virginia, and this time she could not avoid his eyes. "I believe I have encountered him before. He is a troublemaker, of that I am certain."

"I am glad you are a man of the world who understands the vagaries of the female mind. Virginia is an impressionable girl, and she still harbors the belief that this man is loyal to our country. I feel it is important that she learn her error."

David approached Virginia and brought her hand to his lips. His next words were for her ears alone. "So! It was not just a farmer I saw you with that day. He was a special person to you."

Virginia blushed. "You are wrong. I don't know what you're talking about."

David released her hand, but his eyes burned into hers. "Do not pretend with me, my sweet. Remember, I know your secret. I have the power to destroy you, any time I wish." He turned before she could answer and held out his arm to Mother Willing. "Come along. I trust there is room for one more passenger in your carriage?"

The trial started slowly. The names of all the conspirators were read and the crimes of which they were accused. When Anthony Burke was brought before the judge, Virginia leaned forward, eager to hear every word. The clerk read the indictment. ". . . traitorously directing the others in opposition to the will of the general population. As a leader, Anthony Burke bears much of the responsibility for the continuation of the insurrection."

The judge made a remark Virginia could not hear, and Anthony resumed his seat. Virginia glanced around, her gaze resting on the jury. Were these men willing to withhold judgment until the trial was over? Did they share Thomas Willing's emotions? How fair a trial could these men receive, when even the reading of the accusation against them seemed weighted with prejudice?

While the arguments were proceeding, Virginia stirred uneasily. At last she could remain still no longer. She touched Mother Willing's hand. "Mother, I feel somewhat ill. The crowd is so thick. Will it be all right if Angie and I take a short walk?"

Mother Willing spoke to her husband. When she turned back to Virginia, she appeared solemn. "Mr. Willing has suggested that I accompany you as well. You have not been strong."

Virginia dared not protest. She led the way through the crowd toward the barn-like building where the prisoners were being housed.

Before they came close enough to speak to any of the men, a militiaman stopped their progress. "Halt, and state your business!"

Virginia approached him. "I wish to speak to one of the prisoners. Is it permitted?"

"Sorry, no. No one is allowed past this point."

Virginia had difficulty hiding her disappointment. She turned away to hide her tears. Mother Willing took her arm. "My child, do not distress yourself because of this man. He has proven himself to be unworthy of friendship. Don't you see that you upset your fiancé with your preoccupation? How can you treat the man you are to marry with such unkindness?"

"Oh, Mother Willing, I wish you could understand. I do not love David. I cannot, for he has been cruel to me. The man I love is in that jail, on trial for his life. How can I act other than as I do?"

"But you can do nothing, and your love, if it is love at all, is hopeless. I think you would be better off were you to avoid the remainder of the proceedings. I will suggest to my husband that you stay home tomorrow."

"Please, no!" Virginia grabbed Mother Willing's arm in panic. "I must be here. I must see him. at least. Maybe I can testify for him. I know him well. I know how highly my uncle thought of him. Remember last year, when he led the march into the city? Even President Washington congratulated him on his patriotism."

"Yes, I remember hearing of it. But men change. He has shown no loyalty to our government in recent months."

When they returned to their seats, Virginia regretted her attempt to speak with Anthony. She felt certain that Mother Willing would report to her husband and the result might be that any further attempt at communication would be frustrated.

As they drove back to the house, Thomas Willing broached the subject. "Mother tells me you tried to see Burke."

"Yes. I cannot believe he is a traitor." Virginia was determined to stand her ground.

"It is Mother Willing's suggestion that you not come back tomorrow."

"Oh, please, I must return."

David had been silent, but now he took her hand. "Mr. Willing, I realize you wish to be scrupulously fair, and I can understand that you feel my fiancée is behaving improperly to show such interest in another man's fate. However, Virginia is a very special girl. It is possible that her concern for this man lies as much with her political beliefs as with her affections. Maybe she honestly believes him and all the other farmers to be justified in their behavior. We cannot overlook how she was raised, unnatural though it may be for a woman."

"Aye, I fought often with George, her father, to convince him that she should not be permitted to mix in men's business. He would not agree. What, then, do you suggest?"

"Let her attend. See if it is possible for her to visit with the man. I will be with her to keep her safe. Maybe, if she hears him speak for himself and compares his words with those of honest, loyal men, she will begin to recognize her error."

Virginia listened to David with a feeling of elation and concern. If he had his way, she would get to see Anthony. What reason could he have for catering to her desires? She watched him closely, looking for some clue to the cause of his kindness.

As he continued speaking, she began to understand. He was anxious to establish himself as a reasonable man. He was using her to show Thomas Willing how thoughtful and considerate he could be. David was more concerned with Willing's opinion of him than with his relationship with her. It was important to him that Willing like and trust him.

She dared not add her plea to David's. She listened quietly while the decision was made. She would be allowed to attend the trial, and she would be assisted in her attempt to see Anthony.

Permission was not received for the visit until the third day. Virginia held David's arm for support as she walked across the frozen ground to the barn where the prisoners were billeted. She studied the arrangements as she approached. There were far too few guards for so large a number of prisoners. At night, the militia built fires to ward off the cold, and they could be seen gathering around the glow, warming their hands. A prisoner could easily escape without being seen. The realization cheered her.

Anthony was pulled from the barn and led twenty yards out, where he halted and waited for her to reach his side. Virginia glanced up at David. Would he insist on remaining close behind her? He seemed not to notice her unspoken plea. Clearly, he had no intentions of allowing her to be alone with her lover.

He did stop two yards away and allow her to move forward alone. She stumbled as she advanced, and Anthony reached out to keep her from falling.

She clutched his arm, and pulled herself to him. "Oh, Anthony, I had to see you."

He frowned toward David. "You should not have come. You open yourself to too much unhappiness."

"Oh, but you must listen to me." She lowered her voice. "I have studied the guards these last few days. They are placed too far apart to be effective. You can escape. It would be so easy."

"Speak up!" The guard, who had stepped beside David, called out to Virginia. "No secrets permitted."

Anthony raised his voice. "No, my dear. What you suggest is not possible. I am with my friends. I have been with them throughout the entire difficulty. I cannot accept special treatment now that will separate me from them."

"But you must not be executed." Virginia spoke quietly again. "Anthony, can you forget the love we shared? I cannot live without you."

"You will learn. Do you not see that what is happening is inevitable? No country can survive if its citizens maintain the right to oppose its laws. We must be sentenced to death as punishment for exercising the right of freedom. If we escape judgment, others will follow our lead in the future, and the government will never have the power it feels that it must have."

"Oh, Anthony! Don't be so bitter. How do you know you will be found guilty? You may all be freed." She spoke up. "I have volunteered to testify on your behalf."

"I forbid it! You cannot expose yourself in such a manner." He turned toward David. "You must not allow her to do such a thing. Why did you bring her here?"

David seemed taller than usual as he stared down his nose at Anthony. "She is suffering from some sort of misapprehension. I thought she might be relieved of her errors were she to see you as you are—a traitor among traitors. Now that I have heard you speak, I know I am right in my judgment of you. You have no respect for our nation or our laws. You have no faith in our system of justice." He stepped forward and took Virginia's arm. "Come, we must go. I was wrong to bring you here. But, maybe, since you have seen what he is, you will no longer be concerned for his life."

Virginia held tightly to Anthony's arm. "Please, do as I ask. I will send Jonathan to help you." She lowered her voice to a whisper and bent close to his ear. "Tonight!"

Virginia slept little, for she was listening for the sound of Jonathan's return. The night was still, disturbed only by the wind and the occasional crunch of wheels on the snow-covered cobblestones. Once she heard a horseman, and she wondered if it might be Anthony. He paused for a moment, and she visualized him gazing hopefully at her window.

He was gone before she could rise and look out. She was certain he was safe, and so when she returned to her bed, she slept soundly.

Jonathan was grooming a horse when Virginia entered the stable the following morning. She ran to his side, her face alight. "Thank you, Jonathan, thank you!"

He did not look up from his work. "He wouldn't do it, mistress. I waited until almost dawn, but he never came. Maybe they caught him, I don't know." He avoided her eyes. "I deserve no thanks for my work last night."

"He didn't come!" Virginia found herself repeating the words as she dressed for the trial. If he had been caught, he might not even be permitted to appear when they discussed his case.

Anthony was in his usual place, however, as the prisoners filed into the courtroom. Virginia ordered Angie to wait near the door and try to speak to Anthony as he passed. The maid obeyed, but when she returned to Virginia's side, she looked upset. "I asked him, Miss Virginia. He said he could not leave his friends, not even for you."

Virginia was crestfallen. Did he love her less than she had thought? Her answer came when she caught his eyes during the trial. He stared at her longingly, and then his lips formed the words "I love you." Her fears were calmed once more. It was not any lack of affection that had caused him to refuse the chance to escape. He simply could not desert his companions. Silently, Virginia cursed such masculine loyalty.

That night Virginia sat for a long time, staring up at the bit of sky visible through her window. "When he is killed, I will die, too. Some way. I cannot live without him."

She could not imagine what method she might use to end her life, but that did not disturb her. A way would open. Never would she become David's wife.

The thought comforted her. As she surrendered to sleep, she whispered the words once more. "We will be together, my love . . . in death, since life is denied us."

Twenty-eight

"Go to the window, Angie. Find out what all the noise is about." Virginia lay back in bed. The nausea was not so bad as it had been a few weeks before, but she still woke feeling tired. "It sounds as if the whole country has come to Philadelphia."

Angie bustled across the room with a tray of food. "Get up and see for yourself. How am I to know what people do?"

Virginia grimaced. She fought this same battle every day. Angie was determined to entice her mistress out of bed, but Virginia, aware now that there was no hope for Anthony's release, had determined to remain in bed until she died. She played absentmindedly with the food, but she did not eat. At last Angie, her face a study of concern, took the fork and began to push the food into Virginia's mouth.

"Stop that!" Virginia turned her face away.

"Only if you get out of bed." Angie smiled in triumph as she maneuvered another bite of food past the reluctant lips.

Virginia rose slowly, aware that not all of her weakness was pretended. She felt Angie's arm around her waist, and she leaned on her maid as she crossed the room. Two days of fasting had had an effect on her young body.

A mob of people swarmed through the cobblestone streets. Farmers and their wives, sailors in from the wharf, townsmen who normally remained close to their shops—all milled about. These people were somber, and they advanced more like a funeral procession than a group of revelers.

"The court has reached a decision. Many of the women you see have come because their men are to be sentenced."

Virginia stared down for a time in silence. "I must go, too. What if Anthony looks for me as he is . . . ?" She could not complete her sentence, yet Angie understood.

"You must not think such things. Surely, he will be

freed. He has fought all along to keep the farmers from violence. Even Washington knows that. He is not guilty of insurrection."

"God willing, he may be freed. But I must be there, whatever happens. Help me dress, please."

Virginia stood quietly while Angie pulled on her gown and buttoned up the back. She wore a wool dress and heavy shoes to protect her from the cold. Angie followed her to the door, carrying their warmest cloaks. "Miss Virginia, should you not eat first?"

Virginia took the cloak. "No, thank you. I cannot eat now. I must see Anthony. I pray God that everything will be all right."

Angie was pleased that Virginia did not seem to notice that Thomas Willing and his wife had already departed. She had deliberately waited to wake her mistress until they were alone. At least during this trying period, Virginia would not have to pretend a disinterest she did not feel.

They took places far back from the town hall, in the green that had served as the center for the Fourth of July celebration. Though many of the observers at the beginning of the trials had shown an eagerness for blood, none seemed so inclined now. The women who were related to the prisoners were treated with gentleness and respect.

A soldier, still dusty from a long journey, paused and spoke to Angie. "What happens here—a new celebration?"

"No. A sad time." Angie spoke quietly. "Why is it you know nothing of what has taken place here?"

"Your pardon, miss. We come from the fighting in Ohio. A battle is waging near Fort Wayne, at the head of the Maumee River. General Wayne has pushed the savages back. The settlers are in need of supplies to replace those lost during the fighting. We come also to recruit more soldiers to join the cause, men who have no use for civilization that closes in around them . . . men who crave freedom and liberty."

Virginia turned away. Anthony was such a man. But he would have no opportunity to follow the call.

"Aye, there are many here who will listen to your words." Angie stepped away from Virginia. Her mistress had heard enough about the trials already. "We are here today because many such men are being sentenced, after fighting for . . ." Her voice died away.

A cold wind stirred through the bare branches of the trees rattling them together like dry bones. Virginia shuddered at the simile. Dry bones! Would Anthony and all his friends be no more than that when this day was over?

A child began to cry. Beside him, a young lady dressed in linsey-woolsey pulled the boy in her arms. "Hush, my son! You'll see your father. I'll hold you high. But you must not climb the tree to wait. You'll freeze, and you will begin to weep again. You don't want your papa to see you crying, do you?"

The child sobbed, brushed his cheeks with the back of his hand, and stared red-eyed toward the town hall. "I'm not crying. I'm as brave as papa."

"Good." The young mother wrapped her cloak around her son as a stiff wind whipped past.

Virginia shivered. What an appropriate day for so terrible an event. The earth was in mourning for the brave men who were about to die. The frozen ground and gray skies reflected the bleakness within her heart—and the hearts of everyone who had a loved one in prison.

If only she had remained with Anthony! She had begun to wonder about her illness, and now she decided to ask Angie if it might be possible she was carrying Anthony's child. The thought filled her with a mixture of happiness and sorrow. It would be a child who would never know his father. If she let herself die, after Anthony was executed, would the child be born into heaven? She decided she would ask the pastor.

A shout near the hall brought the watchers to attention. The prisoners were coming. The judge was emerging from the hall. Even many of the members of Congress appeared, and President Washington stood watching the proceedings from an upstairs window.

The young mother lifted her son onto a low branch. "Do you see him, Alex? Look close!"

"I see him, Mama! He's waving to me." The lad waved his arms frantically.

Virginia stood on her toes, but she could not see over the heads of those in front. The young mother touched her arm. "You may climb onto the branch. Alex can't stay there any longer. He is too cold."

Virginia waited until the boy was on the ground, then she pulled herself up. She felt a sharp pain, and she gasped. Angie looked up in alarm, but Virginia refused to face her. Now was no time to worry about her own welfare!

She found Anthony at once. He stood slightly apart from the others, searching the crowd. He saw her, and his face brightened. His lips formed her name. She waved timidly, and silently formed the words "I love you" with her lips. Then a militiaman approached him and pushed him toward the other prisoners.

Virginia climbed down, and almost fell into Angie's arms. The angular face of her maid was lined with worry. "Oh, Virginia! I had hoped you would have no trouble."

"You knew?"

"I feared it was a baby. But do not fear. Many times young women lose their first child, especially if they are worried and upset. These are trying times for you."

The barrenness in Virginia's heart grew even more bleak. She had nothing left, nothing at all!

The judge was speaking. ". . . Guilty of treason. They shall all be executed before a firing squad tomorrow, at sunrise."

Virginia gasped and caught at Angie's sleeve. The worst had happened. Nothing was left to her. The young woman beside her pulled her son close. "Be brave, Alex. Your father would want you to show that you are a man. He is dying for a cause he feels is just. We cannot shame him or his beliefs with weakness."

Virginia forced herself to stand. The woman was right. She could be no less brave than Anthony. She whispered the words. "I will be strong, my love. And I will join you soon."

Angie took her arm. "Come, we must go home. They will be returning the prisoners to the jail."

"Washington! He's coming down!" The word traveled up from the hall, starting as a whisper and growing to a shout. Virginia raised her head. Washington appeared on the steps. He was dressed in the uniform he had worn throughout the battle for liberty. The great cloak he had wrapped himself in at Valley Forge was around his shoulders.

A hush fell over the crowd. In the silence, Virginia could hear him speak.

"Friends! I have seen today an expression of legal justice. Men violated the law, and they were condemned to be punished. But a democracy cannot exist in an atmosphere of pure legalism. These men are my comrades. They fought with me for liberty. Is it surprising that our interpretation of that word differs? And should they be condemned to death because the men in power do not see liberty through their eyes?"

A child, somewhere, began to cry and was hushed by his mother. Washington waited until the noise was silenced. "There has been, in the last years, great contention between parties in our land. Some want a strong central government, others prefer that the states be almost powers unto themselves. These men are the victims of that disagreement. But the dissension is over. These states have proven that they will support a central federal law. While the battles to determine how our government was to be organized progressed, these men tried to be heard. When we appeared not to hear, they did the only thing they knew—they fought for their rights. Now they have been condemned to death as traitors."

He paused and looked down at the prisoners. "These are not traitors. They are my countrymen. Thomas Jefferson spoke to me regarding them yesterday. His words have meaning now. He said that there must always be, in a free land, citizens who dissent from the will of the majority. Such dissension is right and proper. Jefferson believes, and I believe with him, that these men who demand a different form of liberty should never be quiet. Our nation needs them. They serve to remind us that the government, no matter how strong or weak, state or federal, exists for only one purpose—to serve the people."

He pulled a paper from his vest. "I have here a pardon for all the prisoners. It is my right as president of the United States to rescind even the sentence of death. I do that now. Men, fellow countrymen, I cannot change the law you have protested, for the majority of the people desire it. But I can offer you a chance to continue the fight for equality in more acceptable ways. Do not again take arms against your lawful leaders. Fight for your rights, but fight within the law. Elect representatives who can voice your wishes. Follow their records when they vote. That is the correct way to gain the kind of liberty you seek." He turned to the officer in charge of the prisoners. "Sir, release these men now. There should be no shackles or chains confining free men in a free land."

A cheer drowned out his final words. Angie grabbed Virginia and pulled her close to the tree, for the press of the crowd was suddenly so forceful it threatened to crush them both. They stood together, waiting. The little boy cried out and ran forward. His father carried him back and then led the young woman away.

When the crowd thinned, Angie released Virginia from her protective hold. Virginia immediately pulled herself up and looked down toward the hall. Anthony stood near the steps, talking with a soldier. Angie tried to catch Virginia's sleeve. "Wait. You are not well. You cannot run about so carelessly."

Virginia pulled free. Her troubles could wait. Now was a time for rejoicing. George Washington had turned a dull, bleak day into a day of celebration.

Twenty-nine

"Why, what a surprise, Virginia! I didn't know you were near." A body blocked her way. David Cavanaugh put his arms out and stopped Virginia's precipitous flight. "Does Mr. Willing know you are here? I am sure he would not approve. You do not look well at all."

Virginia pulled back, but she could not break free of his hold. "Please, I have business."

"There? Down there with the ruffians? Oh, come, Virginia. You are a lady born. You can have nothing to do with such a creature. It was one thing to let you visit him when everyone thought he was to be executed, quite another thing now." He turned her and began to walk back toward the park. "Come along. Mother Willing will take care of you." He turned to Angie. "And you, too, mistress. You overstepped yourself to bring this poor child out into the cold."

"She did nothing of the kind. I brought her." Virginia gestured frantically to Angie. When the woman did not move, she raised her voice. "Find him! Tell him to wait here for me!"

Angie nodded and disappeared. Virginia cast one last glance toward Anthony, and when he seemed too busy to look up, turned in despair and went with David to the carriage. Mr. Willing and Mother Willing were waiting. As he approached, they showed their surprise. He lifted her and placed her on the seat. Then he mounted his horse and fell in beside her.

Mother Willing spread a fur robe over Virginia's legs. "You poor child. You must be frozen."

"She should be." Thomas Willing showed no sympathy for her condition. "Sick in bed for a week, and yet she comes out on this raw day. 'Tis a surprise she has not caught the ague."

Angie was at the house when the carriage arrived. She

received Virginia from Mother Willing's arms and half-carried her up to her room. The worst had happened. If, as she believed, Virginia had been carrying a child, she carried it no longer. She washed Virginia, and put her into a warm nightgown. Only when her patient was safely in bed did she depart with the soiled clothes.

Mother Willing appeared at the door. "Are you all right, now?" She stepped into the room. "David is with me. He seems most worried for your safety."

"I'm fine, Mother Willing. I'm very tired. I'll be better tomorrow."

David insisted upon approaching the bed. He took Virginia's hand in his and pressed it to his chest. "You must not do so foolish a thing again. Had I known you intended to go out, I would have forbidden it. I have agreed to wait for our wedding until spring, but I will change my mind if I feel you need a strong hand to guide you. Obviously, your maid is of no use at all."

"Angie did only what she was told to do. Do not blame her." She wished she could tell him that she would die even now rather than marry him, but she held her peace. She would need all of her little freedom to effect an escape.

When Mother Willing and David were both gone, Virginia called Angie to her side. The woman had returned with a mug of hot rum as the two departed.

"Angie! Did you find him? Where is he waiting? You must help me get ready to leave."

"You have nowhere to go, Miss Virginia. When I reached the hall, Anthony was gone. I asked for him and was told he had departed with a group of other men. I could not learn where they were headed."

"Oh, then I must go and find him. Help me, please!" Virginia raised herself up but fell back weakly against the pillows. She cried out in alarm. "What's the matter with me?"

"Nothing that wasn't the matter earlier. Then, you were too upset to let yourself be overcome. Now you have relaxed. The loss you have experienced was too great. Your body needs rest. It will obey you no longer, until you have slept." She kissed Virginia's forehead. "Do not despair. I will send Jonathan out to search for him. You sleep. When you waken, I promise we will have news for you."

Virginia slept most of the day. She roused herself once when Mother Willing entered the room and adjusted her quilts, but she was too tired to speak. She dropped off again, as soon as Mother Willing left the room.

The sun had set when next she regained consciousness. Angie sat near the foot of her bed, sewing on a piece of lace. She smiled when she saw Virginia open her eyes. "Do you feel better now?"

"Yes. Better and hungry. Could you find me some food?"

Angie leaped to her feet. "Right away. Oh, how good it is to see you interested in life once more!"

Virginia held up her hand. "Don't go yet. Tell me first, what did you learn of Anthony?"

"Food first, talk later."

Virginia fretted until she returned, but the food was delicious, a thick stew that warmed her stomach. She ate slowly, for she was still weak, and she grew impatient for the news. "Tell me now, or I'll throw the stew on the floor."

"I sent Jonathan to search for Anthony as soon as I could. As you know, he has little to do with your uncle away."

"Angie, don't tease. What did he learn? When will I see Anthony? And where?"

"He found Anthony at Braddock's Field, gathering up his gun and his few clothes. He had already saddled his horse. Did you know the farmers near the field cared for the animals while the men were in prison? It was a great kindness. God knows the animals were innocent enough."

"Angie!"

Angie produced a small packet. "He sent this to you."

Virginia snatched it and tore at the seal. The note inside was short, and she read it three times before she spoke again.

Dear Virginia,

I had hoped to hold you after my release, but I saw Cavanaugh approach and felt I would only make things difficult for you if I attempted to interfere. I have heard that you and Cavanaugh have published banns for a wedding in June. Please, my love, do not consent to an earlier date. I must leave immediately on urgent business, for I feel a need to prove my loyal-

ty to a nation generous enough to release me. I will be
back in time to take you for my own forever.

All my love,
Anthony

She stared at the paper. Gone? He had gone without
saying good-bye?

Angie tucked her back under the covers. "You can't
get up now. Where do you plan to go? Jonathan said Anthony departed with a number of other men, and that
young soldier we met before the verdict was given."

"So he went to Ohio! Oh, Angie, he's asked me to be
patient. He says he'll be back in time. How can he think
that fighting is more important than being with me?"

Angie took the note and read it. "He says he wants to
show his loyalty to the country that gave him back his life.
My dear, you must understand. And don't despair. If he
says he will be back, you may be sure he will. You're too
sick to travel about, anyway." She put the note back in
Virginia's hands.

Virginia stared at the paper. Then, abruptly, she brought
it to her lips. She could resent anything that would keep
Anthony from her. No one could deny her that right. But
he was alive! "Angie, tell me again that I can have another
child. Please."

"Of course you can. You are too young to fear any
problems. When you and Anthony are wed, and when you
no longer are torn with worry and distressed by Cavanaugh,
you will carry his child and bear him all the children he
wishes."

Virginia let the words soothe her troubled heart. The
promise was founded on hope, but it was better than nothing.

Angie kissed her forehead. "Good night, little Virginia.
Sleep now. Tomorrow you will feel better about everything." She blew out the light and tiptoed softly from the
room.

Thirty

Virginia took her place at the breakfast table on the fourth morning after Anthony's release from prison. Angie had nursed her well. The weakness that followed her accident had vanished. For the first time in months, Virginia felt optimistic and her normal healthy self.

She missed Anthony. But each time her loneliness grew unbearable, she touched the paper she had tucked into the bosom of her dress. The crinkle told her that he loved her, that he had promised he would be back with her in time.

Thomas Willing rose as she entered the room. "Thank God you are strong again. I have been distressed by the thought that I had been given a healthy girl to care for, and I was returning a sickly one."

"Returning?" Virginia took her seat. "You speak as if Uncle Roy were here."

"Not yet. But you are alert to my meaning. There is a very special ship already sailing toward the harbor. It will dock at nine by the clock. I presume you would like to attend me when I go to meet it."

"Oh, yes! How wonderful!" Her expression grew solemn. "Is my uncle alone? Is Mr. Jay still struggling to complete the treaty?"

"Oh, Virginia! Were you my child, I would be most perturbed by your constant intrusion into men's business. However, I suppose this concern, more than any before, is justified. It is my understanding that Mr. Jay is on board, too, with the treaty in his hand." He gestured impatiently. "Eat quickly. We do not want to be late."

Jonathan and Angie were both allowed to accompany Virginia, for they were as eager as their mistress to greet Roy Salford. They waited in Willing's office, where they were protected from the bitter wind. Virginia stood at the window, gazing out at the approaching ship.

A dusting of light snow whirled about the wharfs. The

278

sky was gray, and the sea reflected its color. Virginia shivered. How cold the sailors must be, she thought, as they climbed about the mast, securing the sails.

When the ship came in sight she saw that it was tacking back and forth against the wind, but its progress was steady. Conversation in the shelter stopped while the final stages of docking began. Then Mr. Willing led the way to the wharf.

Roy Salford was the first on shore. He caught Virginia in his arms and lifted her up to kiss her cheek. She clung to him. "Oh, uncle! Thank God you are home. Was it a difficult passage? Did you complete a good treaty? How is the princess and Percy? Did you persuade him to give you the portrait of grandmama?"

He held her for a moment, and then set her down. "No, the passage was pleasant. The princess sends her greetings. As for Percy, he is married, and he let me take the portrait, for his wife seemed oddly jealous of it. We will speak of the treaty later." He turned to Willing. "Good to see you, my friend. I hope caring for this strange niece of mine has not taxed your patience too greatly. I can never repay your kindness. I thank you, from the bottom of my heart."

Willing smiled broadly, and embraced his friend. "No need for such a show of gratitude. We have had our moments of distress, but that is to be expected with a girl her age. Mostly, she has filled Mother Willing's life, for our own children are too far away to visit as often as she wishes. I fear she will be lonely, now that you have come to take her last daughter away."

"Well, then, Virginia must visit her often." Roy turned toward the ship as Jay approached. "Thomas, you know John Jay, do you not?"

"Yes, very well. I am thankful you have arrived, John."

Willing took Jay's hand. "Was your mission successful?"

John's expression did not change. He pulled his cape closer around his shoulders. "Please, let us get inside before we all freeze to death!" He hurried across the icy stones and led the way into the shelter. When all were settled around the Franklin stove, he resumed. "In some ways our trip was most worthwhile, for we have opened channels that were closed to us before. But neither Roy nor I am pleased with all that transpired. I trust you will forgive me if I do not go into the details at this time. I need yet to complete my report, so I can deliver it to Congress. You must attend that session so you can hear first-hand what has been done, and what has been left for the future negotiators."

"May I go, too?" Virginia watched her uncle. "Even Mr. Willing seems to understand my interest in this affair."

Roy looked deep into her eyes. Then he smiled. "Yes, my dear, don't fret. You may come with us, but I suggest you remain only for Jay's report. You will grow bored if you have to listen to all the debate that follows."

Virginia did not reply. There would be time to settle that question when she was at the hall.

Roy continued to look into her face. "Have you been ill, my dear? You look pale."

"A little indisposed, uncle. But I am fine, now." There was so much she wished to ask her uncle in private. Would he want Anthony to be his aide, now that the insurrection was over?

Mother Willing took Virginia's hand. "Oh, Mr. Salford, we have been so busy, your niece and I, preparing for the wedding this spring! She has worried greatly that you might not return in time to bestow her on the happy groom."

"The wedding? Ah, yes, with Cavanaugh. Then it has not yet taken place!" He looked around the room. "I should have known. He would have been here, too, were he my niece's husband."

Virginia felt a sudden depression. David might insist on an early wedding, now that her uncle was returned. She still had cause for her delay. "I wanted a gown made by Princess Charlotte's own seamstress. One to equal those that were made for me when I was there. We are waiting for its arrival." She looked nervously toward the docks. "Perhaps it has arrived with you?"

Roy shook his head. "I think not. There were precious few packages for individuals in the hold, and I saw them all when they were carried aboard. But it will come soon, I am sure. And if it does not, well, other women have been married in less fancy clothes."

Mother Willing came to her rescue. "Oh, but Mr. Salford, you must not deny your niece this pleasure. A woman marries only once, and she needs make that event as memorable as she can."

Roy shrugged. "If David does not object, why should I?"

David arrived at the house that evening, but Virginia spent little time in his presence. She had no difficulty pretending fatigue, for she was tired from the many activities of the day and from the excitement of her uncle's return.

She was ready the following morning to leave for the Congress. She had, in fact, been greatly frustrated by Roy's silence on the matter of the treaty, but she had not dared to urge him to speak, since Jay had made their stand so clear.

On the way to the hall, Roy took her hand in his. "So you are not married yet. I had thought I would return to find you a married woman, with a child in your belly. However, it cheers me to see that you and David have settled your differences. As I thought about your report of his actions, I came to realize that you could not be expected to see things as they were. You were upset by your parents' deaths and you were alone. I am pleased that your differences with Cavanaugh were not so great as you made them out to be when I first saw you."

Virginia considered his words carefully. Should she tell him how she felt about David? Was this the time to explain that she had reason for not trusting the man, that she felt certain he was involved some way in many of the piracies that had occurred in the last year?

She held her peace. David had obviously decided to keep his activities well hidden until after the wedding. Without any evidence, she would only sound unreasonable.

The gallery was crowded with men eager to hear Jay's report. Virginia refused to be upset by the fact that she was the only woman present. She took a seat near the front where she could see as well as hear.

A hush came over the chamber when Jay rose to give his report. "Gentlemen of Congress, Mr. President. I have spent the last year in London, fighting for time, fighting for an opportunity to speak with Mr. Pitt and with the king. I and my companion have followed the court all over England. We have stayed in Bath, we have visited the sea, we have returned again and again to London. I have carried on diplomacy in the most difficult of situations. I fear that I have little to bring back as reward for my efforts."

A murmur momentarily drowned his words. Washington cleared his throat and held up his hand for silence. Jay continued. "One important goal has been achieved. The British have agreed to evacuate their forts south of the Lakes, as well as any forts south of the border line determined at the time of their surrender. They have agreed to do this by June of 1796."

A cheer interrupted him. When Jay continued, his face was solemn. "Other than that, I have had no true success, though I see a glimmer of light ahead. First, as you know, there has been much pressure on the part of the British to reinstate the debts to English merchants that were canceled by the start of the great war. On this subject, I was not equipped to fight, for the men who suffered were honest merchants who lost fortunes, and the goods they had delivered to us were real." He glanced about. "I was forced, in the end, to agree with such reinstatement."

Virginia noticed that Washington paled noticeably. It was common knowledge that he was among those whose debts were the greatest.

"One other area is far from satisfactorily resolved, though I see here some hope of future settlement. The British government has agreed to stop any waylaying of American vessels by British warships unless they have knowledge that we carry cargo for France. They insist that they are at war with France and are, therefore, entitled to use every means to achieve victory. This means that at least for the present the only ships of ours that will be safe are those headed for England."

Again, there was a murmur. He raised his voice. "However, the fighting with France seems to be coming to an end. When it does, I am certain this matter can be resolved." He paused and turned toward the president. "I regret, sir, that I do not carry more cheering news. I can only assure you that we did not lag in our efforts. I must also add a note of appreciation for the great help given me by Mr. Roy Salford. He made a difficult task more endurable."

Washington rose. "Thank you, Mr. Jay. We share your disappointment in those areas where your success was less than hoped, but we understand. Negotiations will continue. You have paved a good road toward eventual peace and understanding between our two nations."

The debate was short, little more than the drafting of a note of thanks to Jay and Roy for their efforts. When Roy escorted her from the gallery, Virginia was content to go. He ushered her into the carriage. Angie, who had waited in the corridor, climbed up beside her and tucked a fur around her legs.

Roy waited until she was settled. "My dear, I hope you are satisfied. However, I will personally give your apologies to David this evening. I feel it is too much to subject you to so trying a morning and then expect you to remain up late at night. If you are not too disappointed, I will permit him to escort you on a short ride tomorrow morning, if the cold tempers."

Virginia repressed a smile. She had no wish to see David. "Thank you, uncle. You are very kind."

Jonathan flicked his whip over the horses' backs and the carriage moved away. As soon as she was certain they were out of her uncle's hearing, Virginia turned to Angie. "Have you heard anything about Anthony? Is he well? He has not been injured, has he?"

Angie shook her head. "We have heard nothing, and that would seem to be good. But you need not worry. If he sends no message it is because he still expects to arrive this spring."

Virginia was silent. Maybe Angie was right. But what if he lay dead? Would she ever know? Her uncle's return was cheering, certainly, but it increased her worry. He had already said once that he considered a wait for a special wedding gown to be foolish. He might become more insistent. If he did, she was sure David would increase his efforts to move the wedding date up. The delay was costing him money.

Things were closing in on her. She prayed silently that Anthony would come even earlier than he had promised. If he did not, he might arrive too late.

Thirty-one

For Virginia, the months that followed her uncle's return seemed to both drag and fly. When she thought of Anthony's return, she felt the days were far too long and the nights terribly empty. When she considered that each day brought her closer to the moment when she would be expected to marry David, she wished she could hold back the movement of the sun.

Each morning she rode with David, usually through the city or a short distance into the surrounding countryside. He seemed to accept her varying moods with patience when they were with others. When they were alone together, he let his irritation show.

One day, when he stood beside her on the crest of a hill, watching the harbor, circled in the faint greenish hue of spring, he drew her into his arms. She pushed him away and pulled back. He grabbed her and forced her to remain close to him. His voice was cold. "My sweet, you forget that I am no longer just one of many suitors. I am your husband-to-be. Your uncle has given us his blessing. You have no cause to keep me still from your bed. As your affianced, I am your master. Remember that, for I will not allow a lack of affection again."

She held herself stiff in his arms. "We are not wed yet. You may have deceived my uncle and Mr. Willing, but you do not delude me. I know what you are—and I hate you. Don't be too sure that I will live to be your bride."

"Come, now! You expect me to believe you have the courage to destroy yourself?"

"Do you want to take the chance that I do? If you force me to accept you in my bed or if you attempt to advance the day of our wedding, you will learn how strong I can be. Then what will become of your plans to use my inheritance?"

He studied her for a moment in silence. Abruptly, his

expression changed. Virginia glanced about. Her uncle was approaching. David was careful to keep matters between them smooth and pleasant whenever anyone was nearby.

She wondered when she was again alone whether her words had been mere bravado. Would she, in truth, have the courage to kill herself were she trapped into marriage with David? She shuddered at the thought. Only if she received news that Anthony was dead would she take her own life. If matters grew too difficult, if she were forced to set an earlier date for the wedding, she would run away and hope that she would be able to find her lover.

She often thought of her move from Amos's inn to the Freedom's Arms. Something about that bawdy house teased at her memory. When she tried to sort out her impressions, she could not.

She did broach the subject once with her uncle, so he knew the inn was actually David's property. Roy seemed not too pleased at the knowledge, but he recognized that such places were common, and no shame existed in owning them, though the people who actually managed them were usually of a low class. Virginia was a bit disappointed at his attitude. One more possible reason for canceling the wedding plans was eliminated.

March winds were blowing all signs of winter from the streets of Philadelphia when a tattered soldier arrived from the frontier with news that set the city agog. General Wayne had not found it easy to push the British back, despite their agreement to depart, nor had the Indians let up in their harassment of the settlers. He was sending messengers to many cities in the East to ask for more help, both munitions and men.

Virginia listened eagerly as Angie reported on the soldier's plea. "Did he mention Anthony? Please, did you ask him if he knew Anthony?"

"Yes, I asked him, and he does know your Anthony Burke. He has been fighting alongside many of the others who rebelled against the whiskey tax, for he seems not to be the only one who feels he has a debt to pay to his country."

"I must see this soldier now!"

"No, Miss Virginia. I swear I have asked him all he

knows. Besides, he is surrounded by rough men who seem interested in responding to his call."

Virginia paid no attention to Angie's protest. She pulled on her cape and hurried from the house. As she leaned into the wind, Virginia felt elated. Anthony was alive and evidently well. This soldier had come from the fighting line. Anthony could make the trip, too. And if the soldier was planning to return soon, she might even send a message with him.

He was surrounded by a group of young men. As she approached, Virginia heard him reply to an earlier question, "We'll be leaving within three days. The general is sorely in need of men and ammunition. We have been promised gunpowder and shot from the armory. Have you all your own guns?"

One youth shook his head. "I'll find one. There is a gunsmith in town." He seemed to be trying to appear taller than his five feet.

Virginia turned to Angie. "Why, they're no more than lads. They're too young to go to battle."

"Perhaps, but I have seen youths his age fight well under the stress of attack. Often, on the frontier, it is spirit that counts more than judgment. The Indians seem to have respect for men who show no fear of death." She slowed her steps. "Jonathan has spoken of his days in the settlement near Fort Pitt. It was young men who won that land from the savages."

Virginia hardly heard Angie speak. She was studying the young soldier, seeking some way to break into his discussion. As she approached, the young men seemed to open their tight circle. He waved to them as they began to depart. "I will see you, then, at the town hall in three days."

When the boys were gone, Virginia stepped forward. "May I speak to you for a moment, sir?"

His smile was wide and filled with good humor. "Please, miss, I am not a 'sir.' But speak to you I certainly will. I have been a long time away from the company of a lady."

She liked him. "I come seeking more information about Anthony Burke. My woman here spoke to you earlier."

"Ah, yes." The lad turned to Angie. "I had no idea you would return with so lovely a companion. Your Mr. Burke is a good soldier and a fine leader. I served under him for a time. He keeps his men disciplined and ready for battle. He loses few soldiers, despite being mostly in the thick of worst fighting."

Virginia shuddered. "He is in constant danger, then?"

"Well, miss, every man on the frontier is in danger as long as the British persist and stir the Indians to raid our settlements. He might well be in less danger than some, since he is so well prepared to defend himself. Many deaths are caused by carelessness or by ignorance of the best methods of defense. Anthony Burke remains always on the alert."

"Thank God! What is your name?"

"Kirk, miss. I come from the Ohio Territory, where my parents settled when I was a child."

"Does Anthony have a farm there, too?"

"I don't think so. I believe he comes from Fort Pitt, or near there. However, I have heard him speak of moving west into the Ohio country, for the land is most beautiful, and there is much freedom there to grow and prosper."

So Anthony did plan to settle on the frontier. She had hoped he would choose to remain in Philadelphia. She considered her future as a woman in the wilderness and realized she had no fear if she were with her love. "Kirk, I am Virginia Nelson. When Anthony learned that you were traveling to Philadelphia, did he give you a message to deliver to me?"

The lad's smile was brilliant. "Yes, miss! I feared I might have a problem finding you. He asked me to tell you he'd be back. Maybe earlier than he first thought. He ain't quite sure yet."

Virginia glanced quickly at Angie. These were encouraging words—"maybe earlier." Now all she had to do was pray that the gown would not arrive too soon.

Thirty-two

"It's come! Your gown is here!" Mother Willing rushed excitedly through the great hall and up the stairs to Virginia's room. Thomas Willing smiled indulgently at his wife's eagerness, and then vanished into the library.

Virginia rose from before the mirror, where she had been sitting while Angie brushed her hair. She was choked with panic. Now there was no excuse to delay the wedding.

And Anthony had not been heard of since the young soldier, Kirk, had come to the city.

The time had passed far too quickly, and she had as yet no plan to save herself from a wedding she dreaded worse than death. She watched as Mother Willing tore open the wrapping on the package.

It had traveled well, possibly contained in some larger bundle, for the fine wooden box in which it was packed was undamaged. Virginia wondered if it could survive Mother Willing's eager hands, tearing at the paper that encased it. "Thomas separated it from the other shipments, so I could deliver it right away. Oh, Virginia, isn't it wonderful? Now you don't have to wait until June 20, after all!"

Virginia was thankful that Mother Willing was busy looking at the gown, for she could not conceal her distress. May was half over and it had been a glorious month, filled with balmy days and star-filled nights. More than once, David had prodded her with an impatient request that they set the wedding date for the following Sunday. Each time she had managed to hold him off. He still held the same threats over her head but his power was gone, for she no longer feared him as she had in the past. If she could not marry Anthony, she had no wish to marry at all. David might ruin her reputation, but she did not care.

If Anthony was still alive, he would come and save her. If he was alive . . . Since the day when she had talked to

Kirk, she had heard no further word of the fighting. Was it going well? Had the British finally retreated or at least abandoned the fight they no longer could win? Most of all she worried about Anthony. Had he survived the fighting or was his absence proof that he was no longer alive?

Virginia had no wish to see the gown that might force her to flee her home in order to avoid being wed to a man she hated. And then Mother Willing lifted the dress free of the box and held it before her. It cascaded open, like an avalanche of pure white snow. Angie cried out in delight, and even Virginia could not repress a gasp of pleasure.

The gown was by far the most beautiful Virginia had ever seen. Its white silk folds were encrusted with embroidery that wrapped around the sloping shoulders and over the cap of the sleeves. The neck was modestly high, as a bridal gown should be, with an upright collar, thick with hand-sewn birds and lilies. A line of tiny white buttons ran down the back, with each buttonhole surrounded by embroidered leaves, making the buttons appear to be tiny blossoms on a climbing vine. Every thread on the dress was pure white silk. Pearls were encrusted among the heavy embroidery with such impeccable taste that the overall effect was one of utmost simplicity. This was a gown that would need no jewelry, for it was a jewel in itself.

"Oh, Miss Virginia, how beautiful!" Angie stood back, her eyes wide. "You must wear this."

Virginia gave her maid a sharp glance. But it was too late. Mother Willing looked up, confused. "But of course you'll wear it. Yours will be the greatest social event since the country was born."

"Yes." Virginia felt the excitement mixed with her disappointment. If Anthony arrived on time, and if she could break her contract to marry David, she might be married in it, after all. But there were so many ifs! She took the gown and held it before her as she walked toward the mirror. "It is lovely, isn't it?"

"You knew it had to be. The princess Charlotte's own dressmaker. Just think! What an heirloom you have to give to your daughter."

Virginia smiled at the ease with which Mother Willing

leaped from the present to some unknown future. "Yes, I suppose so." She pulled at the waist and turned to see the results. "I have not thought of such things yet." She held the gown out toward Angie. "Hang it up, please, so it will lose its wrinkles. I'll try it on later."

Mother Willing shook her head. "You're a strange girl, Virginia Nelson. How can you not put on that lovely dress? Why, if it were mine . . ."

"I'm sorry, Mother Willing. I don't feel too well." Virginia leaned against the back of a chair.

"Oh!" The rebuke was forgotten. "Is it the same trouble you had through the winter?"

Virginia wished mightily that Mother Willing would depart. "I don't think so. Probably just the excitement. It came on suddenly."

Mother Willing kissed her cheek. "Don't fret, then. But do let me come back another day and see you in it. Oh, you must be so happy. Now nothing can interfere with your nuptials."

When Mother Willing had departed, Virginia stood staring at the box that still lay open on her bed. "Angie, what am I to do? Neither David nor Uncle Roy will accept any further delay."

"Didn't Anthony say he'd be back early?"

"He said he might. Oh, Angie, I wish this gown had been lost at sea."

"Don't say such a thing. Think of the lives that would have been lost, had that happened. Surely you did not mean it."

"Please, don't lecture me. Of course I have no wish that a ship had gone down. But I don't know what to do." She stared at the blossoming trees that brushed against her window. How could she have thought this was a good day? There would be no more good days for her.

She moved suddenly. "I can go to him. Quick. Get me a valise."

"Go to Anthony Burke? Where is that? And how do you expect me to bring a valise to your room without being questioned?"

Virginia dropped to the bed, pushing the box to the floor. Angie was right. She would have to go with nothing but the clothes she could wear. "Prepare food for me, then."

Angie did not move. "You plan to ride out alone? Miss Virginia, stop and think. The same people who assaulted you before still wait outside the city. Do you want to ride back into Gregory's clutches? Besides, you might ride past your Anthony on his way here to get you, for you would not dare show yourself on the road."

"But I can't stay here and marry David." She threw herself into a chair. "If only my father were here. He'd never have forced me to get engaged to David."

"Had your father been here, you would not have gone through what you did at the Freedom's Arms or at the other inn."

Virginia stared ahead, struggling again with the strange feeling she had had when first she entered the reception room at the Arms. What was it that had triggered her memory that day?

It had been a chair—a large, imposing, upholstered chair with ornately carved decorations on the back and arms.

Why did that memory come now? What had it to do with her problem? She struggled to recall the details of the carvings. Something there was important.

Suddenly, she rose to her feet. "Angie, do you remember when my father ordered that great chair from China? Remember how carefully he went over every detail with Mr. Willing?"

"Who could forget? There's never been another like it. Don't you recall what Mr. Willing said when he returned from the journey to the Orient, where he placed the order with native craftsmen? He told your father he made them swear they would not use the pattern again."

"Angie, I saw that chair!"

"We all saw it in our imaginations. But you know as well as I that the ship went down with captain and crew aboard. There was no trace of any of them."

"That may be, but I have seen the chair." She began to pace the floor. "Angie, do you see what that means?"

"No. You had best get back in bed. You told Mother Willing you felt ill. She will wonder what is happening if you march around like this."

As she spoke, there was a knock on the door. "Virginia, are you all right?" David spoke impatiently. "Angie, let me in. I must see my bride."

Virginia climbed into bed as Angie walked to the door. When David entered, Virginia was resting on her pillows, her eyes closed.

David crossed to the bed. "Angie, what has been going on up here? I swear, it sounded as if you were running races."

"Nothing, Master David. Miss Virginia was resting, and I was hurrying to clear the room before she woke."

" 'Tis a miracle you did not wake her with all your noise." He stood beside the bed. Then, suddenly, he bent and kissed Virginia on the lips.

She opened her eyes. "David! When did you come in?"

"Just now. Mother Willing tells me your gown has arrived. I have come to set the date. Now we have no need to wait nor any excuse for delay." As he spoke Roy Salford entered the room and stood behind him. "I understand the gown is most beautiful, well worth the long postponement."

Virginia did not need to pretend enthusiasm for the gown. "Yes, it's lovely. I've never owned so exquisite a gown before."

"Well, then, we must set a wedding date immediately. I cannot be patient any longer."

Angie stood across the bed. "My mistress is ill. She has no strength for a wedding yet."

"Ah? The old weakness returned?" David's eyes made his position clear. He did not believe she had ever been sick.

"Possibly." Virginia spoke softly. "Time alone will tell."

"Aye, but we have run out of time." He spoke gently, but his eyes still burned into hers. "My sweet, we have delayed our marriage too long already. Now that the gown has come, now that there are no more causes for delay, I insist that we proceed. We will be married this Sunday. I'm sure the guests will be glad to see us united as soon as possible."

"But the reception! The invitations! People will not be ready."

"They will understand, nevertheless. No groom has been more long suffering than I."

"But what if I am not yet recovered?"

"Why, then, we will have to continue your nursing after we are wed, won't we? I will find you a better woman to care for you. I know one who is highly skilled in keeping young females on their feet and active."

Virginia thought immediately of Bessie. Was David threatening her? She closed her eyes.

Roy stepped forward and took her hand. "She feels feverish. I'll send Jonathan for a doctor. Come along, David, you are right about the wedding, but now we must let her rest."

Virginia sat up as soon as they left the room, struggling to understand the significance of the chair. Suddenly her eyes lit up. "Angie! We must get Mr. Willing to visit the Arms."

"Miss Virginia! A man of character does not enter such establishments."

"I know, but we must get him to do it, nevertheless. But how?" Again, she settled back to think. "There were many objects of great value in that inn, all from the Orient. Surely Mr. Willing would recognize more than one. There is only one solution. I must run away."

"But we have already decided that is fruitless!"

"No, you don't understand. I must be captured by Gregory and you must return here to bring my uncle and Mr. Willing to rescue me!"

"But that is dangerous. And how would I know you had been captured by Gregory if you run away?"

"You're right." For a moment, Virginia seemed despondent. "Of course! You must let me know when David departs. Then I will speak to Mother Willing and suggest that maybe a short ride in the fresh spring air might strengthen me. You and Jonathan will come with me."

"But—"

"Please, do as I say. I will explain everything when we are on our way. Now get me some food."

In spite of her bravado, Virginia felt a tremor of fear as they approached the Freedom's Arms. What if her plan did not work? David would know, then, that she was aware of how he made at least some of his money. He would marry her still, of that she was certain. But when he owned her as his wife, he would not let her live long. And with her pretense of illness, she had already provided him with an explanation for her early death.

The buildings of the Arms had not changed since last she saw them. They still shone with fresh paint, and they were in good repair.

Many people moved in and out of the courtyard. Some, she knew, were travelers pausing for a rest from the rigors of the road. She prayed she would not see any man she recognized among the patrons of the brothel.

Jonathan stopped the carriage at the rise of a hill, just within view of the inn. At Virginia's direction, he turned there and appeared to head back toward town. When he had retraced the road a short distance, he stopped and leaped to the ground. Angie took the reins and held the horses still while Virginia climbed down.

"You know what you are to do?"

Angie was obviously displeased. "Yes, Miss Virginia. But what if something delays me? You could be in danger with no one to rescue you." She pursed her lips. "This is foolishness."

"Believe me, it is the only way. If it comforts you, I will wait here with Jonathan until we see you returning. Then I will proceed with my plans." She tugged at Angie's skirt. "Muss up your clothing, so they believe you struggled to get away. And remember, ride as fast as you can, so that the horses are exhausted when you reach the city."

Angie unlaced the front of her bodice just enough to give herself a disheveled look. She pulled at her hair. Then she lifted the reins. Virginia stepped back and watched as the horses galloped away. Angie, at least, was playing her part well.

Virginia turned to Jonathan. "Come with me to the top of the rise but keep hidden from the inn. I will slip ahead in the woods and wait closer to the entrance. Stay on this side of the road so that you will not be seen by anyone but me if you step out and signal. I must know when Angie is approaching, for what I have to do will take a little time."

Jonathan nodded. Virginia waited until everyone at the inn seemed busy, and then she slipped across the road and into the woods. She moved cautiously down the hillock until she was directly across from the inn. From where she hid, she could still see the road where Jonathan would give his signal.

Dusk was gathering when Jonathan waved his arms. As he vanished again into the woods, Virginia rose and crossed the road. She entered the tavern boldly, her cape thrown back to expose her face.

Gregory stood close to the door, as was his habit. "Good morning, mistress!" He bowed slightly. "May I serve you? Will you and the master require food as well as drink?"

"Neither." She stepped past him. "I have come to see Miss Bessie."

Immediately, he was in front of her again. "Ginia? You have changed. Are you alone?"

"Yes." Her voice was calm. "I must talk to Miss Bessie. May I wait in the other room?" She knew her heart was beating wildly. If she could not get into the reception room, her entire plan would be for naught.

A sly smile crossed his face. "Ah! So you have learned how difficult it is for a girl alone these days. You've come back to beg her to let you stay. No one wanted you, eh?"

She grasped at his explanation. "That's right. They were ashamed to see me. I have no place to go now, except here."

"Come along, then." He led the way across the common room and pulled the heavy curtain aside to allow her to enter. This had been far easier than she had expected it would be.

The room was just as she remembered it. The jade pieces still stood on the table. The line of chairs against the wall was partially filled with girls, some of whom she recognized. Gregory led her to an empty seat and spoke to the nearest girl. "Call Miss Bessie. I'm sure she'll be glad to see her visitor."

Virginia sat down and gazed about her. The large carved chair was still in its place of honor at the end of the room close to the door from which Bessie would emerge. It faced the door to the tavern, as it had in the past: Bessie's favorite seat, from where she could see every man who entered and the girls they chose. She could demand additional pay from any man who remained upstairs longer than she felt was proper.

Bessie was as overwhelming as she had been the first

time Virginia saw her. She approached the line of chairs without glancing at anyone but her unexpected guest. "Well! So you have come back. What makes you think I would have any use for you?"

"Oh, but you must!" Virginia was trembling. "My uncle has thrown me out. I have tried for over a year to find other lodgings, but no one will keep me for long. Please, take pity on me." She overcame her fright as she spoke, and now she felt pleased with her ability to lie. It was a good story, and she had told it with feeling.

"Well . . ." Miss Bessie pursed her lips. "We'll see. Much depends on what Cavanaugh has to say. He might not have any use for you—here, or anywhere else. He is not pleased when a woman runs from him."

Virginia thought quickly. Evidently, David had not told Bessie of his plans to marry. She uttered a silent thanks, for her way seemed easier because of David's unwillingness to talk to his hired hands.

A noise in the common room drew her attention. She stepped closer to the curtain, as if interested in who might be arriving. "You need me, Miss Bessie. Listen to all the noise out there. Surely, you will be crowded very soon."

Bessie stepped beside her and pushed the curtain aside. Virginia peered around her. She had timed her entry well. Angie stood close to the door, just behind Roy Salford and Thomas Willing. "Help!" Virginia called so suddenly she took Bessie by surprise. "Help! In here!"

The curtain fell back into place and Bessie had her by the shoulders. She felt herself dragged across the room, and she cried out again. Then Roy was through the doorway. Thomas Willing pushed behind him, followed by five men in the uniform of the militia. One of them had Gregory in tow.

Roy caught Virginia as she broke free of Bessie's hands. "Are you unharmed? How foolish you were to ride out this far."

Virginia stood proudly beside him. "Uncle, I'm fine. I was not in any danger—I did not enter until I knew you were coming." She saw his frown and hurried on. "Please forgive me. I had to get you and Mr. Willing into this place." She turned to Thomas Willing. "Please, sir. Look carefully at that chair and those pieces of jade and this carpet. Do you recognize any of them?"

Bessie stared at Virginia in alarm. Her face was red, and she gestured toward the pieces. "They are all gifts to me from Da—from an admirer! What concern are they of yours?"

Mr. Willing had not moved. He studied each piece in silence. At last, Virginia grew impatient. "Do you not remember the chair my father ordered, and the carpet and jade pieces? Remember, you told him you had the pieces of wood used in the chair branded with his initials, so it would be marked as his when it was finished?"

Thomas Willing nodded. "Aye, but it was lost at sea."

"I don't think it was. Look at these things."

Willing strode across the room. He pulled the chair from the wall and turned it onto its side. When he rose, he faced Bessie. "Mistress, you had better tell me the name of the man who gave you this chair—unless you wish to take full responsibility for a piracy on the high seas."

Bessie stared back at him. For one terrible minute, Virginia feared she would remain silent. Then she said, "The chair was given me by David Cavanaugh. I have other evidence, if you need it, to show that he has been party to many other piracies." She turned to Roy Salford. "He forced me to supply him with information on shipments of value which my girls acquired from certain customers."

"You will testify against him?" Roy fingered one of the jade pieces. "These are part of the shipment?"

"Yes. I'll testify." Suddenly, Bessie was herself again. A crafty look came over her face. "On one condition. That I not be punished for my part of the affair, and that I be given the Freedom's Arms when Cavanaugh is sent to prison." She turned toward Gregory. "He must go free, too. He has had no knowledge of any of this."

Virginia started to protest, but then changed her mind. She no longer cared if these two were punished for their part in her suffering. What mattered was that David be caught and imprisoned for his crimes, and that she be relieved of the contract to marry him.

On the road back to town, they stopped to pick up Jonathan. Roy turned the reins over to him and settled back beside Virginia. "You realize, do you not, that you did a very dangerous and foolish thing. You might have been killed. You're still in danger, unless the militia find David when they reach the city. How do you know that one of his henchmen hasn't warned him already?"

"I know, uncle. But how else was I to persuade you to come here?"

"Possibly you are right. Still, I will never get used to such behavior in a woman. You are most extraordinary."

Virginia smiled contentedly. For the first time, her uncle seemed actually pleased with her. She turned to Thomas Willing. "Sir, did David always show interest in your business? Did he only begin after he received uncle's consent to our marriage?"

"Now that I think back, he was around my old office far too often for a man with a business of his own. I am ashamed to say that I was never suspicious of him. I confided freely in him much information about my cargos. I had no reason to distrust him. We were, after all, in the same business."

Roy chuckled. "More so than you ever thought. Tomorrow we will send for those pieces. They are part of Virginia's inheritance."

As they approached the town, Virginia touched her uncle's sleeve. "Please, uncle, may we drive past David's house?"

Roy leaned forward and tapped Jonathan. "Do as she asks, please. I, too, would feel more comfortable were I certain he is in custody."

Jonathan drew the carriage up to the curb, only one door away from David's residence. There was no room in front of his door, for a special wagon, used by the militia to house prisoners, occupied that place. As they watched, the front door opened, and David emerged.

He was surrounded by soldiers, young men with serious faces and weapons in their hands. David paused for a moment on the stone step and gazed up the street. When he caught sight of Roy's carriage, he started. His eyes burned into Virginia's. He saw her, and he knew she had been the cause of his downfall.

She felt a chill run up her spine. And then a flood of relief swept over her. It was truly over—at last!

Roy Salford accompanied her to the trial and stood beside her when she testified. She knew she was admitting to having been inside the Freedom's Arms and that some of her less loyal friends might surmise that she had lived a life of shame after her father's death. But she did not care. Her uncle had faith in her and so did Anthony. They would defend her honor, were it ever threatened.

The entire court rose when the judge entered to announce his sentence. Virginia cast a covert glance toward the dock, where David stood beside his lawyer. And then the judge spoke.

"I have learned, in my years on the bench, that men steal for a multitude of reasons. Some rob others because they are hungry, or because they have never received proper moral instruction. But there are a few who steal because they are too indolent to labor for themselves. These are the men who choose to use others for their profit. The testimony I have heard these past days convinces me that David Cavanaugh is such a man. And for him, and others like him, there is no cure. I sentence you, David Cavanaugh, to be hanged by the neck until you are dead." He paused and looked directly at David. "Sentence will be carried out Monday week, at daybreak."

Virginia was shocked. She had hated David and feared all he represented, but she shuddered at the thought of him being hanged. She buried her face in her uncle's shoulder.

As they left the courtroom, she turned to her uncle. "I do not wish to see him die. Oh, uncle, he was unkind to me, and he even might have harmed me, were we to have married, but I still hate the thought of—" She could not continue.

Roy patted her hand. "My child, do not think that you are the one responsible for the sentence. That is the price of piracy, and he has been connected to many cargos that were lost on the seas. Your testimony only contributed to proving his guilt. There was young Francis and Bessie. And the tale told by the man you saw on the road. He seemed unable to stop talking, when he realized his life was at stake. Do not let the punishment dealt out to David hang on your conscience. He committed the crime. He is the one who earned the punishment."

Virginia nodded. Her uncle was right, she knew that.

Nevertheless, she pitied the man who had caused her so much distress.

It was Angie who reminded Virginia of David's joy when he thought Anthony was to be executed. And that memory brought peace to Virginia's mind. David had played a dangerous game—and he had lost. She had no reason to feel responsible for his end.

Thirty-three

"Come in, Virginia." Roy Salford stood before the fireplace in the study. "It is time we discussed your future." He waited until she was seated opposite him, in the large chair they had brought back from the Freedom's Arms. "I have at last come to recognize that you cannot be treated like most women, for your father raised you to be independent. Therefore, I will not again insist that you see suitors of my choice."

"Thank you, uncle. Father said he would be content only when I found my own husband—as my mother did."

"Yes. Well, I accept his decision, though I have always considered it a foolish way to raise a woman. However, we would not now be enjoying these beautiful pieces were you an ordinary woman." He opened a drawer in the secretary and pulled out a book. "This is your father's account book. As you have suspected, he was a wealthy man, and you have inherited his wealth. It will belong to your husband if you marry. If you do not, I will remain your guardian. I do suggest that the latter is not a satisfactory solution to your life, for I will not live forever, and you will have no one to manage your estate for you when I die."

"Please, uncle—"

"Do not interrupt me. And do not act surprised at what I have just said. No one is immortal."

"Yes, Uncle Roy."

"So, then, I must know what you have in mind. Is there a man whom you have considered as a spouse? Are there any among the suitors who attended you before David whom you felt drawn to?"

She clutched the carving on the chair. "Yes, uncle. One. Anthony Burke."

"But he is a traitor. He betrayed all my trust in him!"

"He was released from his sentence by the president himself. And he has been fighting with General Wayne on the frontier in Ohio for many months, to show his appreciation for the gift of his life."

"Oh? I had thought he left town because he was too ashamed to speak to his friends whom he betrayed."

"Please, uncle. He did not betray you. You knew all along that he was an anti-Federalist. He never pretended he did not sympathize with the farmers in their protest against the whiskey tax."

"Where is he, then? Why has he not presented himself to me and asked for my forgiveness? Why does he remain hidden?"

She held her peace until she was calm once more. "Uncle, he is not here because he is still in Ohio. I had news of him when the young soldiers came to town to recruit more fighters, but I have heard nothing more since then."

"Do you think he is still alive?"

"Oh, he must be!" Virginia clasped her hands together. "He sent word he would return before June. We had planned to marry before the day I was pledged to David, and then to flee to the frontier to escape your wrath and David's vengeance."

"And I thought you were willing to accept my decision regarding David. Tell me, why did you distrust him so? What was it he did that made you suspicious?"

She told her uncle, at last, of David's treatment of her after her father died. "He took me, uncle, when I was too upset to object or to know whether what he did was good for me. I know now that he intended to use me for a time and then to turn me over to Bessie. If I had not listened to the old hag, if I had not tried to run away, and in my attempt, met Anthony—I would have been lost. No one would even have known I was still alive."

Roy pulled her into his arms. "I am thankful, my dear, that your father raised you to be the woman you are. A less spunky female might have accepted her fate. Maybe there is some merit, after all, in instructing females in more than cooking and embroidery and the fine arts. You are an unusual woman, my dear. But, then, so was your mother. I am ashamed that I have not been able to admit your value before."

Virginia touched her uncle's sleeve. "Please, do not rebuke yourself any longer. If Anthony lives, I have no reason to be angry with anyone. And if he does not, then I will need you very much, for I will not wed any other man."

"What shall we do regarding your wedding plans? Mother Willing is very distraught. She sent word to me that she was ready to notify all the guests that there would be no marriage."

Virginia gazed out the window. A bird settled on the limb of a tree and began to sing exuberantly. The sweet fragrance of spring filled the air. This was the time for her to marry. She would not abandon hope yet.

"Tell her to wait." She paused. "No, I will go and speak to her. She has worked so hard on the preparations. I cannot give up my hope that Anthony is alive and will return as he promised." She kissed Roy on the cheek, and then, her heart still heavy with trepidation, hurried from the house. Mother Willing would be glad to know that, at least for a time, there would be no need to cancel the plans she had made with such loving care.

Thirty-four

June entered gently, bringing with it more blossoms and birds that filled the air with song. Each morning, Virginia awoke with a prayer that Anthony would return that day, and each morning she dressed with great care, for she wanted him to see her at her best when he arrived.

She followed the same pattern. Breakfast was eaten early, with her uncle. When he departed for Congress, she had her horse saddled. She rode alone into the countryside, always remaining on the road that led to the west.

She grew to know every farmhouse, every fence, every tree she passed. Occasionally, she stopped and spent some time talking with a farmer, resting from his labor in the field. More than once, she remained through much of the morning with the farmer's wife, watching the woman work at her duties. If Anthony returned, these would be her tasks, for on the frontier servants were out of place.

When she spoke of her hopes to the farm woman, she expected to be greeted with derision. But the woman showed surprising understanding. "You have never done such labor? Then, maybe, you had best persuade your husband to remain in the city. This is not work for the unskilled."

"Can you teach me some things? I learn quickly. Please. It means much to me. I am Virginia Nelson. I hope to marry Anthony Burke, the man who led the farmers' revolt."

"Anthony? Why, he did speak of a girl he wished to wed. So you are she." The reserve the farmer's wife had shown before vanished. "Forgive me for my coldness. I thought you were some fancy lady seeking relief from city boredom. I am Helena Whitehead. My husband and I have known Anthony Burke for many years. He is a good man and an honest one. He deserves a wife who can be a help to him."

"Then you will teach me?"

"What I can."

Helena was as true as her word. And Virginia, with a purpose for her rides, made arrangements to stay the day with her new friend. She was careful to return to the city in time to dine in the evening with her uncle, for she doubted he would fully understand her new project. And, with Angie's help, and the cooperation of the cook and Jonathan, she kept her secret.

For the first time in her life, Virginia ground flour and made her own bread. She was delighted with the tasks set for her by her teacher, and she thrived under the exertion. Most of all, she found the exercise reassuring. If she were ready to move with Anthony to Ohio, then surely he must come for her.

There were times when she heard pounding hoofs on the road and hurried to the window to watch some rider pass by. Helena stepped beside her as she turned away, disappointed, as usual. "It does no good to fret. If you are to be a frontiersman's wife, you must have patience. There were days when Fred and I were out near Pittsburgh, when he was gone for weeks at a time, and I never knew whether he would return alive."

"But he has to come back. What good is it for me to learn all these things if he has been—" She could not complete her sentence. Anthony had to return! She would not accept any other conclusion to their separation.

When she arrived at Helena's farm on the eighteenth of June, she was growing desperate. No word had come from the frontier.

She forgot the leavening in the bread, and had Helena not been watching, would have put it to bake without rising. And then, just when she was ready to return home in despair, she heard the thunder of many horses on the road.

She ran to the door. "Helena! They've come!" She was out on the road, her hands still covered with flour, an old apron covering her gown.

The men filed past slowly. Some had arms in bandages, and one rode his horse awkwardly, for his left leg was cut off at the knee. Virginia ran alongside the road, searching every row for a face she remembered. Suddenly, she called out, "Kirk!"

The young man looked up. He had been riding with his head down, and his crown was wrapped in a bloodstained cloth. He saw her and pulled his horse off the road. "Virginia Nelson!" He did not look happy to see her. "I had not expected to meet you."

She grasped his saddle. "Please, do you know? Is Anthony Burke among those that return now?"

He did not reply immediately. When he did speak, his voice was almost inaudible. "I think not, Miss Virginia. He was badly injured only days before the fighting ended. I do not believe he was strong enough to make the journey with the rest of us."

She stared at him in disbelief. "But, there are men accompanying you who are most grievously hurt!" She stopped speaking. Anthony would not return. He had been killed in battle.

She dropped her hold on his saddle. "Thank you, Kirk." She felt hot tears burn her eyes, but she held them back. "Did he leave any message for me?"

Kirk refused to meet her eyes. "He said not to despair. He would return."

She turned away, too overcome to speak. But she withheld her tears until she was alone once more in the privacy of her room.

Thirty-five

She refused to leave her bed on the nineteenth. Angie carried a tray of food up, which Virginia left untouched. She lay unmoving, staring up at the pattern of lights on the ceiling. The noises of the street meant nothing to her, and even the sweet fragrance of a red rose that bloomed just outside her window failed to rouse her interest.

Angie fussed about the room, but she made no attempt to speak until she had finished her chores and sat beside her mistress, on the edge of the bed. "Miss Virginia, you must not stay so alone. Mother Willing has been twice to see you. And your uncle has sent a messenger back every hour since leaving for the Congress to learn if you are recovering." She took Virginia's hand in hers. "You must not lie in bed like this. The best cure for bereavement is work. Let me help you dress, so you can ride out to visit with Helena. She has been through many hardships and can give you much help in bearing your burden of sorrow." She pulled out a gown and carried it to the bed. "Did you know she had a son who was killed by Indians?"

Virginia sobbed. "The frontier! Why do men have to go to the frontier? Why aren't they content with what land we have?" The floodgates opened, and she threw herself into Angie's arms. "Oh, Angie! Why did he have to go to Ohio?"

"He did what any man would have done. He had a debt to pay to his country." Angie stroked Virginia's back. "Oh, my baby! I would give anything if you could be spared this sorrow. I wish I had died, instead of him."

They remained together until, at last, Virginia's sobs quieted. Finally Angie urged again, "You must get up, my dear. You'll feel better if you are busy."

"I wish I were dead. I don't want to live without Anthony."

Angie did not reply. Instead, she helped Virginia to get up and dress.

Jonathan had a carriage ready when Virginia reached the front door. Virginia backed into the entryway. "I don't want to go for a ride. Please."

"My dear, you must get out. The sun will do you good."

They rode for a time about the city. Virginia sat for a while watching the children at play, thinking of the baby she should have borne Anthony. The thought only increased her sorrow.

She turned at last to Angie. "I want to go out, up the road a way. I can't believe it, Angie. He has to come. He can't be dead."

"You must accept life as it comes. Such clinging to lost hopes is not—"

"Please! Just this once. If we do not find him, I will admit that he is . . . gone."

Angie did as Virginia asked. She directed Jonathan to head out on the road that led west from the city, the road the soldiers had taken the day before, when they returned.

They traveled slowly. Jonathan had no reason to expect to find anyone on the road other than travelers, but he agreed with Angie that a ride, any ride, was better for Virginia than for her to remain indoors. Angie tried to chat, but Virginia seemed uninterested, and so she stopped, contenting herself with looking at the rich farmland.

They reached a rise from which a long valley could be viewed, and there Jonathan paused. He knew they ought to turn back, but he hesitated to do so without a specific order from Virginia.

As they sat quietly observing the peaceful valley, a cart appeared over the distant ridge. The man who was driving sat hunched forward, as if some pain kept him from holding himself erect. Behind him, three forms lay side by side on the bed of the cart. Even from the distance, Jonathan could see that the driver was holding the horse back, so the rough road would not disturb his passengers.

Virginia leaned forward. "Angie! Jonathan! It's him! I'm certain. Oh, thank God! He's alive."

Angie pulled Virginia back onto the seat. "Please, Miss Virginia. Don't build your hopes. Kirk told you he was dead. How can you still believe he's alive?"

Virginia was beaming. "Oh, but he didn't. He said Anthony was very badly injured, but he didn't say he had been killed." She tapped Jonathan's shoulder. "Hurry! I must see him!"

Jonathan looked at Angie and they exchanged a look of despair. If this were a dream, if the men in the cart were strangers, Virginia would never recover. Yet, there was nothing to be done. Jonathan raised his whip, and the carriage moved forward.

As they came closer to the cart, Virginia could see that the men were all dressed in rough frontier clothing. One had his musket tied to his leg, to keep it straight as it healed from a break. Another wore a bandage over half his face. These men were not able to travel by themselves. The driver of the cart seemed no less injured than the others.

He sat with his head down, as if searching the road for rocks, and he carefully guided the horses around those largest ones which he saw in time. He looked up as the carriage approached and pulled the reins so as to lead his horses off the road and out of the way of the racing carriage. Jonathan realized he was attempting to avoid the dust that rose behind the carriage as it sped forward.

He looked up, and then pulled his horses to a halt. He was not leaning over now. Instead, he strained forward, his eyes searching the interior of the carriage. Then, suddenly, he let out a shout. "Virginia! Oh, thank God! Virginia!"

She heard him call, and she threw herself forward. Jonathan pulled his horses to a stop in a cloud of dust that billowed around the carriage, obscuring it from view. Virginia did not wait for the air to clear. She was on the road and running before Angie had gathered her wits about her. "Anthony!"

She stood for a moment beside the carriage, and then she clambered up beside him. "Anthony! Oh, Anthony!" She was weeping uncontrollably, and she buried her face in his shoulder.

They clung together in silence. Virginia could feel his lips caressing her cheeks, her ears, her neck. He took her hands in his and held them against his face. "Oh, my love! I have missed you so!"

"I—I thought you were dead." Virginia at last recovered her voice. "I thought I'd never see you again!"

Angie stood near them. "Master Anthony, can you climb down? Jonathan will drive the cart the rest of the way to the city. You must ride with us." She held out a hand. Anthony nodded. He moved slowly, but Virginia could see that he had all his limbs. His injury was to his chest, close to his shoulder. One arm was tied close to his body. He had lost a great deal of blood and his face was pale, and he staggered when he moved, but he did, at last, reach the carriage and climb in beside Virginia. Angie settled in the driver's seat and picked up the reins. "I will drive the horses slowly. We must take care not to open your wound."

Virginia leaned close to Anthony. "Why did you leave me after the trial? I wanted to go with you!"

"I explained in my note. I had to repay my country for my life. Had Washington been less generous, I would have died a traitor. He gave me the chance to redeem myself. Surely you understand."

Virginia kissed his cheek. "Of course. But I missed you."

He sagged against her. "Where is David? How did you manage to get away from him today?"

Virginia told him what had happened. When she spoke of entering the Freedom's Arms alone, he pulled her close and kissed her tenderly. "My brave Virginia! What a wonder you are. You have the courage a woman needs to live in Ohio."

She lowered her head. "I don't know. Oh, Anthony, I'm so ashamed. Yesterday, when Kirk returned with most of the men, I assumed that you were killed. I felt like dying myself."

"Ah, but you didn't. You came out to search for me."

"Only because Angie urged me to. Oh, Anthony, please let's not go to Ohio. I will be worried about you all the time."

His face grew solemn. "Darling, I love you dearly. But you must understand me. I belong on the frontier. Listen! Before I left Ohio, I spoke at length with General Wayne. He is eager to have settlers come to occupy the lands vacated by the Indians. And oh, my darling, the land is so beautiful, miles of virgin forests, rivers leaping with fish, birds that fly in flocks so large you cannot see from one end of them to the other, and skies so blue you will never believe that soot exists."

She watched him in fascination. "It sounds so wonderful! But—it is dangerous, too."

"Not anymore. Not like it used to be. My dearest, I learned from the whiskey insurrection. President Washington and Thomas Jefferson were right. There is no place in this nation for armed revolt. All such an act does is harden the opposition to the cause, no matter how right it may be."

"But why should that influence you? Surely, you can stay in Philadelphia. Uncle Roy will give you work again."

"No, my love. I know now that the way to change unequal laws is through legal action. Our system has been constructed to provide every citizen with the opportunity to receive justice. But"—he took her hand in his one good hand and held it tightly—"for me, such a process is too slow. I want freedom—liberty—now! I cannot survive in the closeness of city life, where my rights must be tempered by the rights of others who live around me. I am happy only when I am my own man, free to live my life in my own way."

Virginia brought his hand to her lips. "I suppose I knew that was how you felt. But I had to ask. I expect that there will be times, when we are in Ohio, when I will be frightened. Will you comfort me?"

"Oh, my love, you have the courage and strength. And you will have our children. They will bolster your determination to persevere. You have all the makings of a good frontier woman. It has only been hidden beneath the veneer of city life."

Virginia smiled. Maybe Anthony was right. One thing she knew. She would prefer life in the wilderness with Anthony to any other life available to her. "May we stay here at least until you are well again—and until we can be married? I have the most beautiful wedding gown that has ever been made. I want to wear it for you!"

He chuckled. "Such a delightful mixture of grand lady and down-to-earth woman. Oh, I love you." Again, he pulled her close. When he let her go, he leaned back, exhausted from the exertion.

Virginia grew solemn. "Anthony, Washington said something else, remember? He said it was the duty of all citizens of the land to pay attention to their government so as to assure their freedom. If we go to Ohio, will we not be neglecting that duty?"

"I think not. I have no intention of abandoning my country. Even on the frontier, I will be a citizen. If the day comes when our new home needs representation to Congress, I will be ready to take a place here or wherever the government is established. I suspect, as I grow older, I will feel as your uncle does, satisfied with all I have done on the frontier and ready to contribute in a new way to my nation."

The carriage drew up before the house. Angie dismounted and hurried inside. Roy Salford emerged moments later and lifted Anthony from the seat. When they reached the door, Anthony stood up beside his friend, and, together, they walked inside. Virginia followed behind. When Anthony was settled in a bed, she remained beside him.

Roy repeated much of Virginia's story about David to Anthony. "He was captured. I suppose she told you. And he has paid for his crimes." He stood for a moment, looking at his guest. "I hope you will forgive me. I misjudged you, and I failed to see the obvious. My errors almost destroyed Virginia."

Anthony held out his good hand. "Please, my friend. You were sincere in your beliefs. But you have always been the kind of man most needed here. You are tolerant of opinions other than your own and you listen to arguments. We can be thankful that men like you are here to guide our new country through the years ahead. As for Virginia"—he felt her hand on his shoulder—"she has no resentment toward you, for she has never ceased to love you. We will miss you when we return to Ohio."

The prenuptial ceremony began early in the afternoon. Virginia sat through church without hearing a word of the sermon. Her thoughts were on the wedding and the gown she was to wear. When the midday dinner was over, she hurried to her room to dress. The wedding was to take place in the garden, and she could hear the murmur of the guests and the rattle of their carriages as they arrived.

Anthony waited at the altar that had been set up under

the grape arbor. The pastor stood facing her as she moved toward him, leaning on her uncle's arm. Roy leaned down as they advanced. "You're beautiful. Your father would be so proud of you."

Virginia smiled. She was thinking of Anthony. How strong he was to stand so erect as she approached. Three days of nursing had renewed his health, though he would need more rest in the days to come.

A small ensemble of strings began to play as she took Anthony's hand in hers. The pastor opened his book and began to read. "Dearly beloved, we are gathered . . ."

Virginia felt Anthony's fingers tighten around hers. It was beginning at last, their life together. She knew that wherever they went, whatever hardships they faced, they would be at each other's side. And she would be content. For she was wed to the only man she could love.